BLOOD RAIN

On St. Mark's Square

—

A novel by

GAITHER STEWART

Author: Gaither Stewart

Cover art: Anatoly Krynsky
Back cover article and book editor: Rowan Wolf
Preface: Christofer C. Black
Poem: The Thunder, Petar Penda
Technical Consultant: Carlo Merlini

Cyberwit.net
ISBN: 978-81-19654-31-4
First Edition: 2024
Rs. 325

Cyberwit.net
HIG 45 Kaushambi Kunj, Kalindipuram
Allahabad - 211011 (U.P.) India
http://www.cyberwit.net
Tel: +(91) 9415091004
E-mail: info@cyberwit.net

Printed at Repro.

"Memory of people behaving magnificently gives me the courage to act as I believe human beings should act in defiance of all the evil around us."

Howard Zinn

Unglücklich das Land das Helden nötig hat.

(Unhappy the land that needs heroes.)

Bertold Brecht

PREFACE

Christopher Black

Gaither Stewart's new novel *Blood Rain* lives up to its title, for a central theme throughout the play of events, is rain, lots of rain, falling on a once great city, Venice, now fallen into desuetude as a beautiful but tragic shadow of its glorious past, the rain symbolising the drowning of reason, integrity, knowledge, care for others, in the flood of self-interest, corruption, ignorance, cruelty and brutality that inundates the modern world, that threatens to drown and destroy us all, with Venice a stand-in for the entire West.

The novel opens with a poem, *The Thunder*, that sets the stage with images of deep disturbances shaking the world, warning of the storm that threatens, and leads the reader into the complex lives of its characters trying to do their best to make sense of the world, live their lives and stay true to their conviction that there is a better way.

The opening chapter is an homage to Venice and its past glories, an homage to the past generally, of age and aging, the loss of friends with passing years, the loss of identity in the modern age of mass consumerism, mass media, and mass ignorance.

We are quickly introduced, by Stuart, the main protagonist and narrator, to a man, Gulliver, who is 102 years old, full of history and experience but weary of the world who acts as an anchor for the narrative that follows, a narrative that blends action with stream of consciousness reflections and thoughts on the state of the world and the characters, with references to the literature of James Elroy Flecker, his famous play, Hassan, and Samarkand, to Thomas Man's Death in Venice, while the date given for the opening of the story, November 1, brings to mind the opening of Moby Dick; the need to go somewhere to seek escape from the ennui that envelopes the soul when the weather matches its despair. Literary and cultural references abound throughout the narrative, an essential part of it; an education for the unenlightened, a reminder to those who are, but have forgotten.

The central characters are all refugees, fleeing war, crime, corruption, danger, gangsters and Freemasons, their own pasts, looking for a refuge in a world where refuge is difficult to find, a world in which communism, the hope of humanity, once again fights against the rise of Fascism, where common decency is a waif lost in the darkness of brutality and cynicism.

The colour red appears in the narrative throughout, signifying on the one hand the blood spilled as the plot evolves, and on the other signifying the red flag of the working class and its struggle for justice for itself and the world, the symbol of resistance to western imperialism, a symbol of sacrifice, and hope. But red is also a symbol of passion and love, for the other essential thread connecting the characters and the story is love, its complexities, its promises, its disappointment, its despair.

Stuart, Sophie, Helen, the principal actors we meet at the opening, are involved in a fluid arrangement where love is shared among them as perhaps love should be, where jealousy is absent, though confusion about what their relationship is and means, what love means to any of them and us, is a constant source of reflection.

The sexual-love relationship among them becomes more complicated with the appearance of a Ukrainian man, Vasily, who competes with the Italian cop, Marcello, for Helen's affections, while the old relationship between her and Stuart is ever present.

All this takes place against the backdrop of Venice with occasional references to Turin,

Florence and Amsterdam, the Jewish Ghetto; in which Venice is the stage on which is played out scenes of the wars provoked by the West against Ukraine, against Russia, wars in Africa, and Venice is a hotbed of arms dealing and smuggling, Ukrainian and Italian intelligence agencies, spies, and the activities of secret Masonic lodges and fascist organisations acting in concert to form a complex web of plot and counter-plot. It is a world of loose loyalties, uncertain attachments, greed and betrayals.

The reader of Gaither Stewart's novels can expect a rich menu of stimulation for the mind, for thinking about the world and in this novel he does not disappoint. The discussion in an early chapter between Stuart and the old man, Gulliver-Jonathan Swift would appreciate the reference-about the merits and faults of Hemingway, Tolstoy, even Gore Vidal is followed by conversations about the immorality of the arms trade, then an essay about the crisis points in life, the growing dangers of nuclear war, climate catastrophe, our attempt to live lives of illusions created by the elites and their media, about probabilities, possibilities, our place in life; and all the while the rain continues to fall, and one hears in the background, or at least I did, while reading it, Bob Dylan's *A Hard Rain's A Gonna Fall.* And in later chapters, we are exposed to the ideas of Sartre, Foucault, Cioran, the chaos and disarray of the capitalist society, its constant undermining of Marxism or anything else good for the working class.

The novel is divided into two parts. The second part opens with a discussion of the role of masks and what they represent in various cultures, the masks of the Carnival of Venice, of masks in ancient Greek theatre, their role in the culture of Mexico, with references to Camus and the Myth of Sisyphus, to Octavio Paz, even the Italian actor Marcello Mastroianni, to Oscar Wilde, to Nietzsche and his work on morality, *Beyond Good and Evil*, to the fate of those who expose the truth, like Giordano Bruno, burned at the stake in Rome, the dangers of speaking the truth, the masks every writer wears in his work.

A continuing motif connected to masks is Helen's attempt to complete a self-portrait, which proves difficult as she struggles with her own identity, and this in turn leads to discussions between her and Stuart about what art is, what purpose it serves. Stuart asks the same questions of himself; what is the purpose of writing, what is the role of the writer in a world where nuclear war threatens, where extinction threatens, which leads to reflections on the labyrinths in which we all become trapped in our lives, of the Minotaur, of Ariadne, Troy and the Helen that launched a thousand ships, the labyrinths of the world politics, what it means to be a communist when communism in the West has lost its force and struggles to survive and rise again, the labyrinth of intrigue and aggression by the West against Russia, the world war taking place. This leads to a reference to Euripides famous anti-war play *The Trojan Women* and lessons not learned.

But finally, the novel is also a detective story, as the Italian police, all interesting characters, with the help of a sympathetic agent of the Italian intelligence service, try to solve several murders, and Stuart becomes involved along with Sophie and Helen, against the dark forces involved.

Their involvement and the consequences forces Stuart, to think of leaving the West, to go east. He asks the mourning Helen to go with him, to find a place where they can revive themselves in body and mind and they finally settle on the ancient city of Belgrade, itself a city bombed heavily by the Americans and their allies, but which, for them, is now a refuge of light in a darkening world.

Blood Rain, a novel rich in action and ideas, drama and pathos, is a novel of our time.

The Thunder by Petar Penda

The thunder took away
Our generosity, compassion
And self-control.
We are not who we were,
And the thunder isn't what it used to be.
We hardly speak the same language now.
But we know the thunder rages
and rumbles the warnings
Of the times to come and
Of the division within one's self.

It forebodes ruins in place of cities,
Fear in place of inner peace
And death in place of life.
The thunder rolls stones in the sky
Ready to hit us with the fiery truth
Of our nothingness and futility.
There is no hope of redemption and
The peace which passes understanding
Is just an unreachable echo.

The Narrator says:

I'm at the end of this fragmented relation about our life during a compressed period of time and circumscribed by the tight spaces of the Italian peninsula. I hope to have reflected each of our individual attempts to find what we have sought, and I continue to wonder if the struggle between the feeling of one's existence and my subjective narration of it ever ends. For I still ask the question of questions: where do I come from and what is the purpose of my existence? This aspect of the story affects me in a peculiar way: it sharpens my nostalgia for more of life itself, a desire which jolts me back to the reality of my mortality and my sense of loneliness. The sentiment of my story has been that pervasive sensation of loneliness of many of us and the consequential nostalgia. Nostalgia for persons we have loved and places we have been, nostalgia for places we have never been and the loved persons lost along the way.

Then when I read the words I have just written, I start and regret that I fail to express the spark of my original idea. My uncertainty explains my inclusion of the words of Erich Auerbach that "The man who finds his homeland sweet is still a tender beginner; he to whom every soil is as his native one is already strong; but he is perfect to whom the entire world is as a foreign land."Although today I too feel like Auerbach's homeless stranger in the world, I should feel beatific. But I do not. Nonetheless, feeling like a stranger everywhere is a familiar sensation, an invasive sensation of alienation and of estrangement.

And so life goes on; it continues to be an endless search for that lost self. My greatest hope is to get at least a glimpse of a me that I will recognize as authentic and that I will come to know that I am not only what I seem but what I am.

I observed most of the events recorded here of our journey. A journey filled with love and fear, intrigue and discovery, death and mourning; therefore, I consider our life voyage a quest for a meaning in what happened—in the good and in the evil—and at the same time trying to remain free of illusions. I have related why my friends and I fled from Rome to Fiesole, from Fiesole to Venice, and from Venice to Belgrade where I now live with Helen, the great love of my life.

I think that it's because I know so intimately much of what happened to this small group of people that I feel like a survivor, for several of them have been lost along the way.

This story remains as true as the ambivalence of our times allows—a political story on the one hand, a love story on the other: everything is political and life is not life without love. My conclusions confirm the maxim that in the unoccupied space between stimulus and reaction anything at all can happen as it did in our case. I have narrated here the unabridged and still incomplete story as I have lived it. (Stuart Stuart)

RAIN

1

November 2

In the moment my attraction to this isolated district was born, cascades of a vicious rain drummed against the window panes. The wind was berserk in its comings and goings, and the cobblestones of our street reflected a mystical reddish light. There was something cynical in the air of Cannaregio that day, a suggestion of woes and ills to come concealed in the rainfall, a whisper that first impressions reflect the peril itself.

Sophie and I had arrived on All Saints Day and our day two in the city of Venice was All Souls Day, when Venetians were visiting San Michele Cemetery on its own island off the coast of our quarter. Whether an inexplicable quirk or some atavistic east-European memory was stored in my hippocampus, ancient landmark cemeteries have always fascinated me: the Poets' Cemetery in Rome where John Keats is buried—*Pale warriors, death-pale were they all*; '*La Belle Dame sans Merci Thee hath in thrall!'* I once saw the antique Jewish cemetery in Prague. And Novodivichy in Moscow to visit Chekhov and Gogol and the Novo Groblije "open air museum" in Belgrade. And soon we too will visit Joseph Brodsky, Ezra Pound, Sergei Diaghilev and Igor Stravinsky at San Michele.

Sophie and I came before the others in order to prepare the house for their arrival. Even though she came along with me on this last leg of our journey reluctantly, Sophie Berardenga was a real striver, experienced at new starts, of which she had undertaken many in her life. When I met her ten years ago, she was a Tuscan waif lost in Rome—the kind of girl you met in those times on Campo de' Fiori or in the back alleys of the Old City. Since then our life together has changed many times, although whether by chance or will is unclear. I am her husband, Stuart Stuart, third generation Scottish-Italian.

We are arranging three apartments of an abandoned, five-story building in the more obscure Venetian Sestiere of Cannaregio. Sophie inherited the apartment house from her filthy rich parents who had a nasty tendency to give their daughter the leftovers.

Still, it was because of the existence of this building that when the period in our preceding stay in Fiesole ended badly, we fled north to the island city on the lagoon. For us, Venice, the former Queen of the Seas, La Serenissima, is an ideal hideout in our underground life, no less hidden from the public eye as was the house in the liana-infested jungle hanging on the hill above Florence. There, the jungle. Here, the rain. All our hideouts! Sophie laments. We run from one to the other like along an underground escape line. Our kind of exile can be exotic, but it is not a life for everyone. However you get used to it, however like getting used to living in temporary five-star hotel suites. Yet when I jest about the infectious rhythm of our gypsy life, Sophie looks at me like I'm crazy. She wants to go home. Sensitive to change even before our zigzag journey began, she'd wanted to stay in our original home in the Rome outskirts. She says that I'm a romantic; she a realist. In fact I still find it striking that she has always seemed to know herself so well. Today she too seems to feel atmospheric similarities between the rugged nature of the Rome-San Nicola countryside, the jungle-like setting in the Fiesole that we had just abandoned, and the narrow building wedged snugly between the tourist-infected ghetto and the Ca' Foscari University branch in Cannaregio. While the definitive escape route of the nearby Santa Lucia rail station with its receptive wide white steps and its trains heading east and west transmits the sense of security that the more fortunate hunted people like us may come to feel. After all, there are other places to go in life, also the unfamiliar and unknown places, places that people on the run encounter, sometimes by choice, sometimes by chance. Still, I am already coming to feel our house on Calle di Solferino in Cannaregio as the center of our world. Sophie thinks me fickle because I had also perceived Rome and the hamlet of San Nicola as the center; then I felt Fiesole and the Ho Chi Minh Trail leading to our hideout as our center; and now there is Venice where our recent past seems to meet our future— the center of our existence today. I felt for each of those places and those times what our friend Oriana's current subject, Emil Cioran, wrote in his *A Short History of Decay: The source of our actions resides in an unconscious propensity to regard ourselves as the center, the cause, and the conclusion of time.* Oriana said that the philosopher thought that if we were to recognize our true position in the world, the revelation of our infinitesimal presence would crush us.

November 3

The streets, the roofs and every uncovered surface are covered as if by a carpet with a distinct reddish tint. When the rain relents to a drizzle, I like to explore the forgotten streets of the Venetian *sestiere* of Cannaregio. Today it is cool. And walking under the drizzle is surprisingly pleasant. However as they do many days the meteorological experts this morning warned of a Siberian cold front moving south, a cold which for mysterious reasons usually comes to a stop in central Europe. Yet the short gusts of wind promise general disorder in *la Serenissima* too. The skies are pure clouds, uniform, evenly spread like a deep gray blanket. Though November mornings are like November mornings everywhere, *this* non-stop rain differentiates Venice today even if some Venetians continue to claim that it seldom rains here in November. Besides, the humidity is so fierce it makes you think it's raining when it's only misting. It perspires. It drops. It drips. Then the drizzle falls—or is poured sparingly—until finally the malevolent rain returns and as if on a different wavelength intermittently turns to the same invasive reddish hue.

Nothing uncovered is dry in the city this November, and you see red reflections everywhere. The skies over the Adriatic Sea out beyond the beaches of the satellite islands of the Lido and Malamocco rumble and tumble ever closer to St. Mark's Square where I have not yet dared to go but which seems to draw the rain. And I am beginning to feel the familiar and unsettling end times atmosphere hanging over the world. Optimistically I believe that too will pass.

Somehow, the most desolate areas of Cannaregio remind me of Sophie's "abandoned spaces" back in the hamlet near

Rome. This time however it is different. Maybe it means that our life on the run will end here. And after us, time will speed on its way as it did after Galileo who once lived here in Cannaregio, he also a man on the run. My feelings are a mixture of repulsion and disappointment at the signs of surrounding decadence, the same decadence reflected in films shot in Venice—but none that I recall set in big and lonely Cannaregio. For who wants to live here? Not many since Galileo left five centuries ago, although real Venetians still come here and look around curiously in search of the authentic Serenissima that once was—that was before the year-round mass tourism that smothers classic Venice. Though the city's picturesque canals and luxury hotels actually lie within walking distance, it all seems so far away from us: a dream city. At least it does to me. A place you might come to love. The nearby ghetto remains the ghetto and the Ca' Foscari University is the university but Cannaregio as a whole seems like somewhere else in place and time. A water land of marshes and no trees and parks. No benches along grass-lined streets. No sidewalk cafés. Maybe therefore my feeling of physical security here even though I can't explain the real reasons why I feel that way. Sophie insists my optimism is a misplaced mystery. Cannaregio is accessible but as the city's second largest district it is ignored by tourists. Still, in the city where the myth of the opulence of the former Queen of the Seas remains, so also that of the whole of the lagoon city as a place of decay and obsolescence and corruption.

Like Thomas Mann's old Gustave von Aschenbach, enamored of the boy, Tadzio. Aschenbach—portrayed in Visconti's cinematic masterpiece by Dirk Bogarde—dies because of that love.

Or he was a victim of cholera-infested Venice.

Or because of his old age, he too withered in the waning and dying society on which it must have rained in November. Maybe a red rainfall.

That city didn't count anymore. Anything but the Queen of the Seas. An evil, infected city whose magnificent Opera Theater, La Fenice/ the Phoenix, resting on capricious foundations of lagoon water—waters of the stormy Adriatic Sea— for mysterious reasons was a victim of a public burning, a victim of corruption, questionable shipping laws, flimflam in general.

We know the story: In 1996, it burned to the ground. Then in 2004 it arose from its ashes more beautiful than ever before.

Tenacious, these Venetians, miserable and distressed without their Fenice. La Fenice—the last of the great city's once-upon-a-time eleven opera theaters—had already burned down the century before … and was rebuilt. Each new version more beautiful than the destroyed one. For theater lovers, a jewel comparable to the "cursed" Hope diamond or Marie Antoinette's pinky ring with the letters MA in diamonds and a lock of her hair inside. Makes you wonder what is going to happen to it in the end, like what will happen with our hearts.

Diamonds, diamonds, and more diamonds! The symbol of European colonialism. Ever spreading colonialism. Maybe that's the reason the Fenice burned in the first place, not because of negligence but lit by aesthetic madmen forcing the city to react. The former Serenissima, the Queen of the Seas, once had 175,000 people, every one of whom must have been opera lovers—with the exception of an alien handful of anti-lyric opera arsonists hooked on burning down opera houses. Ten-down-one-to-go feelings.

Today the 55,000 population plus the rest of Italy suffice as an audience for one of the world's most beautiful theaters. Now, the waning away of the city, the former city-state, has ceased. The turning point has been reached. A case of time measured in epochs. The great swerve has occurred. So above, so below. I somehow feel that I am leading the way toward renascence—of ourselves, of Sophie and me, of Oriana, Helen and Marcello—as well as of a new city. My wife Sophie thinks I am nuts, blind to the reality of what is happening in our lives.

I take off my cap, throw back my head and let the cold Venice rain shower me. I stand there and I drift. The drops pattering my face remind me of a recent dream of a sandstorm on the way to Samarkand: I had to reach that dream city but the camels wisely refused to plod another sandy step until the storm was over, and I in my dream recited *The Golden Road to Samarkand.* James Elroy Flecher's beautiful words: *How sweet to ride forth at evening from the well. When shadows pass gigantic on the sand.*

No matter the stubborn cowardly camels now full of water. No haste to get to Samarkand. Pronunciation here was the disturbing dream problem. Surely in exquisitely named Samarkand, with ans 'a' as in *ah* conditions the pronunciation of the word sand, which had to be another, to rhyme with that broad 'ah' too. But who says 'sahnd?' So in his English language rhyme scheme Flecker was obligated to think of the ugly 'a' as in sand. Once on the southern shores of the Caspian Sea in Iran looking northwards in search of Samarkand, 'a', 'a', 'a', I stumbled over the poem's word, 'sand'. I gave up. Struggle was useless. That “a” was greater than my aesthetic. I pronounced it with the same distaste as the poet Flecker had to: *the sands of Samarkand.*

The broad ‘a’ was impossible in sand.

No matter.

Nor what does it matter if over on St. Mark’s Square they are preparing the elevated boardwalks that would soon crisscross the piazza so artistically? Venetians know. They know the great rains are beginning … and together with the rains, the high waters from the Adriatic. Lines are forming at stores selling green knee-high rubber boots. St. Mark’s, the huge square people dream about. Where reality lives up to childhood dreams and imagination. The first glimpse of St. Mark’s Square does that to you, more than fulfilling your expectations. But today the city’s one hundred twentieth Doge is likely testing the MOSE flood barriers now underwater out in the lagoon to block the high water. It helps, I read. But it’s not enough to stop the high tide, scientists claim caused by the same Saharan winds that brings red rain to Italy. Man-made objects are no match for the power of nature’s rains and the high water. Venetians knew in advance that the rain was coming but nobody knows when it will stop. Some pessimistic forecasters predict that this time it is coming to stay. To stay? For how long will it rain? Forty days? Or can it really rain forever?

Everything ends. That’s what we’d thought back in the hamlet. It has rained a long, long time, they said. Summer is truly over. And in *The Crow*, the song goes: *It won't rain all the time/ The sky won't fall forever.*

And God said of the rain: “I will remember my covenant between me and all living creatures of every kind. Never again will the waters become a flood to destroy all life. Whenever the rainbow appears in the clouds, I will see it and remember the everlasting covenant between God and all living creatures of every kind on the earth."

But there is a rainbow-less period of indeterminate length during which evil runs rampant in Venice: when the rain turns to blood and when it seems it will never stop, and man commits all manner of evils like happened at Academia one night. A shoot-out and three bodies lay side by side on the banks of the canal … victims of a bloody massacre.

But in the city of Venice, every thing seems unknowable. Everyone mysterious, impossible to comprehend. *Calles* and *rios* but there's no real waterfront. Here, lagoon waters threaten to overflow the little piece of *lungomare*. Few streets. Many canals. Canals instead of paved streets. Optimists sing that Venice is greater than the waters, everlasting, like in the lands behind the First Emperor, Shih Huang Ti's great stone wall—*He, whose long wall the wand'ring Tartar bounds*—with its towers reaching for the skies like the Serenissima's *campanile*. Shih, who burned all the books before him, an attempt to abolish the past—even all memory of the past—terrifies me; yet that one man alone undertook all that was magnificently god-like. Yet time promised him nothing; healed nothing.And now the churches of the city on water dedicated to their dead god serve as museums to preserve every sign of the magnificence that once was, is, and will be until the day the city and its great *campos* and bridges and it water-barrier MOSE are covered by the raging unstoppable high waters of the great raging sea, it too turning red.

Cannaregio seems far away from dreamy Venezia. Under such a rain Cannaregio becomes a separate entity from the rest. It rains. It rains heavily, monotonously from a deep, leaden sky that you know has never been really blue since the creation. Its name refers to the great expanses of wetland reeds, the watery fields of cane of this area long before it was populated. A waterscape of tall, slender grasses fed by the waters of the great lagoon. A *canneto* is where cane grows: *canna>canneto*>Cannaregio. But the former cane fields have little relation to what the Queen of the Seas once was. Former wetland Cannaregio is distant from the great luxury hotels, the Daniele and the Gritti Palace. Distant from the tourist-infested Caffé Florian and Harry's Bar where Hemingway worked on his novel *Over The River And Into The Trees* at his corner table and journalists fought to get into Harry's and see the man rumored to be first in line for the Nobel Prize. Far from the great palaces lining the Canal Grande. The Lido island facing the great sea where foreign submarines maneuver and the renowned Venice International Film Festival comes each September is another world. To me, the Lido across the lagoon seems like overseas. My new world is desolate and secure at the same time, menaced by the red rain. Locked between the ghetto and the Santa Lucia train station we lead a watery life in Cannaregio, to the ceaseless rhythm of the cascading rain. That unpleasant undercurrent of blood-streaked rain striking any exposed surface gradually vanishes and you lose consciousness of the sound of rain until you hear nothing but the one compound sound: the rainfall. What was once so pleasant has become evil. It is the malevolent madness of the times.

The story unraveling in and around me is not a tourist story; it is a story of survival. I tell you that sadly. And that's the mystique of this city floating on flimsy islands scattered across the deep and agitated waters in an inlet which is the great lagoon of the Adriatic Sea—beyond which to the east lie solid Slavic lands. It's not the mystery children feel in haunted places or of UFOs and aliens and angels and jinn or of people who are not who they seem; it is a mysterious mystery that people like myself try to comprehend while I know that people who were born here on the island city and who grew up on its canals, rios and calles comprehend. The mystery is in them, inherent in being Venetian, which they in their historical disillusionment perceive as cold, cruel reality.

I stood on the corner of our canyon-like street, Calle di Solferino. It was mid-morning. The red flakes of sand insinuated in the crevices between the cobblestones supported my suspicion that the winter drizzle would continue until spring. The street was quiet and sad. No people. No cars. It contained only shadows, today, dark reddish rain and cold stone. I nodded to a frail-looking old man sitting on a straight chair protected from the rain under a slanting roof. Overhead a neon sign blinked on and off. He'd been watching me again … as he did yesterday. This time I spoke up. I asked him if he believed it was going to rain forever.

He did.

He said he sat here on the corner to see it. To feel it lasting.

"To escape," he said clearly.

I stopped dead and began examining him. A strange word to describe coming downstairs to sit on a straight chair and watch the evil rain and a blinking neon sign. He was wearing a black cap with a long bill, *PIRATES* written across the front. He had a cavernous, lopsided face partially covered with a gray beard, one cheekbone more prominent than the other, a long nose, small, deep-set eyes, one blue the other colorless, the thin shoulders, bony chest and stick legs in the empty baggy pants of the aged. I was perplexed by his eyes, the colorless one of which seemed fixed on me.

"To escape?"

"Not really escape. I don't walk well so this is as close to movement I'll ever get. You have to do something to change the humdrum of life upstairs. Create a counter rhythm."

"The mysterious counter rhythm," I muttered.

He looked at me with a puzzled expression, rapidly opening and closing his right eye.

"Yes," he said, but poetically..

"People don't realize the things others do in their private lives," he said. "Repeating the same personal actions every moment. Taking dozens of medicines, slowly, slowly washing and dressing. Why, I'm wearing fifteen different pieces of clothing, four just to cover my feet. Makes me wish I were like Louis XIV with valets to dress me. Takes me half an hour to dress to come down here to sit in the rain and hope to see someone I used to know. Now I've seen *you* ... tall above me. Something new in my life ... my life of memories. "

"How old are you, if I may ask?"

"Old."

"Ancient?"

"I'm one hundred and two …or soon will be."

"Your birthday coming up! One hundred and two! Incredible!"

"I barely remember birthdays or my age … the weeks and months and years fly by and there's no one to remind me of my unimportant birthday. But on the other hand so much goes on in my mind. This morning I looked at the person in the bathroom mirror looking out at me that did everything I did, pretending to be me. I blinked. He blinked in the same way. We both have glaucoma, I in the right eye, he in the left. The old man there in the mirror was a stranger. Arrogant and obnoxious. I refused to have anything to do with him … even after I saw faint familiar signs of recognition of someone I once knew.

"But that's neither here nor there. That's the present. In my heart I look backwards like that Swiss painter's angel. I recall how after the Habsburg era the same aura hung on long after they were gone. But what a wonderful time that was though! Tough time too. But splendid. And we Venetians literally again sailed the seven seas. We also passed on to the Empire ancient Venetian qualities: things like the art of the lie and the art of bribery as a means to thwart the bureaucracy—we showed the Austrian officialdom that intelligence could accomplish many things but that everything could be accomplished with money."

No one to remind him! I felt a shiver run down my spine—the sensation of time struggling to move ahead, ahistorically drawn by the past.

One hundred and two years and there he was right in front of me, sitting alone and chasing memories and feeling a sort of essential vulnerability while waiting for something to happen. Maybe he sometimes would just like to close his eyes and let life go. That man was a poet, I knew.

"Then, *auguroni* for a happy birthday," I muttered weakly.

"The only one who remembers. And I hope you're not being ironic. So *mille grazie!*"

"I saw you here yesterday too. We seem to be neighbors. My name is Stuart."

"Stuart?" he said, blinking his right eye.

"Third generation Scottish-Italian …and a Roman too."

"People have always called me Gulliver because I once was a big man like the giant Gulliver in literature. Physically! Before I shrunk. But never as tall as you up there in the stratosphere. But I was never big professionally either. I was, that is, I am a writer. Some Venetians once knew me and read the writer I was but they're all dead now. So I'm alone … except for my housekeeper and my memories."

"Well, Signor Gulliver as soon as I get settled here I hope we can sit together and talk about your memories. I too am a writer by the way and I would like to hear your ideas about what's going on."

"What's going on? In the world you mean? I don't generalize—or try not to—but I can speak of what has occurred here. This vibrant city has always been beautiful. They say it still is. I can't confirm it or deny it because all I see is the corner of Calle di Solferino. Sometimes I like to sit here on the corner, close my good eye and view things through the tunnel vision of my right eye: you can't imagine the difference when you zero in one object down at the end the tunnel. It's like seeing the world through binoculars. I don't even see all the others rooted in a home on some private island or the other, their windows closed and blinds lowered. I don't go to St. Mark's anymore either because in such places I turn into a ghost; I don't know anybody and people simply look straight through me. No, I don't go to such places anymore. My housekeeper, a lady of about fifty years, keeps me abreast of what she sees; she says the Rialto market is still ours, but that tourist-occupied St. Mark's Square is an alien shithole … as she expresses it in her colorful language. The city once had a mission: its ships sailed the seas and brought to Europe the riches and the beauty and some of the knowledge from exotic faraway places. Our city was a gateway to this continent. Most certainly the city was richer then ... and people read books and painted pictures and built museums and palazzos. And the word tourism hadn't entered our vocabulary. It didn't yet exist. Oh, some very rich people—the early jet set, visited *in* places like Kabul or the Taj Mahal or Shanghai. But not the masses. They didn't tour; they died without seeing Piazza an Marco. Now they all come in those massive cruise behemoths and dock right at St. Mark's Square raising the water level in the whole city."

Gulliver has offered me a gateway to this astounding city but for now what I really wanted to know from him was if it was worth the candle to live to the age when you are alone, when everyone you once knew is gone and you are condemned to live like an alien with another species who do not see the real you ... only a wavering, floating outline of you and you depend on a housekeeper to see slices of reality for you. The age when you might stop and wonder if you are really you and what you're doing here.

I would never ask him such things but I suspect he will tell me anyway.

"You must live in that fourth building down the street, abandoned since the years when Venice had degenerated and was only the ghost of itself ... like me today. Anyway Stuart, talk like this is an echo from the distant past to my old ears."

Distant past! I should say so. The survivor remembers the aura of the Habsburg domination of the Queen of the Seas while my memories of the hamlet near Rome and the underground biolab and the cypresses and the Ho Chi Minh Trail in Fiesole of only months ago are already fading. I need to speak with Gulliver as much as he desires to speak with anyone besides his housekeeper.

2

November 5

Marcello, Helen and Oriana arrived in the dead of night. I met them at the Santa Lucia Station with rented trolleys to carry their stuff to Calle di Solferino. Even in the dark and the pouring rain, they loved the complex of apartments at first sight. The five-story building was narrow and deep, the apartments big and sprawling, identical tall and wide windows on each floor. Small shops lined the dark and narrow cobblestoned calle, all alike with their shutters down. A trattoria in the middle of the block was named *da Manin*. Our house was just opposite it. Sophie and I occupied the first- floor. Oriana had the second and Marcello and Helen the third, the rear room of which had abundant natural light which created a perfect studio for her painting. How I wish you were here!

There's a certain charm in living in a historically named street that bestows on you the sense of being a small part of the phenomenon of destiny, that force that I think controls what happens in the future despite people's efforts to change it and despite Gulliver's predilection for the past. There's a poet in that man. Maybe in every man.

Solferin, Solferino, Calle di Solferino, the Battle of Solferino. An historical battle took place on the fields of Lombardy in North Italy near a place named Solferino. A battle by chance fought between the Austrian army and a Franco-Piedmontese army headed by Napoleon III. An act of destiny, that battle. Blood flowed in the battle that neither side could avoid: a total of 30,000 men were killed or wounded in a battle that should never have taken place and the fields of Solferino were soaked in blood. Yet at the same time it was a decisive step in the struggle for the unification of Italy. Napoleon III sought a truce with a nearly defeated Austria. The state of Lombardy—a most important region of Italy today—was annexed to a surging united Italy, the International Red Cross was founded and the Geneva Conventions were signed.

Red Cross. Red for the blood spilled that day of destiny and an historical shade of red—the color of the blood on the fields of Solferino. The color of the rain falling on Venice.

Escape from Florence-Fiesole was more difficult for the late arrivers than it was for Sophie and me. Marcello abandoned dangerous positions but death was still on his trail. Marcello was a cop. He rejected coincidence and believed there existed only the hidden hand of fate. Perhaps that was the reason serendipity remained foreign to him and therefore to Helen. He shot his enemy in Florence but despite the hate he felt for the man, he didn't shoot to kill but to punish … while he was to come to believe that there was nothing crueler than destiny which, he believed, de Tanzi would have to reckon with. Detective Leone de Tanzi was released from the hospital two days after Marcello shot him. Even though he'd wanted De Tanzi to die, Marcello drove him to a hospital and instead of taking the bastard's life, he saved it. When he became the new Chief of Detectives of the Florence Police Department, Marcello Bolzoni went to visit the former torturer at his home. He stepped into a hallucination: de Tanzi had been a rogue among a league of vicious rogues, cops and Freemasons. Marcello found his nude body tied to a straight chair sitting in a pool of darkening blood. He had been razor sliced until the torturers tired. Just to finish off the martyred man his throat had been carefully cut literally from ear to ear. His head was left dangling from his trunk. Marcello said de Tanzi's dead blood spilled on the hardwood floor surrounding him emitted the obnoxious stink of non-life where life once was. Chance? Destiny? Thomas Aquinas saw randomness not as the result of a single cause but of multiple causes coming together. But still by chance, Marcello thought, although he long wondered if it was not the same thing. Because of the ferocity of the mutilation Marcello had no doubts that killers of the secret Freemasonic Lodge had carved him. The Lodge was cleaning up *its* police department in order to show who was the real boss in this city on the Arno River. According to Marcello, Freemasons have always had this tendency: control over the institutions of power. And de Tanzi's fate signaled that he and Helen had to get the fuck out of Florence, t*out de suite*. The Acting Police Chief too—the leftist Oriana Alberti—was in no less danger than he and Helen. So, Oriana travelled north with them. The Florentine refugees thus became five.

I was doubly pleased that they decided to join Sophie and me and even though Marcello had taken the heart of the woman both Sophie and I loved, I looked forward to a closer relationship with him. On the other hand it was Marcello's love that also thwarted Helen's vague intention to return to her second home in Vienna and brought her to our new hideout in Venice-Cannaregio. The portents of a new world were there in Calle di Solferino. Nonetheless, I continued to fear the ambivalence of life's idle promises.

November 6

The ex-policeman Marcello had a contact in the Venice police department, the *Questura.* Detective Nicola Trevisan of the investigative division had his own office along track 1 inside the Santa Lucia Station. A loner by nature, Trevisan had the capability to remain unnoticed … practically invisible. He was the observer. The watcher. Medium sized, bearded and sloppily dressed, Trevisan was the eternal undercover man. No need to check his arrest record; he had none. Few people knew him because he never exposed himself. If an arrest was to be made he sent uniformed cops or young detectives who needed to up their arrest records. Trevisan was of the beyond. He studied the detective craft. His profession. The Venice chief of detectives had absolute confidence in him. The *questore* himself loved his style. Mention the name Nicola Trevisan in Venice police circles and mum was the word. Nicola who? Trevisan? There are thousands of Trevisans in the metropolitan area. Literally. Some names are like that. They strike a chord because of their frequency. But he himself thought he didn't need a common name like his to be anonymous.

Sitting in his glass cage office fifty meters down the quai, his rubber booted feet on the desk and wondering what he would do all day, he looked across the station's twenty tracks and mused about how small his country had become since the fast trains, the *Frecciarossa*—the Red Arrow—came into use. Three hours and you're in another world, in Rome or in Turin. He watched the departure of a sleek low-lying Red Arrow and remembered the long hours his father had spent on slow packed trains on the Venice-Turin line during his entire working life at the FIAT Mirafiori auto plant in Turin, coming home on every possible occasion. Fuck fascist FIAT, Trevisan père said to himself each time he thought of Torino. A member of the Communist Party all his life, his father too had kept a low profile. Nicola adored and emulated him; he too was a Communist and he too kept a low profile … in his work, in life in general. Yet he was widely admired by the local and national police forces as much for his style as for his accomplishments against organized crime and the entangled illegalities that infringed on workers' rights. Love for his father conditioned his life. Operating undercover and alone, after twenty months of investigations into the ring that smuggled drugs arriving by ship to Italy from Colombia, he had pinpointed the boss of the Venetian Lagoon organization headquartered in Chioggia, the Little Venice, at the southern extreme of the great lagoon. Shortly afterwards he was assigned to the case of the murder of three sailors across the lagoon at the southern end of the island of Lido at the cargo ship wharfs of Malamocco that became known in Venice police annals as the *Malamocco Slaughter*.

Trevisan reasoned that if the detective sorts out the physical evidence objectively and then think subjectively from the killer's point of view he could solve crimes that baffle others because of their randomness. Like the almost daily occurrences like that of the modest man who comes home from work one day and suddenly picks up a butcher knife and calmly stabs his wife to death and then slips into his children's rooms and strangles both in their beds. After which he calls the police and sits in his easy chair and watches TV until the squad car arrives. When asked why by a puzzled detective, he just shrugs, his eyes glued to the TV quiz show and says, "I just wanted to do this thing." The detective stares. Trevisan thought that if that whole scene could be reduced to one moment, the asymmetry would be so blurry that some quite normal city policeman might shrug in the same removed way and take out his service pistol and shoot the killer to death on the spot.

Trevisan had not yet solved the Malamocco Slaughter but he believed he would someday.

So when Marcello Bolzoni called and asked for help, he imagined that this was a key moment in which his life was about to change. They'd met a couple of times and had understood one another. He was not surprised when he saw Marcello's vaguely familiar figure meandering down the quai peering left and right. He jumped to his feet and pulled him inside his glass-fronted office.

"A good sign. Not even another detective notes my presence in the station. My hideout! My observation point."

"So you're the don't-call me-I'll-call-you kind. "

"Discretion is my secret method."

As they exchanged personal information, Marcello understood that they were still on the same wavelength. They felt trust one in the other. Marcello told Trevisan of their flight from Fiesole and identified their adversary: the reborn secret Freemasonic Lodge in Florence-Arezzo. Marcello believed that the same secret part of the Freemasonic movement must exist here too. He reminded Nicola of the story of the secret Propaganda 2 Masonic Lodge of last century run by the Fascist Licio Gelli.

"It's back, Nicola. Meaner than ever."

"I've heard about it. I heard also that a certain Bolzoni shot another detective because of it."

"Florence Chief of Detectives, Leone De Tanzi, was in cahoots with the reborn secret lodge. Besides, he was a torturer who deserved to die. And the new lodge is even meaner than Gelli's version was. I punished him but I didn't kill him as I'd sworn I would."

"And I thought Venetians were rough!"

"Nicola, forty years ago Gelli had a dream: a pure Fascist Italy … to be headed by him. The new Duce. In secret he gathered a thousand prominent people—the elite of Italy—who shared his dream. But his dream Italy seemed to die with him and the P2 was disbanded. But in reality the dream lived on, half of which has been realized today. Tentacles of his fascist dream had already reached the core of the state. But today we've got a fascist government in Rome. Elements within the Fascist Party governing Italy are intent on implementing Gelli's programs for grassroots control of all Italians. They've taken over state TV, much of public transportation and right here in your city control of the Venice Film Festival. And they've sent armed troops back to the streets of our cities. Fascist salutes galore in their mass demonstrations. And now Gelli's program is that of the reborn Masonic Lodge in Florence and Arezzo that killed my friend—the anti-fascist Dante expert—Pierluigi Da Molino. Now they want to kill me and some of my friends who migrated north with me. And so we're now hiding out here in Cannaregio ... exiles in our own country,"

"What a story, man. Sounds like you people have things under control."

"I need help. We need a private security force in our neighborhood of the triangle of the ghetto, Ca' Foscari and Santa Lucia. We need twenty-four hour security for our three apartments and for us personally. We need also an all-Cannaregio security force, a secret anti-fascist network that I hope will eventually cover the whole city. For which I need also the collaboration of Venetian leftists … your kind of people, Nicola."

3

November 7

Oriana felt little sense of displacement in her new life in Cannaregio, little more than when she had accepted her appointment as Deputy Police Chief in Florence. She had felt the move to Florence refreshing after a drawn-out divorce. Even though she had no experience in police work as such she was not intimidated by the title since hers was to be a purely administrative assignment. In any case she had confidence in her ability to adjust to new challenges; she could handle it. Had she not shown that quality during her five years as Director of the School for Foreigners in Perugia? Moreover her work there was connected with national security in which cooperation with police and intelligence agents was part of her daily life. Like the intelligence agencies, she was aware that foreign governments sent future secret agents to Perugia ostensibly to learn Italian but which in effect was the perfect cover for agents engaged in the most nefarious activities. Intrigue and undercover work became familiar to her. Because of Ukrainian students at Ca' Foscari University in Venice where she'd enrolled in philosophy courses, she realized that the high number of Ukrainians enrolled in the language program in the Perugia University For Foreigners had not particularly surprised anyone back then—it was merely a statistic. Today that statistic was meaningful. The pro-Ukraine lobby was strong in the fascist party running the country: Italian military weapons to Ukraine—howitzers and cannons—and special dispensations for Ukrainian refugees were no surprise. Oriana was convinced that if AISI—Intelligence Agency and Internal Security, Italy's FBI—had conducted real security vetting of the foreign students, they would have been astonished at the true identity of the recipients of long-term residence permits . Although some of those foreigners came to stay, their loyalties lay elsewhere. Now she was on the run with the others—guilty because she was not of the fascist party that appointed her, guilty by association—although here in exile she in reality had never felt so free. Anyway, people had always said she was too pretty and sexy to be a fascist. Sleek Oriana! I thought of her. Sexy Oriana.

"You're beautiful," the Florence detective Giacomo had insisted.

Though she laughed off such compliments, in her heart she knew that her good looks—and her demanding body—had made her life journey more complex than others realized.

"I know I'm not beautiful", she said when anyone spoke of her beauty. "But I am sexy."

She studied herself—perhaps more than she should—and sometimes she thought she understood. When she read the thoughts of Schopenhauer, she returned to his ideas on our illusions about how things actually are. The world appears to us as something it is not. Life is for suffering: *"The life of an individual is a constant struggle, and not merely a metaphorical one against want or boredom, but also an actual struggle against other people. He discovers adversaries everywhere, lives in continual conflict and dies with sword in hand."* She applied Schopenhauer's pessimism to herself. 'Our erroneous perception of things!' she thought. The golden wrapping for the gift must be removed with consummate care, folded neatly and put away for other times and forgotten. She found that the appearance of the container creates illusions about the possible content. Yet she balked when her thought master insisted that human beings are doomed to the illusion of the good and rich life—forever and ever—an illusion as real as life itself … and she suspected Schopenhauer meant also death. She liked Jorge Luis Borges because he went so far as to thank the German philosopher for "having deciphered the universe" which seemed to her simply his form of Latin cynicism. Be that as it may, she knew that her existential problems were conditioned first by her womanhood and secondly by her great secret. She rejected Chekhov's belief that secrets often fester and die, only to live on in repressed lives. That was not her case. She was not repressed, but she suffered anyway—so Chekhov was half right, she conceded. All her life she had tried to do the right thing about her secret son. But thus far she had felt one impediment after the other to the realization of her true nature because of that unresolved, most likely unresolvable dilemma. Aristotle, she thought, would have emphasized the necessity of unlocking her secret so that she could define who she really was and enable her to be able to live a more meaningful life. But that agonizing, tormenting secret blocked her every venture into herself. No one knew the confusion running rampant inside her. Not one other person in the world. No wonder she felt lonesome! Yet her body and her life did not permit her to retreat and become a hermit either. For there were those physical needs … gigantic at times! Her unfulfilled womanhood.

But above all there remained the huge issue of her secret son to contend with. Her biological son who was not her son. Though he came from her womb, he had never been her son. Her son's very existence was secret. Given away for adoption at birth when she was nineteen when she had made the unholy compromise that she now recognized had conditioned her life:

she'd bowed to the demands of her bourgeois parents terrified of the opinions of people on the hill of Perugia.

Now she knew where her son was. She knew who he had become. He was eighteen, no longer a minor. He was Dutch. His name was Mark, Mark Koning. He lived in Amsterdam, Surinameplein, 12. She had been there. She had seen him from a safe distance. Now that he was legally an adult she could go back there and introduce herself. A mother knocking on her secret son's door! A stranger! She couldn't face it. But she knew she had to go again soon … or never more. To go or not to go was the dilemma. She was always wondering if her having searched for him her lifelong was not sufficient penance for a mother's redemption. Would that reality not stimulate in him a positive reaction to the woman identified as his mother?

Mark knew he was adopted as a baby.

He knew his biological mother was Italian.

He knew he was born in Perugia, Italy.

This stranger at his door was from Perugia.

He resembled her: dark hair and eyes, slender body.

Oriana tried to imagine his perplexity. If he accepted that she was truly his mother what effect would it have on his life? Oriana asked herself that question every day. One day she believed he had a right to know her. The next day she thought his knowing her personally would create a tempest in the calm of his life; it was too late, too late for her to become his mother. That conclusion was the bane of her life. The Marco Polo Airport was a short taxi ride away from Cannaregio, the Amsterdam Airport was only eight kilometers from Mark's home, she could go and return the same day. When and if she went to Surinameplein again! But she couldn't decide. Not yet. Someday, she thought.

No, not yet. The pitiful image of a lonely woman alone on the doorstep of a son who was not her son was not the way to sway an eighteen-year old Dutchman to accept a long-lost mother. Yet she knew that if she procrastinated much longer, circumstances would decide for her and her secret son would vanish entirely from her life like the lost city of Atlantis.

"Mark!" she exclaimed confusedly as she pondered her situation when the front door of her apartment in Calle di Solferino in Cannaregio-Venice suddenly crashed open. "*Ma, ma..* . Giacomo, Giacomo!" She threw herself against him. Before he could take off his coat, she was pulling at his clothes.

His surprise passed quickly. He understood. He had always understood. From the moment he had stepped into her office that day in the Florence *Questura*, he had seen and understood her needs, her pressing desires, maybe even her secret, too.

4

November 7

I was struck by the thought that the Jewish ghetto reflected the universal nature of the city of Venice itself: a tiny area, a microcosm, representative of a worldwide people, like Venetian sailing ships of yore. But the ghetto was not their place either. A home? There was none. It shouldn't matter, as Erich Auerbach wrote. Moreover, the world's first Jewish ghetto lies in a small desolate area in a bleak corner of the city, separated from the rest by the same canal that separates Cannaregio itself from the whole.

Ghetto, from *geto*, the word for the foundry once located here that built cannons for the Venetian Republic. Crazy, how words go off on their own tangents, picking up the wildest of meanings as time marches past. Etymologically, *geto* was no more than a street or a small town. Nevertheless, for centuries the ghetto inhabited by some half thousand people, chiefly German Jews, were segregated as a danger to "Venetian values and way of life". How I hate that expression: *our way of life*. From the start Venetian Jews were tightly controlled. Many professions forbidden, the ghetto's exit-entry points few, and a curfew was enforced. Although the community is still culturally active, few Jews actually live in the expensive touristy ghetto with its museums, synagogues and restaurants.

"Ironic," I said to the others standing in the middle of great square, "that exit from the ghetto was once tightly controlled, but today's visitors must buy tickets to enter … and then try to imagine what it was like.

You learn that in the Fifth century, some refugees from the declining Roman Empire had fled to safety on the islands spread across today's lagoon, an inlet of the Adriatic Sea. By the Twelfth century the city they created had become a rising power in Europe and the Mediterranean World. A city-state. A colonial power, not a territorial power. A city of sailors and merchants like Marco Polo and Gulliver, a city rich and powerful from trade and commerce: it built great ships that sailed the seven seas and carried enormous wealth to the tiny island city-state.

But why did the Jews come here?

"Ok, some did come before the ghetto. But others? Later? They must have heard about the ghettoization. But they came anyway. A big rich city of 175,000 people was intriguing, mysterious and secretive. So they came in growing numbers. Up to five thousand Jews lived here once, eager to participate in the booming Venetian enterprise ... and enterprise it was. However, some greedy and fearful Venetians got the idea of segregating them. Make their life tough and complex. Reduce competition. Evil brewed in their capitalistic minds.

"So the tense and apprehensive Doge-In-Chief found an empty corner in the former cane fields, in the marshes—today's Cannaregio—and built a 'nice' home for their Jews … and locked them in it."

As always happens in empires, underneath the wealth of the Venetian Republic flowed currents of fear and paranoia. This tiny, fragile, so-called empire physically based on its one hundred little islands was plagued by water, dirty rains, mist, fogs and winds sweeping over it in waves from the great sea on which an empire thrived. Small and rich, and fearful of losing what they had.

"Still," I said, "the ghetto never became a Jewish construct like in Palestine. Now that it's over—over for the Jews of Venice but not for the have-not Palestinians of the world—we see the elegant rubble and remains of the Jewish enclave in Venice: five synagogues for the different peoples, the German Jews, Jews from Spain and Portugal, the Ashkenazi and the Sephardi. A Charade community center, a Yeshiva school. Chiefly symbolic stuff. Not a visit to Auschwitz by any means, no reminders of the Holocaust . Bad for tourism."

"In an case, I'm not about to o into one of the museums," Sophie said.

"Actually, it's all one big museum, left here as a reminder to guilty people," I said.

"We're not tourists, Stuart," Helen insisted. "Maybe guilty, but not tourists."

"Right!" I said. "I'm as close as I need to get to the story I already know. I recently read an interview with Gilad Aztmon, a Jew from Tel Aviv, now a resident of London, who compares the Jewish ideology to that of the Nazis and describes Israel's policy toward the Palestinians as genocide. He said to the interviewer, Theo Panayides: 'I don't write about politics, I write about ethics. I write about identity. I write a lot about the Jewish question because I was born in the Jew-land, and my whole process in maturing into an adult was involved with the realisation that my people are living on stolen land.' Atzmon said that his experience in the military of his people destroying other people left a big scar and led to his delusion with Zionism. He is NOT anti-Semitic but he condemns Zionism as a supremacist, racist tendency.

"He writes: 'History is commonly regarded as an attempt to produce a structured account of the past. It proclaims to tell what really happened, but in most cases it fails to do that. Instead, it is set to conceal our shame, to hide those various elements, events, incidents and occurrences in our past which we cannot cope with. History, therefore, can be regarded as a system of concealment. Accordingly, the role of the true historian is similar to that of the psychoanalyst: both aim to unveil the repressed. For the psychoanalyst, it is the unconscious mind. For the historian, it is our collective shame.'

"Well, that's Aztmon, the anti-Zionist. But Benjamin Netanyahu is still there. And now, friends, we can lunch in the restaurant here on the Cannaregio Canal and leave the ghetto to the tourists … and memory. But wait! Speaking of shame one important thing I forgot to mention is Walter Benjamin's essay on Kafka in which he affirms that shame is Kafka's strongest gesture: 'It has a dual aspect, however. Shame is an intimate reaction, but at the same time it has social pretensions. Shame is not only shame in the presence of others, but can also be the shame one feels for them.'

"That said, I confess my own tendency to fictionalize my life and at the same time personalize my fiction. The temptation to fictionalize one's own life is always a power to be reckoned with, especially when you suddenly find yourself looking backwards and what you think you see is exaggeration or lie, that is, fiction ... and by definition unfinished. Nonetheless, the attempt to be honest with ourselves is a good exercise; after all we pay psychiatrists in an attempt to see our true selves. But there's no fiction here. No place for it."

The Ghetto. Main piazza … or campo. Dreamy Oriana and Giacomo arrived. The drizzle had declined to a mist through which an early winter sun occasionally peeked turning the red hues around the cobblestones to blood red. A moment of quasi peace—if not for the awareness that the place where we were standing in momentary confusion had known terror during the Fascist-Nazi era when all the ghetto Jews were deported and few returned. And today it was again marked by blood.

Still too early for lunch, we sat on the covered terrace of a restaurant on the Cannaregio canal to watch the water traffic headed toward the north Lagoon and the satellite islands of Torcello and Murano and Burano. In the drizzle I caught momentary, maybe unreal reddish reflections that not everyone sees—maybe you have to be looking for them. The drizzle was becoming red rain.

The terrace café was deserted except for one lone man bent over a table, writing. I did a double take when I saw it was Gulliver. He raised his head and waved at us. Small world! A few steps from our new home, we step onto the trail of history into the remains of an ancient society and out of the mist of history appears a one hundred and two-year old writer and part of that history. Proves the adage that there is a poet in every man.

We took a table several meters distance from Gulliver, who couldn't keep his eyes off of us. And why not? Who could blame him? Three beautiful women in one place a few tables way from him. When later I joined him, Gulliver's first words were an apology for staring.

"In my long years I've never seen anything like it: three stunning women at one table and I can only think that if I were only at least thirty years younger! Only thirty years … but also the length of one of history's longest wars. You can see that I'm still awake to beauty, but living history dominates my thoughts. And what thoughts for an old man like me!"

“Understandable,” I said. “They’re my close friends and I’m still not used to their beauty. Ah, Gulliver! Women! What kind of history would it be without them?”

“Most of such women-related things are over and done with in my life. But then writing is a substitute … helps me to forget how it once was … when I was young.”

“Positive pessimism or negative optimism! Hard to know how to react to them,” I said, nodding my head toward Helen. “I once wrote an ode to ugly people. I had just visited Caravaggio in Rome's Santa Maria del Popolo church. The interior of this holy site was slashed by rays of sunshine that day, the beauty stunning. Beautiful because of its unique art—paintings, sculptures, moldings, friezes and cornices and rose-windows creating the diffused chiaroscuro play that drives the most cynical agnostics to contemplation. I found it strange that even in the corners of permanent semi-darkness beauty reigned, a beauty completed by the ugliness of the realities its magnificent art contains: the union of both the beautiful and the ugly necessary for the creation of perfection since ugliness is an intrinsic part of beauty—the necessary scars of beauty—like a facial fencing scar on the most handsome face, like the flaws so necessary in real people, of which the writer Czeslaw Milosc once wrote. I recall reading such words also by Giordano Bruno and Charles Baudelaire-influenced critics that ‘the role of art is to subdue ugliness. A subjugation which is bound to appear somewhere in the masterpiece.’ I meant it as a defense of physically ugly humans, that there should be a place where there is no ugliness or beauty … or rather that there should be a quality in humans that appreciates ugliness in the same way as beauty. Like a Persian poet sang, ‘Where everybody’s as pretty as the moon.’ That we should change our perspective. However a brief look around you on a most ordinary day in our contemporary world of gas stations, bill boards, fast food joints, more gas-guzzling automobiles than people and big enough to live in which many people do confirms that ugly vulgarity is winning, a concealed reality to which the humans that the vulgarity affects seem blind and untouched. My beautiful wife read it and said , 'Darling, you're a dreamer.' I still don't know what she meant, but I think she was insisting on the unjust difference between beauty and ugliness. I instead maintain that if there is—as it seems there is—a fixed totality of beauty and ugliness to be distributed, then there should be both unnoticeably less ugliness—a new quality of ugliness, not to be denigrated—and slightly less beauty … that the two should commingle into one. That transformation is what the beautiful red-headed artist, Helen, paints."

""Oh, so she's a painter too. Extraordinary!"

"Why do you say that?"

"I don't know, but you just don't expect that from a woman as beautiful as she is. But who knows how the mind of a beautiful woman works?"

"I think I know but I can't express it in words. They have their secrets. Anyway, what are you working on?"

"Well, this. You may know that Faulkner wrote that good fiction is far truer than any kind of journalism. He says the best journalists have always known it. I think a writer like him realized that fiction was only a step from the so-called New Journalism. You know, where the reporter puts himself at the heart of the story and becomes a participant and not a mere detached observer. It's a free story-telling technique that blurs the boundary lines between fiction and non-fiction. More style than precision. More personal experiences and sensations than facts. You know I started writing late in life and I wrote like that … I like to think I was ahead of my times."

"Yes, you were," I said." But what did you do before?"

"I worked in the shipping world … like many good Venetians."

"Shipping! Well, well! The glory of Venice. By the way, does Venice do a lot of transshipments, I mean unloading the goods from one ship into another to complete the delivery to another destination?"

"That's what we did, a major part of my company's work."

"I suppose that's still done?"

"I should say. Maybe not as much as in our heyday, but enough. Today, ships carry a lot of military equipment, cannons and guns, trucks, occasionally even tanks. We get some grain shipments from Ukraine here in Venice. Some of those cargoes are ten percent grain on top and underneath the rest is military stuff. So when you hear of Ukraine's concern about keeping Black Sea ports open—especially Odessa—and cries and laments about the grain shortage in Africa and starving people, you know what they mean."

"So where is the military stuff going?"

"Africa. That's what I hear from people who know, from people whose own ships deliver to Africa often—East and West Africa."

"The final part is the key of course: Where are the arms shipments coming from?"

"From Ukraine!"

"Ukraine exports arms!"

"Yes, and chiefly by sea. Some of it arrives here in sealed container cars attached to trains. But a lot of such stuff—allegedly destined for Ukraine and not intended for commercial transshipment—are flown to a reserved part of Marco Polo Airport directly from the USA. Ghost shipments. No bills of lading. No official sender and real destinations unknown. Unmarked aircraft then fly it straight to Mali or Nigeria or anti-Assad terrorists in Syria. And no, Stuart, I haven't written a word about this. Too dangerous. The transshipment business going on in the Venice hub is still to be investigated. But for shippers it's all cut and dry … business as usual. We just charge the normal fees and ship it out. No questions asked. That's the administrative aspect. But we know little about the real money part."

"What do you mean, Gulliver? The real money part?"

"Like how much a tank costs. Are you a buyer or a seller? Who pays whom and how much and in what currency and how. Black money. Laundered money. But I can tell you that many billions of dollars are being exchanged in those complex and highly secret arrangements. After many centuries of this activity, we Venetians are smart … and careful. One thing is certain: EU and American gifts of arms to Ukraine are not really gifts and can never be what they seem. No military weapons to Mali or Burundi are mere gifts. And every transshipment there is a clear political statement and an economic transaction.

"Tax payers foot the bill for American and European 'gifts' to Ukraine. An Italian howitzer is 'gifted' to Ukraine and the Italian taxpayer pays the producer. Part of the Italian workers' taxes pays the state's Oto Melara Arms Industry … and most likely more than the market price. The USA announces a gift of five billion dollars to Ukraine. That is, five billion in military weapons. Ukraine does not send the weapons to the Russian front but sells the major part of it to Mali or another African country rich from gold, diamonds and other mineral deposits and gladly pays discounted prices to the USA, Europe and Ukraine for weapons to suppress their own peoples or to make war on each other. The USA and European nations are to be repaid partially by Ukraine someday for the weapons already paid for by taxpayers. This is called foreign aid. *La drôle de guerre*! Who in power wants this to end? And if it does end because all the Ukrainian men are dead, then a new war can be invented elsewhere and the deadly game continues."

"US-EU aid to Ukraine, eh?"

"It has always been that way, Stuart. The rich get richer and the poor poorer. Look at Rome. Each new annual budget means new cuts of health benefits. We're headed toward the American model where the government does nothing for its people, as per Gore Vidal—whom I got to know, by the way, during his annual visits to Venice."

"Gore Vidal! I hadn't thought of him much in a long time. A friend of mine interviewed him once in Rome. He was too supercilious, too arrogant for my tastes. But I loved his message."

"Yes, he was interesting and had something to say about everything."

"Something ugly but critical."

"As a rule, yes. I learned a lot from him. Gore liked to go to the islands like Torcello—where Hemingway went too—but he wouldn't go near Harry's Bar ... afraid of the ghost of Hemingway, he said, because of all the bad things he'd said about him. But you must know English-language literature well, being Scottish and knowing the language."

"Yes, pretty well. I read the main Italian writers when I was at the university in Rome. But then my ethnic background entered the scene so that today I read mostly in English and write English for a Glasgow magazine. Never read much of Vidal … but I pretty much agree with him about Hemingway. I had my Hemingway period. Read everything and thought he was great. But it didn't last. I began to see his simplicity as fake. The only Hemingway novel I find readable now is *Farewell To Arms*. Especially unbearable is his Venice stuff. But no matter. He won the Nobel Prize for a reason: his new writing style changed English-language literary writing. And he was courageous at the end when he killed himself—even though probably for the wrong reasons. Not that I'm for or against the idea of suicide but nevertheless I think it's more prevalent than we imagine. There's a tragic irony in that he did it with a shotgun that he killed animals with. You know, I really hated him in Africa when he actually gloated over his kills. That's a chapter of his life he could have omitted."

"Anyway, there's something compelling about him that attracted both men and women," Gulliver said. "Men like himself or men who would like to be like him. And women attracted to his way of life and his he-man image."

"Yes, but though he wrote about love and sex, he never seemed to understand that it was a two-way affair. I don't think he ever wondered. I think that man loved only himself … or the image he had of himself … and all the rest was fakery. I think of him as the opposite of, say, Tolstoy."

"Tolstoy! Well, though I'm not a Tolstoyan, I love him the writer. The pathos and rage he wrote of. The life instinct. And also the death instinct as a constant tension that is always on the verge of splitting apart. And the most torrid relations gone horribly wrong. The changing frame of reference from one passion to the other, and the intermingling of the orderly and the chaotic. Like the young couple so happily in love can't even imagine the day they will offend and hurt each other … and their former relationship ends so completely, as if it had never existed. All that is missing in Hemingway."

"Maybe Hemingway's women felt such emotions," I said. "But we'll never know since he didn't understand his women—but I doubt the idea ever occurred to him. At least, not until the end. Until it was too late for him to feel the emotions accumulated in his subconscious over a lifetime. That was his tragedy. I've never believed that he killed himself because he couldn't write any longer. You can always write more. You can write on your deathbed! But lived life can break you apart. Nobody can protect you from that. He knew he'd made many mistakes, but after his wandering, his solitude back at home in Illinois broke him. Maybe he realized he'd play-acted a life. That he'd never loved anyone except his own image."

"Well, you have to love … and feel. Hopefully he understood that before he pulled the trigger."

While we were talking about Hemingway, I did a double take and saw Helen's eyes fixed on me. Intense but somehow dreamy. What did it mean? Those times of us together were over and past, done, even though not absorbed and certainly not forgotten.

Her look was a beacon. A disturbing beacon.

November 8

It was still early afternoon when I climbed the three flights of deep blue carpeted stairs to her apartment. Contrary to our house security rules we had laid down together, Helen's apartment door was ajar. Warily, I stepped in, apprehensive about the anomalous situation: her what seemed to me an intentional breach of our internal security practice troubled me less than the significance of her stare at me on the restaurant terrace. Purposefully noisy, I called out if anyone was home. No answer. Down the hallway toward her studio I padded, sliding my hands on the white, white walls, and recalling the nights in Rome-San Nicola when she would come to me late and knock just once, lightly. The single, almost melodious rap identified her. Now that time was over. Again, I called. She waited, shifting objects around her studio. From her doorway the first thing I saw was the darkish rain smashing against the windowpanes and the rivulets of reddish water running down the dark shadow of her face reflected in the window. Smudges on the panes suggested the outlines of buildings similar to ours nearby. The sky hung over us like a blanket. Still transfixed in the doorway, apprehensive about what I might see in her eyes. It had taken all those months of intimacy and love to sense the first inklings of who and what Helen really was. At first, baffled, then staggered when I became cognizant of and saw clearly in her eyes the glimmer of her peculiar form of madness, a madness that I thought accounted for her artistic brilliance, as well as her unexpected childish dependence on others and her willingness to step into convoluted inter-personal situations that to most people would seem immoral. Nonetheless, she had the unusual capacity to make such situations seem normal: seamlessly, it seemed, in that same fluid way she had become both Sophie's and my lover. So that Sophie and I were chagrined when what had seemed to us—as to her—our mutual expressions of love ended so abruptly. Within a period of a few hours, our three-way relationship was broken and cast aside like something of minor import. Marcello! Love at first sight. It seemed she'd been waiting for him. Already that same morning, I saw it coming. She fell in love with Marcello in a few hours sitting in a straight chair near the door looming like an escape route: on the same day she left us and moved into his house.

It was one or the other for her, I thought: the denigration of the nature of romantic love … or dementedness!

Those thoughts careening through my mind, I turned to her now, convinced that the intensity of her gaze fixed on me on the restaurant terrace was my sick imagination, that she was concentrated on Gulliver's words about old Venice, that she was daydreaming and in any case unseeing, or that she was lost inside a new painting as was happening more and more frequently. Now the strange glitter in her eyes squashed such conclusions. Her first words were:

"I miss you."

"I miss you, too," I replied automatically.

She said nothing, the same shining in her eyes.

I hesitated, unsure of how to continue. Then: "Helen, you are truly mad."

"Yes, I know madness. It's familiar. It's in me. Do you find it off-putting?"

"Yes. Or somewhat. But how are you? Where are you?"

"I need you so," she said in a low voice.

She was magnificently beautiful, her damp eyes big and deep.

"That's the problem. I need and miss you too," I said.

"Oh, no! But there's more. I also miss Sophie."

"Have you told her?"

"I'm afraid to."

"But you will tell her?"

"I have to tell her something, don't I? But Stuart, it was a totally different matter with her ... with a woman. The tenderness, for example. I miss the sensation of that tenderness, her fingers and her mouth."

"Helen, we're back where we started."

"I knew I should have gone to Vienna. Not Venice,"

"And Marcello?"

"I'm madly in love with him … the reason I'm not in Vienna. But I'm lonely anyway. Lonesome … because you're missing. I feel your absence. I stand at the easel and paint my feelings. I'm trying to paint my loneliness and when I see it in color I want to throw up because the image is you."

"But there is Marcello. You should repeat it over and over too: Marcello, Marcello, Marcello. Maybe you're still confused about the difference between loving someone and being in love. In any case, Helen, you can't have it all!"

"Your idea, after all! Stuart, what can we do?"

"There's no alternative, Helen. We'll plough ahead—as long as possible. Anything to keep you away from Vienna-Grinzing—your nemesis … and you know it. Thank God, you have your art. Let it absorb your dreams like, well …"

In that moment the front door slammed shut. Marcello shouted. I sat down on a chair at a window and hating myself for my duplicity I automatically picked up a book on Gustav Klimt that Helen and I had been reading a few days earlier. I felt cheap.

Marcello came in. He kissed Helen. A deep amorous kiss. Her arms went around his neck and held him to her.

I looked out at the rain and observed the anomalous green of the drops zigzaging down the pane. Strange the way the color of the rain kept changing. Jealousy lived in me. Red turned to green.

"Stuart, you're just the person I need. Your friend Gulliver told me quite a story … some of it documented. If you have time, I can relate it all now. Then I have to see the detective I told you about, Trevisan, over at the Santa Lucia Station. By the way, Stuart, I learned there are over twelve thousand Trevisans in this area. Incredible! I wonder what it means."

"I think it's just the name of people from the Veneto city of Treviso. I guess many migrated here for work in the distant past."

"No matter. Come on into the front room and I'll fill you in on Ukraine and the arms industry. Excuse us, *Amore*."

I followed Marcello and wondered if in his rejection of coincidence he recognized the madness in perfectly sane people like his wife, the great love of my life.

5

"Stuart, you follow the Ukraine war—or whatever it is—more than I do and you told me about your trip there to see those Russian soldiers dying from botox. So you must wonder about the mass of money and military arms the USA and Europe send there. My question is, what happens to all that stuff? Where does it go? With that huge arms flow from the West, why does Ukraine lose the battles, their men die and kids and old men become soldiers? Their economy is in shambles, dead like their soldiers, yet their President and his cohorts get richer and richer. Zelensky has a big villa in Versilia in Italy and, I read, a huge one in Florida. His personal fortune is enormous, $20,000,000 … or much, much more. The Ukrainian army—if it's an army and if it's still Ukrainian which I somehow doubt with the French Foreign Legion arriving.—doesn't seem to get many of the super weapons the USA sends while the Ukrainian economy gets crappier and crappier. So where the fuck does all that foreign aid go? "

"Marcello, don't forget that Ukraine is the most corrupt country in Europe … maybe in the world. So you can be certain that the foreign aid stays in the hands of the Kievan elite—that's for sure. And no, the USA and the EU are not winning the war. Not do they want to. But they don't want to lose either."

"I ask because I stumbled onto detailed information about the involvement of the Ukrainian government and some shadowy US arms dealers in schemes to resell Western weapons on the arms black market. Steven Sahiounie, a journalist based in

Lattakia, Syria spoke with the Foundation to Battle Injustice—a Moscow-based human rights organization—that documents how a Ukrainian-run arms black market sells that stuff. Former Ukrainian Defense Ministry informants identified the NATO weapons the Ukrainians are reselling and revealed to the Foundation the scale and routes of the bloody business. Ukraine has disposed of hundreds of thousands of weapons and military equipment worth tens of billions of dollars. Here are the numbers: the foundation reported that between January 24, 2022 and July 31, 2023 Western countries allocated $254.36 billion to Ukraine, of which $98.74 billion was for military needs. In theory, the Ukrainian Armed Forces has modern anti-tank systems, grenade launchers and small arms produced in NATO countries, but also expensive artillery and missile systems and high-tech reconnaissance equipment. US aid alone between January 2020 and September 2023 consisted of 60,000 Grad rockets, hundreds of howitzers and mortars and ammunition, HIMAR systems, 2000 Humvees, and hundreds of tactical vehicles. Yet, despite the scale of the arms flow to Ukraine from the West, the Kiev authorities regularly claim a shortage of weapons."

"And people wonder why that is!"

"Because they resell the stuff elsewhere. That's why. Mostly in Africa. To terrorists or governments. No matter which."

"Yeah, and the disgusting secret is that neither the US nor EU governments really care. Their taxpayers pay their arms industries like our Oto Melara in La Spezia. The arms industry has no problems with the arrangement. Kickbacks then seal the lips of US and European Union officials who authorize the foreign aid 'gifts' to Ukraine. Its President, oligarchs and Defense Ministry officials are getting richer and richer from the sales of the military hardware they get free. The only ones to pay are Western taxpayers and the people of poor African countries, pieces of whose mineral-rich earth are leased gratis to Western countries enriching their corrupt, luxury-loving leaders. What a bonanza!"

"I should say! Ukraine is running a veritable black market for military weapons. Its arms trafficking dates back to the 1990s, Sahiounie says. But Ukrainian Defense Ministry officials and generals have never had such an extensive military arsenal as today under the Nazi government of TV comedian Wolodymyr Zelensky. The Foundation to Battle Injustice claims that the illegal arms trade grows in direct proportion to the increase in military aid to Ukraine. This is a threat to the worldwide distribution of high-tech modern weapons with which Kiev's arsenals should be overflowing. Many of these weapons end up in those regions of Africa, Asia, the Middle East and Latin America where the political situation is already unstable ... not on the battle front in Ukraine.

"Nigerian President Mohammadu Buhari says he's concerned about the lack of control over the arms supplied to the African continent via Ukraine because of the subsequent distribution to terrorists of IS and Al-Qaeda to inflame the political situation in the Middle East and Africa."

According to the Foundation to Battle Injustice, Ukraine sells on the black--market large amounts of ammunition and artillery shells from the Czech Republic and the US, helmets and body armor of Norwegian, Polish and American manufacture, night vision devices from USA, military first aid kits, and military camouflage. On the DarkNet there are specialized weapons "stores", and in social media anonymous groups sell weapons by the *stash* method: in exchange for payment in bitcoin or other crypto currencies, the seller informs the buyer of the place where the weapons are hidden. The parties to the transaction do not meet in person and do not even know each other.

"Russell Bentley a former war correspondent from Texas who joined the Donbas militia ten years ago confirmed the existence of such ads in an exclusive interview with the head of the Foundation to Battle Injustice, Mira Terada. I read that he has now disappeared.

"Bentley said there are numerous photos on DarkNet showing American weapons, such as the M-16, available for purchase with cryptocurrency. The geography of delivery is different, but the weapons are coming from Ukraine.

"According to Foundation information, the main routes of re-export of Western weapons are sea transportation from the Ukrainian ports of Odessa, Mykolaiv and Izmail. The loading of Western weapons is carried out at night: arms and grain. In other words, Ukraine has implemented the grain deal for the illegal re-export of Western arms, all under the guise of carrying out a humanitarian mission to provide the poorest countries in Africa with vital grain.

"Russell told the Foundation that the grain corridor is the main way they re-export weapons. They want ships to be able to leave Odessa without inspection on the Black Sea. The Ukrainians put 100,000 tons of weapons on a ship and then 50 tons of grain on top of it and claim it is a humanitarian mission. You can be sure that as long as weapons are going to Ukraine, they are diverted around the world for criminals and terrorists."

"Well, Ukraine's desire to keep the port of Odessa open fits into the logic of selling large supplies of weapons on the black market," I said.

"Sahiounie reports that the Foundation's anonymous Ukrainian source claims that Western arms shipments go also to terrorist groups in Somalia and Iraq. The source reported that in this scheme of re-export of weapons to third countries, the territories of Somalia, Iraq and Lebanon serve as transshipment bases, while the territory of Libya is used for the shipment of Western weapons to Mexican and other Latin American drug cartels.

"You realize how small the world has become when Libya just across the straits from Italy ships arms to Mexican drug cartels."

6

February 9

I am one of those people to whom unusual things happen. I settle down in Rome's most exclusive hunting estate-like suburb, and the secret services build near my house a top-secret underground bio lab producing a toxic form of botox used to kill Russians. I join the opposition and they kill two of my friends, and my wife Sophie and I and Helen have to flee. I find a hideout in Fiesole and am soon swept up in events concerning a conspiracy against the state of Italy by an illegal masonic lodge born thirty-five years after the demise of its first iteration, P2. Again, I and the others run for our lives, this time by chance to the marshlands of the island city of Venice on the lagoon waters from the Adriatic Sea. That is, at first I thought this new life came about by chance but in this moment I'm convinced it was written in the cards from the start: Cannaregio was my destiny. But destiny is an unstable phenomenon, unpredictably volatile. Yet it is also true that such moments in life as ours occur and there is no alternative to flight. In some circumstances, flight is the only word with meaning: salvation. And eventually you come to feel that you've been abstracted from your real life, from your real you. As if you were living someone else's life. But the idea survives in you that somewhere your real home and your real life await you. Strangely, time comes to seem shorter than it had when you were younger. And the years before your flight fade quickly from your memory. As if, like a fata morgana, they never happened. And you were always older than you'd believed. This astonishing confluence of events is the heart of my story. My life is changing again. Maybe I now face the change I've been waiting for. The mother of all changes. I scanned my thought piece for the Glasgow magazine I write for, *Time and Space.* I clicked *send.* Then I re-read it. Everything was clearer. Every tiny error looked up at me. I would make more corrections, straighten false innuendos and delete, delete, delete. The editors knew my quirk and by now they too only scan my first submission and wait for the final final.

TURNING POINTS

Turning points are among the most important moments of our lives. They are the interstices, the breaking points—usually stressful—that section your life, making your past resemble a quilted sequence of disjointed film frames. When you look back on your life, across, through and over the turning points and landmarks, when you consider paths taken or not taken and the opportunities lost forever, you see flashes of yourself, first here, then there, one you superimposing itself on the other. For a brief moment you might see yourself victorious and exultant; then in the same instant the image transfigures and transforms into failure and defeat. And you begin to wonder if you are really you. Before a turning point you are one person; after it, another. As one Arab poet wrote: "the future lies within the walls of the past ... therefore the future is also made up of our nostalgias." The latter appeals to me immensely. You are aware that your life changes along the way, but the exact moment the change comes about eludes you, because though you do change and transform you also remain the same you. Still, you want to grasp the precise moments when the key events happen. Those transcendental moments are what you long for. They are your nostalgias. Some of them you would like to relive and try again and do better; others you want to distort or conceal and finally bury. No wonder nostalgia exists! Nostalgia is the longing you will feel all your life for that one specific but indeterminate moment when you became what you are ... that moment when you could have become (and hopefully can still become)a better you. Sometimes you feel condemned to search for that moment in order to experience it again, to feel the elation and the exhilaration of the transformation, or the regret and the wish you had taken another path. From past to future and back to the present: nostalgia. If you only had another chance!

Not only the moment eludes you but also the very catalyst of the change you once underwent.

Why is this so? What happens?

All the unexpected or predictable turns in life, the sudden expressions of something you never suspected, and then all of a sudden that big thing creates a crisis situation.

A turning point.

In retrospect it is quite easy to perceive that for better or worse at some point your life changed in a fundamental way. Though you are most likely the same, you feel you have become another. And if you are lucky, you are another. You have begun a new life, perhaps your real, your authentic life. Yet even after a personal tragedy, when your metamorphosis gets underway, you may go on living in the dark, as if nothing unusual were happening. You are not even conscious that you have shed an old skin and grown another; then, in later life, in a flash of perception, the awareness strikes you like a thunderbolt. You sit up erect, confused, at first disbelieving the clarity before your eyes. Only if you are very lucky, you might point your finger at it and say: "There, there is where it happened." Or: "Then is when it happened. There is where my real life began. My real story began there." For a person's life does not begin at birth or graduation, or at baptism or bar mitzvah. Sometimes it begins at the end, sometimes, perhaps, countless ages before birth, or, as some believe, after physical death. But for most of us real life begins somewhere in the chronological middle of our lived lives.

You are living your life of joy and pain, victories and defeats, successes and failures, satisfactions and depressions, oscillating between hope and ruin, between belief and desperation, subject to an apparent infinity of occurrences and experiences, when it happens—the great event, the landmark—perhaps suddenly it may seem later. Or maybe it happens drop by drop, so progressively and so gradually that when things go awry you hardly notice the alterations in the confusing panorama of life. Let's say your life is going well, everything like clockwork. You win the prizes and awards. The world is yours. Until they—the gods, destiny, the flow of events, you yourself—pull the rug from under you. Sand blows into your motor. How different are goals for fate and human life! You stumble over meaningless obstacles that once you didn't deign with a glance. Successes and failures are no longer the point. Living your life heroically is the point. But you don't realize it.

Somewhere, sometime, somehow, everything has changed. Where along your way did things go wrong? Or transform? Of the past, condemnation or sanitization?

For a long time you can't identify with life's landmarks and signposts. Yet in a life governed by fate, signs are the most we can hope for: a night train to Paris, marriage, the birth of children, death in the abroad.

There are many unbelievable coincidences and extraordinary meetings in life. In the same moment and place can occur those unexpected and chance events, rebirths, metamorphoses, and radical life changes ... or simply meeting a person on the street you dreamed of the night before. I always wonder if such occurrences are coincidence or pattern? Though coincidence does not prove the existence of a connection between the parallel events, I tend to believe there usually is or at least often there is a relationship, if only psychic. (Stuart Stuart)

.

I stand at a first-floor window and watch the unstoppable rain. With the naked eye you can see the steadily rising intensity of the precipitation and its barely perceptible color changes—red to blue and back to blood red—and wonder if others see those colors as I do. Humidity, mist, rain. It started about an hour ago as I watched: the usual November mist transmogrified first into the drizzle, then into ponderous, multi-colored rain. Since our arrival it had been mist, drizzle and occasional cloudbursts. In this moment I see the difference. The patch of sky visible from my position is black. I now wonder if it will go on forever. Gulliver thought it could. A man of ships, the sea and winds and water, he should know.

The underwater MOSE water barriers out in the lagoon rise and form a kind of dam when the Doge presses the button or pulls the lever: but MOSE can't stop the rain. St. Mark's square still floods and people trudge around in knee-high rubber boots and the intricate, crisscross network of elevated boardwalks is again laid out: but that can't stop the rain. The priests and the rabbis lift their arms toward the heavens and the muezzins call the faithful to prayers; they want the rain to end: but their supplications can't stop the rain. They forget that the rain can also be purifying. After the rain, the promise is rebirth. Random, rambling ruminations while rain watching: Watching and hoping for illumination. Clarification of that uncertain something of my life. Of *das geheimnisvolle Ding*. For sequence change. I have the thought that maybe the answer lies within the enigmatic rainfall. It is out there in the rain, real, but the rain reveals nothing. Not even the thing that can reveal life's secrets. Of how to live life. The anarchic rain is simply running amok. As Gramsci said long ago, "the old world is dying and the new one struggles to be born. Now is the time of monsters." Things are burning like the Fenice Opera Theater did. Still, I watch. I think. I'm too young to look only backwards. But I do. I hold onto concrete things. The things of life that offer infinity. I look around me: the old computer I used in Mexico. The photograph of our kitten, Nina, that had vanished and never returned, I feared eaten by starving homeless. A black and white photo of a beggar in the Santa Novella station in Florence. A Dutch-Spanish dictionary. A boom box I took with me on a trek in the Alps with Irena when I was eighteen, an African face mask a friend brought me from Mali, a page of Iranian poetry. "Some of my things vanish," I muse, "but other objects remain. Some things are destined to remain ... so that I can pass them down to my heirs. I hold onto those things, the objects whose destiny, though different from mine, are also me." Yet it is paradoxical that while I crave for the old things of the *normal,* I may submit to a new-normal that could permanently deny me any chance of returning to the old-normal I long for. I conclude that agents outside our control, foreign agents with their own vested interests—politicians, media, businessmen—construct our reality, much as a film-maker makes a movie or a writer constructs a book or as an artist designs an engraving. They guide our gaze in certain directions and not in others. What we think of as "the real world", the "normal" world, is almost entirely manufactured for us. A look at what it did to me suffices. Clearly our attention is the plaything of others. That "real world" as it is presented to us is merely a set of political, economic and social priorities that have been devised for us. But if you write a book or a song or paint a picture—creating something from nothing—you are you, no longer of them. And you can freely ask where it all comes from. Like my Mexican shaman said, it's a thing from the *mas allà.* The beyond. Beyond dreams. Beyond our very human nature, dreamers and killers alike. That which is beyond what words can express, beyond expression and thought. *Mas allà* is a kind of nothingness. A shadow. It dangles before us like a temptress, just out of our reach. It can free you of human limitations. The shaman said the intangible nothingness we reach for is the ultimate intoxication of our life of dream. Beyond all that in our search for our real self and fearful of what we may find there in the beyond.

Watching the rain. Rain, rain, rain.

Cognizant of the brutal reality that you need strength of character to live life, the outcome of which may be already determined by destiny—but if so, why this thing we speak of at times so lovingly: free will? When Marcello the cop repeats that he does not believe in coincidences—though he acknowledges the possibility of destiny—I feel the shakiness of my position—like searching for a foothold in the tenuous cane marshes of Cannaregio where no olive trees grow.

No olive trees with their roots fixed in the depths of solid earth: trustworthy, reliable, dependable Marcello, olive tree solid.

On the other hand I am like the wetlands—rootless, searching, inquisitive, watching and waiting and hoping for the unknown which however seems limitless and ungraspable.

Marcello knows the meaning of limits. I saw that quality in him in Florence when Sophie's disappearance swept him into the Freemasony affair. It was destiny that brought us all together.

But then how to explain Marcello's doubts? Though he admits the possibility of destiny, he flatly refuses to discuss probability as a philosophy. Maybe he is right, for no one understands for sure what probability means; mathematicians and statisticians have complex theories but they really do not know. Thomas Aquinas saw randomness not as the result of a single cause, but of several causes coming together by chance. Like the two Greek servants whose masters send them for a bucket of water—unbeknownst to both—who meet each other on their way back, each with a full water bucket and find it a strange coincidence that each of their steps occurred simultaneously—all by chance. Some people consider probability merely a hunch, an expression of something that might or might not happen. That's

Marcello, the cop. For him probability is nothing more than an estimate. The estimated measure of the *possibility* that an event will occur is thus more scientific. You see it in police films, the decisive "possibility" that fingerprints or DNA match can clinch a death sentence handed down by prosecutor and jury. Then there is the mathematician Claude Shannon, the so-called father of cybernetics, who developed an equation to calculate coincidence and chance predicting the unpredictable, theories emerging from his Mathematical Theory of Communication. Imagine! Pure chance reduced to predictability. Stuff you could use to make safe bets on horse races, football games or boxing matches.

But back on the solid ground and without the use of mathematical equations, since *apparent* impossibilities sometimes really do occur, the safest approach is to distinguish probability from what is possible and what is plausible, without forgetting the terrifying consequences if the improbable does happen. Because a thing is possible does not mean it is necessarily probable; yet in the example of a US nuclear attack on any one of its targets today we have the following factors to deal with: American possession of—in the words of the US President—the best military in the world, a huge nuclear stockpile and the possibility-capacity to deliver a nuclear bomb wherever he desires—combined with the unknown X factor of the nature of man and his propensity to harm others and himself. So what seems improbable to many people because of its very enormity—e.g. nuking the ancient country of Iran—is possible. No wonder Hedayat the poet wrote "*My heart has gone crazy* ..." Or even more remote, I recall the 'butterfly effect' plaguing the already precarious predictions of weather forecasters: the smallest variation in the universe, a sudden red sandstorm in an African desert or, in this case, the flap of the tiny wings of a butterfly in Brazil sets off an insane wind that crosses the Atlantic, cuts through North Africa and the Mediterranean Sea, lifts fragile house roofs in Calabria and blows away the clouds over Venice-Cannaregio; the rain that was predicted to go on and on, perhaps forever, instead stops and the MOSE water barriers return to their underwater home in the lagoon.

As for Marcello—the ex-cop who rejects coincidence—he admits that improbabilities occur more often than we think, like the case of the two voyeuristic killers in Florence who sneaked around the Florentine hills in the night, peeping in cars parked in secluded places, killed couples and excised female sexual organs.

Fifteen times they did it.

Just for kicks?

For their collection of female body parts hidden away in a cellar room?

They were on a roll and couldn't stop?

Or like the madman who explained that he killed his wife and children "because I just felt like doing it.'

"Man," Marcello comments, "has always had that unpredictable evil stain."

"…and he can't distinguish between what is real and natural and what is artefact."

Therefore, our uncertain future: cybercrimes of gigantic proportions, disastrous floods, financial market collapse, or devastation by a terrorist nuclear attack must be considered as distinct possibilities, in fact, in the long run, at one time or another, probable.

For now, there's the rain. And rain—as many persons will attest—is philosophical. Rain is cold reality … the illusive reality writers search for. In this very moment it is beating against my windows. Not just a possibility. Or a probability. The Saharan blood rain too comes and goes, real and unstoppable. After its shaky start earlier—mist and then drizzle—it has become a heavy rain, methodical and monotonous, falling with a measured intensity. That black patch of sky overhead has never been blue. Optimistic weathercasters emphasize that heavy rains are the norm after the middle of August; the more prudent now venture that prospects look brighter for next week. I doubt that anyone really knows. Yet that random butterfly in Brazil may flap its wings once more, more vigorously this time.

Meanwhile, butterfly flutters or not, this is more than just rainfall. This is nature in revolt. Chaos of the elements. Venetian rain. Red rain. Blood rain.

Anything can happen while the rain falls. An earthquake or a great flood or a mudslide to cover the world.

Gulliver was wrong. There is not enough water stored up in the heavens to continue at this intensity. I remind myself that there is an equilibrium between earth heat and vapor, between the oceans and the skies. And rain always ends ... or always has until now.

7

Sophie went out earlier than usual. I think she's in search of solid ground: a grain field, a large garden, a park, a place with real trees. She misses the sky-reaching pines and the droopy magnolias of our villa in San Nicola and the majestic slim cypresses of Fiesole hills looking over Florence. As a rule, she pushes her tree obsession to the back of her mind and dreamily meanders along *la Strada Nuova* , at four-hundred meters, the Venice's longest street.

What is she doing? She looks into the shops and boutiques and compares them to her own shop in Rome-La Storta. She feels lost. I know she does. And displaced. I think her lostness began when she was sixteen on Campo de' Fiori. And lost again in Fiesole the day she was stuck on the Ho Chi Minh Trail, hemmed in and surrounded by killer lianas.

She now finds shelter in a café when the mist turns into rain. Shelter. A haven. I can see her. She wants to be in San Nicola. But for now entering art galleries, she thinks of Helen, once *her* Helen but now so distant from her, from us, now up in her third-floor studio during the day and in Marcello's arms at night.

Oh, Helen, won't you ever come back?

Sophie, Sophie. Something has thinned and diluted, in our former togetherness.

The rain poured. Torrential now. I called up the stairs if anyone was at home. Sophie would return soon … or she wouldn't. Marcello was somewhere with Trevisan—maybe they were on their way to Chioggia and the transhipping company.

A faint echo sounded from the third floor, from Helen's studio in the back, through the wide open front door and down the blue stairs. In the same moment, Oriana on the second floor unlocked her door and stepped out onto the landing.

"Stuart, come on up and talk to me! This wild rain is driving me mad." I ran up the steps, chased by my life-size shadow on the wall. "I've already missed my ten o'clock class—it was cancelled because of rain. As if a lecture on Schopenhauer were a football game! Can you imagine? And now the eleven o'clock seminar is doubtful."

"Too bad you can't live at the main campus."

"Dormitories are full with thousands on the waiting list. And who wouldn't like to live in such an historic palazzo? But how can I get my degree if I can't even reach Ca' Foscari? Oh, if Giacomo could only get transferred here. I would just wait till the rains are over."

"If ever! Some people believe it will never stop."

"Stuart! Killjoy! Thing is, many professors don't really mind lecture cancellations. But students go crazy. Well, I'm older and have other resources but for these kids it is a life. Therefore the suicides. And the rain doesn't help. Demoralizing, this red rain…"

Suicides? I let her vent her frustrations before asking about the suicides. Who, when, how?

"You didn't hear about the depressed twenty-two year old grad student who jumped from a palazzo window into the Canal Grande … and never came up. Because of the pouring rain they hardly searched. Ca' Foscari hides it. Police bury it. It never happened. A few days later the press mentioned that a drunken tourist had jumped off a vaporetto on a bet that the canal was shallower than people believed , that he could walk to the quai. The man was 1.80 meters tall."

"And the canal is seventeen meters deep," I said. "Strange that the rumour of alligators in the canals didn't spread again. The press loves to interview the few people who swear they've seen them. It's like the monster of Loch Ness—and pictures of Nessie as she's called circulate. Then she just disappears for years. Magic!"

"Well, hardly anyone believes in alligators here but the few fearless canal swimmers are careful about putting even a foot in the Canal Grande. Anyway, this will interest you, Stuart. I learned that two Ukrainian grad students were admitted into the Philosophy Department. The first Ukrainian students here in centuries ... but they won't be as young as the dead boy. You know that I was the director of the School for Foreigners in Perugia for several years. There were Ukrainians there. Many of them. That was before the war with Russia. And many of them stayed in Italy."

"Oriana, that does interest me, enormously. Whatever you can learn about them. Marcello and I have our suspicions. Now you confirm what I've always thought: spies love schools. In this case, it's the where that's interesting. Ukrainians in Venice can mean only one thing."

"What do you mean?"

"I believe Venice is a transshipment point for delivery of Ukrainian black market sales of the arms they get free from the West. Ask Marcello! He knows the story. It's not speculation. Italy donates a number of howitzers to Ukraine. Our government pays the Oto Melara arms factory with taxpayers' money. But instead of turning them against Russia, Ukraine sells them on the black market and the Nazi oligarchs in Ukraine pocket the money."

"For heaven's sake, Stuart! What's going on in the world?

"Look at Africa to know. Africa. Chiefly Africa."

"Africa! Why Africa?"

"To ex-colonial countries, the artificial creations by France and England. Today a lot of adjusting of people and borders is going on down there, like in Europe after World War One. Nascent dictators and new armies need weapons. And they've got money from their minerals, gold and diamonds. Listen, Oriana, since you can't get to your classes today, why not come with me up to Gulliver's now. Only a few doors up the street. We'll get there, rain or not. We'll talk about the transshipment business. Your two Ukrainians are perhaps involved. Or useful to Kiev … in one way or another."

Gulliver's dark-skinned housekeeper showed us in. The old guy stood up with surprisingly little effort to greet us. He had said before he was not tall. Now I saw he was slightly hump-backed. Still, he looked strong and fit. He'd been sitting at a front window on a straight chair like the one he used down on the street and probably like me staring at the rain phenomenon and thinking random thoughts, most likely about his long past and the absence of all his old friends.

His floors were deep red marble, the windows framed in blue velvet drapes, and the furniture scarce and non-Venetian. A huge mahogany desk filling the equivalent space of a grand piano was covered with papers and books, a desk computer and a typewriter, I suppose in memory of former days.

"Giacomina," he said to the housekeeper, "would you please bring us coffee and the, uh, cognac for our guests." When she tilted her head to one side and looked at him ironically, Gulliver waved a hand and added, "or whatever liqueurs you think adequate for our beautiful guest."

Oriana smiled beautifully.

Giacomina nodded.

Gulliver sighed in relief that his hosting part was done. Now we could talk.

The youngish old guy seemed torn between recounting and reliving events of his long past and his desire to be a participant in the present. Maybe he thinks about his life that way. Most certainly he shows no signs of having given up in life; I think his having met new people from the world outside who were curious about his Venetianness gave him a new lease on life, a taste of the immortality that people desire in secret in order to exorcise the parallel unrelenting fear of death. Not today—but soon—I know we will speak of this too ... and of the spark in his eyes in the presence of Oriana, a spark which must fade when he sits alone with himself on the straight chair down on the corner of Calle di Solferino and recalls that when he was born the Habsburg reign over Venice had just ended with the Armistice ending the Great War and that the bloody battle of Solferino was recent history for him and part of his high school curriculum. And he accepts reluctantly the reality that he will not likely experience the disastrous end of the European Union experiment.

Meanwhile, the unexpected occurred. I hadn't imagined Gulliver would have strong feelings about Ukraine. In his lifetime Central Europe had always been messy turmoil:

Galicia, Bessarabia, Bucovina , Moldavia, artificial creations, shifting borders according to the whims of the great powers, indistinct peoples who go to bed of one nationality and wake up of another. In my mind, he was cosmopolitan, a man of the seas and faraway places, so I was surprised that when I asked his opinion of the Russia-Ukraine-NATO conflict, he noted—as if the seventy-five years of Soviet Communism were just another link in history, or like the Habsburgs or the French in Italy and the Battle of Solferino only one generation before his—that he had never thought of Ukraine as a real country. No more than was Bucovina real.

"Little Russians!" he said, waving a hand dismissively. "Russia begins where Poland ends —even though Poles reject such limitations on their territorial aspirations in the East. Their ambitions have always exceeded their capabilities ... ambitions greater than geopolitical reality permits. Polacks-dreamers!"

I drifted geographically onto the subject of Ukraine's black market sale of weapons gifted to its army in its war with Russia—a proxy war for NATO-USA against Russia. I noted that those black market weapons had to be sold, payments made, then re-transported to the buyer's country, a system for which Venice is an ideal transshipment hub and which at some point would require Ukrainian presence or representation in the former Queen of the Seas.

"Signor Gulliver," Oriana said, " two Ukrainian graduate students have recently enrolled in the Philosophy Faculty—where I'm working on my Doctorate. In a seminar on Schopenhauer in which the Ukrainians participated, they spoke excellent Italian. And they do not behave as typical foreigners. They have been around somewhere in Italy a long time. Anyway, I called the University For Foreigners in Perugia—which by the way I once directed—almost certain that they had studied there. They did. Under the same names they use today.

"Then you must have been a teenager-director at Perugia!"

"I was there five years!"

"Good Lord! You're still a kid. A beautiful one, but just a kid."

"Why, Signor Gulliver! You claim to be one hundred and two years and look at you, still young enough to run a shipping company today."

Outflanked for a moment, he retorted: "Let's stay in the realm of reality, young lady! But still, I do know the shipping business inside out. And I've told you what I think is going on. Venice is becoming rich again, but not from the shipping business this time. We modernized. Tourism is our thing today. The switchover took place in the age of rockets reaching for the stars. And all in my lifetime."

"Pardon me, Signor Gulliver, " I said, "if I stray far from our subject—for just a moment—and ask if it has been worth it? Have you seen so much that you regret the past and try to forget it? Or do you still want more?"

"Oh yes, it was all well worth it. My past is me. I do not want to forget it. And its richness. Yes, yes, indeed, a rich past. And my remembrances of its richness and leaving behind a very minimum of empty, unoccupied spaces ... the regret you would feel for such a loss. Looking back and seeing only empty spaces and darkness means non-existence. You see scrapbooks with records of your exploits, the old photographs of how the body that still belongs to you once looked. Its beauty. Its power. Memory is the power to remember what happened; remembrance for me is the act of remembering; and recollection is the conscious ability to remember how things actually went in the past. The stronger the memory, remembrance and recollection, the greater the role the past plays in your daily life. Ah, yes. Remembrances. A throbbing thrill. And an aching torment. Yet the future is problematic … the where-I-am-headed, slowly, with consummate care. But no matter! You might wish you had done things differently, better. Taken another road at one of the forks you met. No departure excludes a return. Departure is not final separation. Only temptation. And what confusion! At times you become sick and tired of remembrances and their shadows and imitations and your useless attempts to change fixed realities of the past and permit new unimaginable destinies. It's enough to make you want to declare yourself out of the running and accept your simple straightforward self. Enough! Basta such ruminations. As others have noted such musings would be like discovering that the consciousness of life is superior to life itself and the knowledge of the law of happiness superior to happiness. When I was in my eighties or maybe it was my nineties—a long life gives you a different perspective on time—I became aware that it all had to end sometime. Armageddon was around the next corner, across the next bridge, just across the lagoon. I remember that when I was very young, time passed slowly, slowly. Anything could happen in one month: a new war, the end of a love affair, a baby born, a life snuffed out. But a year! A year was interminable. You could become another person. Then as time moved on, everything began accelerating. Things happened faster and faster, leaving me breathless. And my body shrank faster and faster so that my fear grew that it was nearly over. I considered a suicide exit from life at the proper time. Not the usual mentally sick person's suicide, nor that of a life prisoner, nor a financially ruined person's compulsive and spontaneous, spur-of-the-moment *Selbsmord.* I mean, old-age suicide, a planned, things-to-do act. A tired-of-life, get-it-over-with kind of thing. But then, suddenly it now seems, I put such thoughts behind me: I think I got used to the idea of my own mortality, of my natural death, as you get used to anything. And so here I am still, no longer plagued by a death wish nor the fear of death. I recall from Borges readings that Emperor Shih Huang Ti forbade all mention of the word death and searched for the elixir of immortality. He secluded himself in a figurative palace of many rooms in the belief the many walls were magic barriers to halt the advance of death. I think the Emperor believed that immortality was intrinsic and that corruption could not penetrate a closed sphere. Hoping to recreate the beginning of time, he dreamed of founding an immortal dynasty; ordering that his heirs be named Second Emperor, Third Emperor, Fourth Emperor, and so on to infinity ... and he condemned those who worshipped the past to work on a wall as vast as the past. Shih Huang Ti walled in the empire because he knew it was fragile and threatened to collapse just as the MOSE, since it cannot stop the high waters of the sea forever, threatens to let the water submerge Venice. And even though he's not my cup of tea, I like Cioran's words that, *Against the obsession with death, both the subterfuges of hope and the arguments of reason lay down their arms: their insignificance merely whets the appetite to die. In order to triumph over this appetite, there is but one method: to live it to the end, to submit to all its pleasures, all its pangs, to do nothing to elude it."*

Breathless, Gulliver stopped the flow that had seemed unstoppable. Silence fell. Giacomina stared at him as if hypnotized.

"My God, what a rare testimony that we were fortunate to hear from a person who has been there and back." I had the thought that Gulliver was an unusually great man, at one hundred and two and unafraid of the death awaiting him.

"I wrote a short piece on old age and the fear of death which I will show you someday if I can find it," he added. "That mess on the table over there is indicative of the order of my files. Now, kids, let's get back to the Ukrainians!"

"Yes, let's do. And sure enough," continued Oriana, "according to data of today there are plenty of Ukrainians around Italy. A young lady in the Registrar's office at the School for Foreigners in Perugia checked names from 2015 till now. Nineteen Ukrainians, fifteen of whom enrolled since 2022. They will send their names by post. Then yesterday I convinced a young man in the registrar's office here to check the graduate students' files. Two Ukrainians came up. Here they are," Oriana said, reading from a note on Ca' Foscari labeled notepaper: "Andriy Kravets and Vasyl Tarnovsky, both thirty years old. And I would wager that the two names are the same as the ones from Perugia! So where have they been since Perugia?"

"Maybe Africa!" I muttered. "Anyway, that's what our detectives will now uncover."

Colonial French Africa wants arms. Anything and everything. Colonial *Françafrique* is aflame. Françafrique is crumbling one coup at a time. French are abandoning. Ambassadors return to Paris. Military coups follow one after the other in France's colonies in West Africa. Armed bands roam around freely, killing and pillaging. Hate reigns. French Africa. Hate for everything white, Western, French. Curfew in Mali. The streets of Timbuktu are empty. Chaos has emerged. But out of the chaos, historians say, will step another Africa. An African Africa. Rich Africa. They have gold and silver and diamonds to pay for arms and power. No more free gold for France, no more uranium, coal, iron ore, tin, phosphates, molybdenum, gypsum, salt or petroleum for France. France wants to disarm them and restore French peace. But the US master commands vassal Paris to send arms to Ukraine which via the black market will re-arm Mali and Niger and Burkina Faso. Ironically, black market weapons also from the *douce France* arm French Africa and empower the rebel troops in the former colonies to oust the French. Military arms of the "gentle France" sung of by *Carte de Séjour* –the Frencified musical group from the former French colony of Algeria—with no small dose of irony.

Douce France
Cher pays de mon enfance
Bercée de tendre insouciance
Je t'ai gardée dans mon cœur.

Parisians know little about the colonies: they only complain that Africans continue to pour into France and that most head for Paris. Some French fear many unforeseen events will mark the fall of their colonial empire, as *la douce France* falls deeper and deeper into vassalage to the also teetering empire of the United States. So if France and Europe fall deeper into the hole of vassalage at the same time its master collapses from excess, the destiny of the earth itself will be sucked into the same bottomless pit in a long contagious avalanche of disaster.

8

November 9

Oriana had experienced how history has become more and more concentrated, multiple events, she said, on diverse levels happening all at the same time. Catastrophic events crammed into ever shorter periods. The element of time seems to have been modified, it too compressed like a computer file. Yet time—the same history shows—is immeasurable. The collapse and fall of an empire is preceded and accompanied by seismic pressures resulting in volcanic eruptions and earthquakes, sending out vibrations and tsunamis unpredictable distances from the epicenter. Some persons like herself or like Vasyl the presumed Ukrainian spy want to get a handle on time as it speeds past in its mad flight.

The first time she spoke with the two Ukrainians, Oriana and dark Vasyl Tarnovsky—who continually stroked with thumb and forefinger his Trotsky-like goatee—spoke of the vagaries of the future arriving quickly and violently in his country, to the sounds of cannon fire and threats of super weapons.

"Truly hard times for the human race," Vasyl said.

The three of them were sipping tea at a table in the Ca' Foscari student lounge shortly before noon. The reserved, studious-looking Vasyl, and his big and handsome extrovert friend, Andriy Kravets, were as enticed by her beauty as she was drawn by her suspicion of their likely secret mission in Italy; nonetheless, she felt an instinctive attraction to soft-spoken, introverted Vasyl. Like people from the North, the two lifetime friends from Kharkov had loved Italy at a distance long before coming to learn its language and culture. And they already spoke nostalgically of their three years in the international Italian language school in Perugia on a Ukrainian government student grant.

"But since things were changing so dramatically in our country in that period," Vasyl explained, "we stayed in Italy, wandering from north to south, working at various odd jobs, until ending up here in Venezia where as refugees we got scholarships at Ca' Foscari."

"Yours has been one long skein of good luck … in Italy at the right time, good schools, and …"

"And a lot of lovely women," Andriy Kravets added, making no secret of his admiration for Oriana.

"My friend's weakness!" Vasyl said in a tone that rang more as an admonition than a friendly remark—a hint that things were not harmonious between the two.

"I've long wondered what Kharkov is like, " Oriana said, "Ukraine's second city, I read, practically on the border with Russia."

"My parents used to say it WAS Russia," Vasyl said. "It was Kharkov then, not the Ukrainian Kharkiv. We spoke Russian at home and on the streets and the language used in the schools was Russian. Still, in theory everyone is supposed to speak only Ukrainian today. Actually, most people speak both. Andriy and I speak Russian together. And the President's first language is Russian so it's natural that he thinks in Russian—as do I, as does Andriy. No matter how much he might deny it, the President had to study and practice to make a speech in Ukrainian. Learning Ukrainian for a Russian speaker seems to be harder than for a

Ukrainian to learn Russian. Actually they're fundamentally the same language anyway."

While Vasyl spoke, Andriy's eyes skipped back and forth between Oriana and the tables of people chattering about study issues, their professors andupper level scandals, each group both aware and unaware of and uninterested in what was going on at Oriana's table.

"Yes, I see," Oriana said, purposefully shifting the conversation away from the personal to the academic. "Well, languages aside, I'm here to get a doctorate in philosophy and right now Schopenhauer, Emil Cioran and Jean-Paul Sartre interest me more than comparative Slavic languages. I read their writings and decided that my doctoral dissertation would include my views of all three.

" Listen to this for example, written by the right-winger, Cioran: *Persistent fatigue leads to the worship of silence, because when you are exhausted words lose meaning and hammer your ears, reduced to empty sounds, to exasperating vibrations. Concepts diminish, the force of expression diminishes, everything said or heard empties until it appears sterile and repulsive. It seems useless then to express an opinion, to take a stand or to impress others; after having forcibly worked to solve all the problems, after having tormented yourself to the maximum extent, at the time when it is necessary to give definitive answers, you end up finding in silence the only reality and the only form of expression."*

While she repeated Cioran's surprising words from memory, Oriana heard a snicker from Andriy, though when he turned his handsome face toward her, it was blank, except for the irony in the corners of his eyes.

Vasyl too heard his friend's snicker and read the critical vacuity in his face. He shrugged as if he knew that look and was sick of the carelessness written there. Although she barely knew the two men, in that moment Oriana had the fleeting thought that a showdown between the two was imminent and that it was an existential question between them, not ideology or even patriotism.

"Yes, and that is the case in many Slavic lands today … including ours," Vasyl said, on which Kravets frowned and looked away—for Oriana marking clearly the crack in what at first had seemed an unbreakable friendship between the two Ukrainians.

With that information in mind for Marcello, she continued: "I remember Cioran's words in **A Short History of Decay** that *scaffolds, dungeons, jails flourish only in the shadow of a faith—of that need to believe which has infested the mind forever. The real criminals are men who establish an orthodoxy on the religious or political level, men who distinguish between the faithful and the schismatic.*"

Ignoring Cioran's obvious reference to the Communist faith and its followers, Vasyl shifted directions and said, "Yes, the unexpected similarity between Italic and Slavic peoples is amazing. Both have problems with nationality and faith. As we've learned in our travels, Italy is composed of Germans and French, Greeks and Catalonians, Slavs and ancient Italics and is glued together by Catholicism and Atheism. And our home country called Ukraine is composed of Poles and Czechs, Romanians, Ruthenians and Hungarians, Belarusians and Russians and further divided by Russian Orthodoxy, Eastern Orthodoxy, Catholicism, Eastern Catholicism … and Atheism."

Hoping to keep the conversation alive and somehow stimulate meaningful reactions from the two Ukrainians, Oriana opened her bag and withdrew a sheaf of papers and notes, thumbed through them and pulled out a single sheet with one longish text. "Listen, in my doctoral dissertation draft I discuss two distinct worldviews which some literary people like the *nouveaux philosophes* in France, par example, interpret as the same thing Cioran speaks of: Communism and Fascism. I personally am neither, but I do not agree that Russian Communism in action is tantamount to German Nazism. They are not the same."

"Absolutely not," Vasyl said.

"The infuriating thing is that modern philosophers carry social thought far beyond the work of the classical school we study most. Like Jean Baudrillard or Michel Foucault. Baudrillard literally announced a rupture in history: post-moderns entered into a new era in which social reproduction replaces production. Labor is no longer a force of production. It is not primarily productive, but a sign of one's social position. Wages bear no rational relation to one's work and what one produces but to one's place *within* that system. Political economy is no longer the foundation in which other phenomena can be explained. People live in the hyper-reality of simulations in which signs replace the concepts of production and class conflict as the key constituents of contemporary societies. Baudrillard's postmodern world is one in which previously important boundaries lost power such as a divide between social classes, genders and political leanings. The social and even sexuality implode into each other. 'In this mix,' he says, 'economics is shaped by culture, politics and other spheres, while art is absorbed into the economic and political—and sexuality is everywhere. In this situation, differences between individuals and groups implode in a rapidly changing dissolution of the social and the previous boundaries and structures upon which social theory had once focused.'

"Anyway," Oriana said, "I've made copies and your reactions would be of particular interest—a godsend that I met you. I will also leave with you this copy of the excerpt from my dissertation. I borrowed the content from a Stewart novel, *The Hamlet.* My different point of view and my emphasis being different requires my retelling of the story of *Dirty Hands* and *The Scarlet Letter*."

TWO WORLD VIEWS

Dirty hands results when a leader encounters a conflict of duties with values and must choose between alternatives, none of which are entirely satisfactory. In Jean-Paul Sartre's play *Les Mains Sales* (Dirty hands), Communist leader Hoederer explains his view to the bourgeois, Hugo, who has joined the Proletarian Party in the fictive East European country of Illyria at the end of World War Two. Despite his love and admiration for Hoederer and the model he makes, Hugo is steadfast in his refusal to "dirty" his hands:

Hoederer*: You hold so tightly to your purity, my lad. How afraid you are of dirtying your hands. Well, then, stay pure. But what good will it do, and why bother coming here among us? Purity is a concept of fakirs and friars. But you, the intellectuals, the bourgeois anarchists, invoke purity as the pretext for doing* *nothing. Do nothing, don't move, clasp your arms tight around your body, put on gloves. As for me, my hands are dirty. I have plunged my arms up to the elbows in shit and blood. And what then should one do later? Do you imagine it possible then to govern innocently?*

Hugo is in total admiration of this man. *Ecce homo*, he apparently thinks. Hugo, the bourgeois convert who hangs onto some of his fundamental bourgeois values, nonetheless approves of the Nietzschian element in his hero Hoederer whom he professes to love more than he has loved anyone else in his life. Hoederer is the philosopher's "man". He is the full human being. More than a Christ. A man who can say: *Hear me!... and above all do not mistake me for someone else.*

The reality is that Hoederer loves other men with all their faults; Hugo loves the image of men as they could become.

But like Hoederer, Hugo too must distinguish opportunists from those who become infected with the disease of corruption through their sincere efforts to govern well. Hugo recognizes that self-serving opportunists rationalize their dubious measures through self-deceptive references to "the good of the whole," or that "the end justifies the means". So, for him, egocentric opportunism differs conceptually from dirty hands. The question thus remains open: Does corruption in the political realm arise as a result of the very nature of governance and morality? Do rulers simply have more opportunities for temptation and therefore succumb more often than do private citizens? Or does good governance sometimes require the sacrifice of moral standards as Machiavelli suggests and Hoederer believes?

We see in nations worldwide that when corrupt governmental leaders are detected, society tends toward leniency in its "punishment" of them. But I don't believe this leniency reflects recognition of the problem of dirty hands, in which setting people forgive and forget so easily the crimes of their governments. I think the reason for leniency is fear and awe vis-à-vis power. They don't want to risk punishment for dissent and social scorn for being "different". Yet, yet, Italian political leaders since Machiavelli have recognized that power truly corrupts.

So we have to wonder about the historicity of morality. "Moral relativism is the doctrine that affirms the relativity of what we consider good or evil." (Rizzoli Encyclopedia). That conclusions about matters like abortion or euthanasia are impossible Moral relativism is the view that ethical standards and positions of right or wrong are culturally based and therefore subject to a person's individual choice. Each of us can decide what is right for ourselves. Moral relativism is the idea that moral principles have no bias-free standards. No hard and fast rules on what is right and what is wrong. Relativism thus contrasts with the absolutism of religious fundamentalists according to which there exists one truth. Like for some fundamentalists when speaking of morals, it is a principle that sex before marriage is immoral. Relativism means different opinions, as many truths as there are cultures. Authoritarian fundamentalist governments like the United States of America, harp on values—"family values, traditions and the future of our children." Values are the line of attack of American fundamentalists, of radical Islam and of the Roman Catholic Church. All claim to possess the true truth: everything is permitted at one extreme and everything is forbidden at the other. In western society there are two opposing views on moral relativism: One: It's time to jettison the nonsense of moral relativism, which emerged in the social upheaval of the 1960s, responsible for the dysfunctional society of today. You cannot have half-rights and half-wrongs; there is only right and wrong. Two: The belief that there is only one moral truth is the source of all bigotry and hatred, in religion, politics. It allows you to demonize others as evil, refuse to see their point of view and refuse to accept that moral standpoints are based in culture.

"Realists" like Sartre's Hoederer maintain that dirty hands are inevitable. "Idealists" like Hugo on the other hand hold that the problem of dirty hands is merely an excuse adduced by the morally weak to do what they want to do. So in that sense power is directly linked to morality.

It is an amazing curiosity that writing one hundred years earlier about the American Puritan society of the 1600s Nathaniel Hawthorne in his novel *The Scarlet Letter* approaches a moral theme similar to the modern one illustrated by Sartre in *Dirty Hands* ... however from a different angle. His character, the Reverend Arthur Dimmesdale, in his life of everlasting guilt and penance for a previous violation of the severe moral code of his times in a moment of enlightenment feels driven to commit "some strange, wild, wicked thing or other, with a sense that it would be at once both involuntary and intentional: involuntary in his human rejection of an unfair social-moral code; intentional in that after seven years of suffering the pain of his penitence, his most ardent desire is to say NO."

Dimmesdale thinks: "No man, for any considerable period, can wear one face to himself, and another to the multitude, without becoming bewildered as to which may be true."

Dimmesdale's penance is transformed into an accusation against an entire bigoted, hypocritical and mendacious Puritan society of the New England of the 1600s, which remained branded on subsequent generations of its descendants, including those of the Nineteenth century when his creator Nathaniel Hawthorne wrote, and so on until today as seen in the American reverence toward corrupt power, one hundred and seventy years since he wrote *The Scarlet Letter.*

Clearly, POWER has always been the question of questions. For man and beast—power, power, power. Power, causing family, tribal, social, national, international, cosmic change. In the Sartrian play the question is political power and how to acquire it. In the Hawthorne novel, power is of a bigoted moral nature and how to acquire and exercise it, subjecting a whole society to its severe sanctimonious Puritan rules. Political power and moral power thus become one and the same, with the same ultimate goal: control of common man.

We see in both Sartre and Hawthorne that high-power groups will resort to most any means to acquire power; they love holding it and using it. Power groups use their style of propaganda to justify their having power and are capable of the most nefarious acts to keep it. They pay little attention to low-power groups, and have a natural will to dominate. However, by their alienation of those with little or no power, high-power group actions elicit resistance. Discontent is often projecting blame onto the less powerful than themselves, thus undermining their ability to empower themselves through cooperation and coalition building.

Power plays a role in most conflicts. Within the social sciences there are various perspectives on power: "power over", or the ability to compel someone to do something; “powerlessness and dependence”; and "power to," as in the power to act without constraint. Hoederer conceives of a mutual interaction between the characteristics of a revolutionary leader a la Machiavelli and the particulars of a revolutionary situation often through using various strategies of influence and if necessary plunging his hands in shit and blood to accomplish it. Puritan leaders did the same and with the same dirty hands to exert power via a false morality of bigotry, privilege, religion, order and reverence for the law they themselves declared.

Personal factors include different cognitive, motivational and moral orientations regarding power. People adopt various perspectives vis-a-vis power. Some people have an authoritarian orientation that stresses obedience to authority. Others are motivated to pursue personal power, or power for their group. Peoples' moral orientations toward power vary with their degree of moral development, their degree of egalitarian sentiment, and with their perception of the scope of justice. Understanding situational factors thus requires an examination of the structural and historical context. Significant aspects of a situation are the role a person plays and the individual's place in the hierarchy.

Both Sartre and Hawthorne emphasize power's demands for reverence from its adherents: acceptance of and reverence for its values and nature. That is, reverence for that one power, imposed, or, as a result of cooperation with and opposition to outsiders. Therefore the need of some level of the divine to justify that particular power. A society in which also political power is within the grasp of Hawthorne's priest, Dimmesdale. Sartre's divine instead is that great majority of guileless men.

Hawthorne makes an interesting remark—almost as an aside—that I have never noted elsewhere. One hundred and seventy years ago in reference to the severity of the Puritan society of the 1600s in which *The Scarlet Letter* takes place, he writes: "... *the generation of Americans next to the early emigrants, wore the blackest shade of Puritanism, and so darkened the national visage with it, that all the subsequent years have not sufficed to clear it up. We have yet to learn again the forgotten art of gayety.* Stewart finds that last sentence perplexing, expressive of something he had long felt though never articulated. Gradually, while on visits in that country, he realized that he had concluded something similar to Hawthorne: except for perhaps short periods in American history and in certain confined places, the gaiety there has seemed forced and false, the kind of wild and unreal gaiety surfacing during the pestilence in a spirit of the end times. A society of seeming. Seeming to "have good time". A society where seeming replaces the concept of being. A narcissistic society in which the false self replaces the true self as introduced into psychoanalysis by Donald Winnicott in 1960 who saw the false self as a defensive façade which leaves its holders lacking spontaneity, behind a mere appearance of being real. Thus to maintain their self-esteem and protect their vulnerable true selves, narcissists need to control others' behavior as in *The Scarlet Letter.* (Paraphrased from Wikipedia entry *True and False Self.)*

Sartre's Hoederer says plainly that what interests him in men is their self, the way they are, men with all their vices. Their voices, their warm hands, their bare skin and their desperate battle against death and anguish. He loves men the way they are in life. He wants to change the world in which they live.

The bourgeois Hugo instead claims that men as they are hold little interest for him; he is interested in what men can become.

In the two books, *The Scarlet Letter,* set in the seventeenth century and *Dirty Hands* set in the twentieth, the two self-sacrificing social leaders, Hoederer the Proletarian and Reverend Dimmesdale the Moralist feel they are the chosen, the elect destined to perform the supreme acts for which they are willing to die, acts beyond the reach of common man.

And Emil Cioran who in his euphemistic manner—saying and not saying—writes that Communism and Nazism-Fascism and his native Romania's Iron Guard are all the same—without ever using the ugly ism suffix. Instead, he uses circumlocutions like *nightmare, hallucination, drunken gods,* the *night's dreams* and the *day's mediocrity, insipid problems* and other such. Cioran, beautiful writer that he is, never plunges his arms into shit up to his elbows. He is above that. He prefers that nice un-nice way, one of the most cynical, lucid condemnations of the Communism of the Soviet Union ever written, his poisonous delight concealed within his philosophical exposition:

There are something like material limits to our endurance; the scaffolding of a nightmare requires a nervous expenditure more exhausting than the best articulated theoretical construction. How, after waking, to begin again the task of aligning ideas when, in our unconscious we were mixed up with grotesque and marvelous spectacles, we were sailing among the spheres without the shackles of anti-poetic Causality. For hours we were like drunken gods—and suddenly, our open eyes erasing night's infinity, we must resume in day's mediocrity the enterprise of insipid problems without any of the night's hallucinations to help us. The glorious and deadly fantasy was all for nothing then; sleep has exhausted us in vain. Waking, another kind of weariness awaits us; after having had just time enough to forget the night's, we are at grips with the dawn's. We have labored hours and hours in horizontal immobility without our brain's deriving the least advantage of its absurd activity. An imbecile who was not victimized by this waste, who might accumulate all his resources without dissipating them in dreams, would be able to disentangle all the snags of the metaphysical lies or initiate himself into the most inextricable difficulties of mathematics. After each night we are emptier: our mysteries and our grief have leaked away into our dreams. So long as man is protected by madness, he functions and flourishes; but when he frees himself from the fruitful tyranny of fixed ideas, he is lost, ruined. He begins to accept everything, to wrap not only minor abuses in his tolerance, but crimes and monstrosities, vices and aberrations. Everything is the same to him. His indulgence, self-destroying as it is, extends to all the guilty, to the victims and the executioner. He takes all sides, because he espouses all opinions; gelatinous, contaminated by infinity, he has lost his "character," lacking any point of reference, any obsession. The universal view melts things into a blur, and the man who still makes them out, being neither their friend nor their enemy, bears in himself a wax heart which indiscriminately takes the form of objects and beings. His pity is addressed to existence, and his charity is that of doubt and not that of love; a skeptical charity, consequence of knowledge, which excuses all anomalies. But the man who takes sides, who lives in the folly of decision and choice, is never charitable; incapable of comprehending all points of view, confined within the horizon of his desires and his principles, he plunges into a hypnosis of the finite. This is because creatures flourish only by turning their backs on the universal . . . To be something—unconditional—is always a form of madness from which life—a flower of fixed ideas—frees itself only to fade. Nostalgia for a world without "ideals," for an agony without doctrine, for an eternity without life . . . Paradise. . . . But we could not exist one second without deceiving ourselves: the prophet in each of us is just the seed of madness which makes us flourish in our void. Ennui is merely the beginning of such an itinerary. . . . It makes us find time long, too long—unsuited to show us an end. Detached from every object, having nothing external to assimilate, we destroy ourselves in slow motion, since the future has stopped offering us a raison d'être.

Silence. Soothing, those twentieth century Nazi non-ideological ideology images. Careful with Cioran, lest you miss the mark. In Oriana's mind, the suspicion that the two men were agents of the Ukrainian Nazi government did not exclude them as readers. By no means.

She searched the faces of both Ukrainian black marketers for confirmation. She was good at comprehending others. Not herself, but others. It seemed it had always been her work, the Perugia school, the Florence police department. Now here, strangers and silence. One face a total blank that she, the note-taker, she, the searcher almost understood.

Maybe Andriy *wanted* to understand what was going on in the world, but he realized the shallowness of his own mind.

Vasyl instead both understood and understood nothing. Again, she shared his bewilderment and understood.

'All is all,' she said to herself, thinking of Giordano Bruno. 'Everything is one. A particle vibration due to the sound when you speak can affect a molecule inside a star at the edge of the universe instantly. Man's greatest illusion is the illusion of separation.'

Oriana considered a flirt with one of the Ukrainians, but after she saw the gulf widening between the two men and moreover detected a mean streak in handsome Andriy and his freely exhibited ambition to get ahead, she decided that rather than fuel the fire between them, a friendly relationship with both was preferable.

Vasyl with his goatee a la Trotsky was hesitance personified and in certain moments he turned his head away, embarrassed at the other's haughty behavior.

She thought that deep down Vasyl must feel trapped in whatever his ambiguous connection with official Kiev was; obviously. he was searching for a way out of an impasse that he himself could not explain. Clearly he was no run-of-the-mill functionary-spy. An intellectual relationship with him seemed to hold the hint of revelation of at least who they really were without risking jealousy on the part of Andriy. If their job was in the black market arms field, they worked for the Ukrainian government and Vasyl, not Andriy, was the one who might reveal details as the price to be paid for escape and freedom from the distasteful idea of allegiance to something evil, even though he seemed to be thinking in terms of justification for acts that he had already performed mentally.

Oriana recalled a similar man—an Arab—in the Perugia School for Foreigners: though he spoke excellent Italian he registered in the beginners course every second year which guaranteed him Italian documents. Meanwhile, he belonged to both anti-Syrian ISIS and was an informer for AISE, Italy's foreign intelligence. All to no avail. For his intelligence went from AISE to CIA to NATO and straight back to ISIS.

When shortly before Oriana left Perugia and the Arab's assassination in the hills above Assisi, he had admitted to his local Carabiniere control the useless banality of his double life and recalled the adage that "what goes around, comes around."

Reading about that period and thinking of that Arab intellectual, Oriana concluded that the books of fiction about western-manipulated terrorism she had read offered the clarification of modern man's dilemma that historicism can only strive for.

9

November 10

Marcello woke up early. He lay on his side with his eyes closed and recalled his dream about the Malamocco Slaughter which Trevisan for some reason had not yet solved. The dream reminded him of the Monster of Florence murders, cold cases of time past. Maybe someday he would return to Florence and apply the Trevisan solitary, scientific method to clarify the murders in the hills of Florence. With such gruesome thoughts racing at breakneck speed through his mind, he opened his eyes and met those of Helen.

She was propped on an elbow, her chin in the cup of her hand, the upper part of her beautiful body only inches away from him and her eyes speaking of love. Goosebumps ran up and down his body.

"Are you glad to see me?" she said.

"See you! I'm already in you."

"You looked like you were elsewhere."

"Forgive me, I can't control my dreams. And mine were ugly, not to be shared with beautiful you."

Helen kicked off the covers. Her naked legs twitched. She'd been waiting. Now she was all arms and legs around him. Face to face. And inside each other. Marcello marveled: they loved each other and they were free to do whatever they liked with or to each other. They were truly free. They didn't have to ask questions first.

Later, they spoke of love. He kissed her fingers one at a time. She bit his neck and kissed his ears.

"You have lovely fingers," he said.

"You have strong Tuscan ears," she said.

Later, Helen invited him to the daily unveiling—her incubus—a dreadful moment that she dreamed of and also looked forward to. She said it was like stepping into a new world each day. They would view the "sketch" of a new work, a new theme, vaguely related to her beauty-ugliness series: her "shadow self".

She opened the studio door hesitantly and held his arm tightly. She perceived both curiosity and fear of what waited under the cloth covering. Then, casting trepidation aside, she reached for the gossamer black cloth covering the canvas on its easel, a covering so delicate and flimsy that the form on the canvas underneath the cloth was also dark, flimsy and gossamer.

Marcello stared.

Helen watched him watching her work; she knew he was seeing the outline of her shadow self.

Marcello thought: embryo, not yet a fetus. It looked as if she had first painted a figure, then somehow blotted it still wet, removing the definitive lines and leaving the embryo.

"What do you see?"

"I see the dark ... ah ...embryo of a person. And I think, the person must be you … that is, the becoming you."

"Right. Discerning viewer! My only viewer. Well, yes, this sketch is the embryo of a painting. The embryo of what I'm looking for in my shadow self. It comes and goes but it's always there … though only sometimes visible. Now, Marcello, I know this sounds silly, and useless too. But it's not. Shadow self means other self. Or maybe first self. Or core self. Maybe soul self. Our shadow that we see on a wall is like this …unimportant as such. Yet you cannot say it's unmeaningful, can you? You don't believe in coincidences. Because you're a cop? No, I don't think that's the real reason. I think because you search for reality. You want nothing to do with illusions. Never. Better that way … to avoid disillusionment. And I'm doing the same: searching for reality in what at first seems unreality.

"Look, Marcello, look at that canvas standing in the corner. What do you see now that it's as finished as it will ever be?"

"I see you. But another you. Not quite you. Nearly you. Your you. Your inner you. But the woman there is different."

"Exactly! And that's what I'm looking for in the shadow self. It's me … and it's not."

"Oh, ok Helen, now stop it. I've got to work now. Work with reality. And I can't take this esoteric world along with me."

"Fine. But anyway, let me tell you where this real shadow resides … besides in me. It lives in the hall outside this door. Keep in mind that the hall leading to the studio from the front is illuminated only by that one wall lamp half way between the studio door and the bedroom door. There are white walls on the sides and also at each end of the hall. That's the critical space within which my shadow flourishes. When I edge down the hall from the bedroom door and look back at the wall facing me I see a huge dark blurb, formless and lifeless. Then as I move slowly toward the studio, after a moment of lull and hesitation the blurb follows me along the wall to my right, assuming different forms as we move. Then, as I reach the wall light now behind me, shadow becomes my exact size at the very same time it vanishes only to soon reappear on my left, moving faster, then ever faster. Growing exponentially before again becoming gradually smaller and more shapely. For a moment, shadow stays in that small but larger-than-life size, then it shifts form and size to a distinct person.

"Helen, please!"

"Yes, it's scary. As I approach the wall facing me I begin to realize it IS me. But me only in shape. No features whatsoever. That's what I must unravel and represent on canvas: my features *within* the shadow.

"Dreamscape!"

"Not exactly. Not for me. I see it, I believe it, the shadow."

"You painted in Vienna. Then you stopped painting to become a chemist. Helen, you were an intellectual before you began painting again. It shows. I don't understand if you're asking me if you are in the shadow, or if the shadow is in you. Or perhaps you think the shadow IS you or that the real you is hiding in the secrecy of her shadow."

"I think this, Marcello … and no, I am not an intellectual. I'm an artist looking for the right way. Here however in such moments with shadows and secrets being revealed, a new world opens up if you can convince yourself that every person, every object, everything around you is hiding secrets … secrets that can reveal the true nature of things. The secret that everything that passes between the spiritual and the material worlds is connected by vision and words perhaps speaking to you. When I think of communication with other people, I wonder if they think spiritually as I do. I wonder if others even realize that I am thinking spiritually. Actually, I know the answer. Most people find speaking of the spirit embarrassing even if they do think of it. When I think of communication with inanimate objects, I wonder if they are truly inanimate or part inanimate and part animate. I wonder if they too are not filled with the inspiration of what has been named *Duende*."

Marcello heard but he did not react. He stood as if spellbound in the now phantasmal hallway, pressed against Helen. A lost look crossed her face. Lost, he thought, in desperation. 'Hers is the lost look of one searching for herself within herself ... or perhaps,' he thought, 'in her intellectual-artistic self in her shadow.'

As he saw the present begin to return to her, Marcello reached out curiously and spellbound touched their shadows side by side on the wall where she usually sees hers alone.

Lonely shadow, he thought, needed its companion. And his mind wandering between shadows and seas and ships and Trevisan and Chioggia waiting for him, he held his finger on the wall shadow and imagined the dark sounds of the mysterious dreamscape in which her art is born, dum dum dum, surging up from the soles of her feet to life in her veins.

'It's creation,' he thought.

'It's the spirit of the earth.'

In their hallway, his finger on their shadow, he recalled his German professor quoting Goethe: "It is not doing the thing we like to do, but liking the thing we have to do, that makes life blessed."

"When I studied philosophy in Florence I never realized the role it would play in my life as cop and lover," he said.

Helen smiled.

Trevisan drove his non-descript civilian car down to Chioggia for their noon appointment with the General Manager of Transworld Shipping. Marcello felt honored that Nicola brought him along. Now a civilian—though he still felt like a cop—he knew his presence was not an infraction of Trevisan's rule of working alone. During the hour's drive, he told him about Oriana's two Ukrainians and filled him in on his own research about the destination of the arms shipments.

The three-story Transworld building spread a hundred meters along the seafront facing northwards across the lagoon toward Venice, the Lido and Malamocco, by speedboat about an hour away. The offices occupied the top floor, the rest were warehouses separated horizontally by three cargo loading canals entering directly from the lagoon. The street entrance was small: a desk and two elevators and walls decorated with pictures of famous ships:

La Santa Maria

Titanic

Bismarck

Old Ironsides

Pequod

Underneath the latter, appears the famous first sentence of the Herman Melville novel *Moby Dick* : "Call me Ishmael"—who is the narrator. Obviously the decorative idea work of Gulliver! Did Ishmael survive the fate of the *Pequod* and Captain Ahab out for vengeance against the ferocious white whale, Moby Dick? There are two answers: yes and no. But that is another story.

Through an open rear door a canal and several docked speed boats were visible. The male receptionist telephoned their names and sent them up to the offices. On the third floor, they stood outside the elevator and looked over the vast area of work cubicles, glass enclosed offices and many wide-open spaces. A cat walked up to them, looked up at Marcello and meowed twice. It was a Soriano. Marcello stroked it affectionately.

The whole place reflected power, wealth and the polish of experience; yet silence reigned. They saw no one until a tall middle-aged man dressed in blue jeans and a black leather jacket ambled toward them, a self-satisfied, devil-may-care expression on a lightly bearded, red-cheeked face, and in the depths of his eyes flickered the haughtiness of superficiality. A delicate lift of his chin to the left, struck Marcello. Something to keep in mind, he thought, as the man stuck out his arm vigorously only to offer a limp hand, slightly moist.

"My name is Blasio Santin and you must be the *Signori* Bolzoni and Trevisan. You are policemen, I believe," which he pronounced with a certain restrained distaste.

"I am an investigator of the Venice Police Department," Trevisan said. "My friend, Signor Bolzoni is a former detective from Florence."

"Our former director, Robert Gulliver, asked me to give you full assistance ... in a delicate international matter regarding shipments to sub-Sahel Africa ...some very popular destinations there in recent times. He didn't explain the subject of your visit. So how can Transworld Shipping assist you?"

"Well, since the subject of arms shipments to Africa is sensitive," Trevisan said, looking around purposefully, "we will need a little of your time."

"I see," Santin repeated. "Then please come with me to my office, gentlemen. We'll be more comfortable and private there."

They wound their way through a maze of desks and cubicles to an elegant office of modern furniture, hardwood floors, Persian carpets, and wide windows looking out onto the Venetian Lagoon with a northern view toward the company's chief docks and warehouses at Malamocco. Trevisan and Marcello sat on a plush soft leather couch and Santin on a red lacquered chair, a low mahogany coffee table between them.

"May I offer you our famous Venetian coffee or a Florian cocktail … or both?"

"A coffee would be fine," Trevisan said. Marcello took the same. The cat pranced across the table, stopped and fixed his eyes on Marcello who felt somewhat embarrassed … for no particular reason. Being a fanatic cat lover, his first thought was that somebody should feed him. At the same time he noted the disappointed look cross Santin's face that both of them asked for coffee. That man is a drinker, he intuited, and this is his hour.

Marcello both loved and hated drinkers—having been one once. 'I understand him better than he might imagine,' he thought. That limp hand had marked his insecurity. Blasio must be a sensitive person. 'Right now, he's a bundle of nerves. Police interest in the two Ukrainians troubles him because he doesn't understand the political-diplomatic background to the story.'

"Look, Santin, the shipments your company makes to Africa, Asia, or Latin America, or wherever, are NOT a police matter as such. We are not investigating Transworld Shipping. But Signor Bolzoni and I are somewhat curious as to why you—among the many shipping companies in Venice—how Transworld came to have this relationship with Ukraine that as a rule is anyway an importer, not an exporter. You see what I mean?"

Trevisan paused when a white-jacked bartender served the coffee and put a glass of a pure white liquid in front of Santin, who for some time didn't touch it; he just stared at it as if evaluating its content.

Marcello remembered well that look. He once did that too. He smiled when he recalled how he used to examine a shot glass or a bottle and ask himself which was the most effective: a fast series of, say, four shots or an immensely long swig from the bottle? I even did tests, the results of which in my case were inconclusive. No matter, he'd thought then. Neither would change his life? Or then on a good day, he would swear that this one drink was his last. He understood Santin's misgivings. His uncertainties about what was to be done. The drink question was piquing his conscience this very moment, Marcello believed. Mornings were always the most critical times which then set the tone and the timing for the rest of the day. Still, he envied Santin too. He could almost hear his hesitations, his inner debates, his suspensions of respiration … so breathless in his anticipation of the instant the drink would hit his stomach. The momentary satisfaction when you feel the state that you've ached for near. And how easy it was to swear in that moment that it was his last drink. The problem now was that in life there were drinking times and places and non-drinking times and places too; the problem was knowing which was which.

Santin started to turn away as if to conceal the act, but instead he boldly looked at them watching him and drank it off with a shrug … somewhat proud and perhaps thinking that this last one hardly counted anyway. Probably nothing in that man's life had ever been stable, Marcello thought, recalling that his own desperation had arrived late. Maybe it began arriving when he came to realize that one thing doesn't lead automatically to another and that most things like drinking or not drinking were only potential or conceptual and easily modified or erased.

Marcello watched Santin and—though not tempted—he felt something … a flicker of the old 'I don't give a fuck' urge. He determined that Santin was hoping for a drinking roll on which both daring and caution are necessary. It's not simply three sheets to the wind and fuck'em all—a drinking roll has its own rhythm. Santin had momentarily lost that rhythm and was searching for it.

When Marcello asked him if he'd seen the two Ukrainian students recently, Santin literally sprang from his Oriental throne—he was trying to return to reality. Direct mention of Ukrainians shattered his already shaky nature.

"Ukrainians, what Ukrai…", he started to say, stopped and sat back down. "Yes, they're … uh, at least one of them is still here, signing documents, I think. They come here, they come often … too often."

Santin rambled, suddenly wanting to tell all. "But a crisis emerged this morning. Rather confusing. The smaller one—I forget their names—the dark one suddenly said 'basta'. He wanted no more to do with the shipment. Both of them began shouting in their language. Raving and yelling at each other. And he left, the smart one. The big one stayed. He would sign shipping documents and falsify the other's signature. What a mess!"

"Well, I'd like to meet them … or him," Trevisan said. "And for non-shipping reasons also. We're curious about who those two are. They've been in Italy too long, traveling like tourists around our country. But theirs is not tourism—up and down the peninsula, back and forth across the northern regions, and frequently telephoning their old Aunt in Kharkov. For what? we wonder. Money or instructions?"

"I'll introduce you," a confused Santin said. "But you should know that this shipment to Mali is not as simple an operation as it might seem. The official exporter is Ukraine. But some of the freight that leaves our ports for Mali arrives here by train or truck from France or Germany… and some by air from the USA. Prices must be converted to US dollars and totaled and billed to Mali which must be paid before the voyage on our ships even begins. International banks, currencies, exchange rates, payment terms, discounts: that's what's going on in all this silence around us. And all the freight lists to be inventoried, check lists controlled: cannons, troop carriers, tanks, ammunition, thirty thousand tons of deadweight.

"Yesterday we found a bill for three British tanks. But there were only two in the cargo and one of them tiny and old-looking. Why, this war is also a story of freight weight, which readily translates into force, then power. Surprising to me too, but there's nothing like the sound of a M198, 16,000 pound howitzer hitting the steel floor of the hole of a four-hundred meter long cargo ship. That's power!"

"Cheapskate arms industry," Marcello said, stroking the cat that had chosen his lap for its nap.

"We know as well as do Ukraine, the exporter country, and Mali the buyer, that it's all a cheap ruse anyway," Santin said. "The only ones to actually pay are taxpayers and the mineral-rich soil of Mali. Well, perhaps not only. Anyway, our voyage ends at Abijan in Cote d'Ivoire that serves as landlocked Mali's port. Then the cargo makes its way on riverboats the 1,300 kilometers to Bamaku, on the way some of it being sold off to Burkina Faso,

Guinea, Sierra Leone, Benin or Nigeria. But the ones to make money are the American-EU arms industry and Ukrainian oligarchs. And we shippers get our fee. Seems to me that the system is an indirect way to finance a bankrupt Ukraine."

"Hey, man, you sound like us." Marcello couldn't hide his pleasure, thinking it unfortunate that Stuart wasn't here. Just listening to Santin in his political innocence was enough to unleash stubborn resistance to brainwash and discover your capacity to see through the black curtain of fakery. This guy Blasio Santin thought in the same direction as Gulliver, but the corruption and ubiquitous propaganda today was much greater than during the old man's time. Surprising, Marcello thought, the number of people walking around in disguise, undiscovered, but anxious to rip off their masks and show their real selves.

"No wonder NATO and Ukraine want to prolong their war against Russia," Santin added. "Money, money, money. And the skim! Skim left and right. Every step along way someone is skimming. Laundered money and many pockets lined with the gold of Mali—the country's chief resource, paying again for the arms that NATO countries' taxpayers already paid for."

All three of them were looking across the seemingly endless corridors, cubicles and glass enclosed offices, when Santin exclaimed, "Hey, wait! There he is, on his way out," the tone of his voice revealing that he'd really departed on his daily journey and in this moment was headed toward his secret place where he wanted to be.

Marcello looked Santin in the eyes, saw himself reflected there and from his own experience perceived clearly his battle. The daily contest. Every day the search for the proper balance. Too many glasses made you drowsy; too few left you nervous, your requirements unmet, still in search of the missing part of yourself. Like Helen painting herself!

Santin touched a name on his phone. He said to keep the man at the bar, he had to speak with him.

"Jesus Christus," he said, "this place is huge. Sometimes I forget it myself. It's a hike to the bar. What we need up here is a metro system. Who invented all this anyway? Gulliver? What do you think, Trevisan? Why are things the way they are?"

No one said a word. Santin knew he'd exaggerated but was already thinking of the right thing to drink at the bar—not too much, not too little. After all he had to go home sometime. They were waiting for him and wondering which Blasio would show up.

Handsome Andriy Kravets was sitting at the bar with a glass of beer in front of him and a shot of vodka in a huge hand. He looked completely at ease, the type that enjoys hurting women Marcello thought spontaneously, looking at that huge hand.

The Ukrainian was in no hurry to leave. He stood up and greeted Santin in an off-hand manner, as if he didn't take him seriously. But he looked closely at Trevisan and Marcello. He understood they were cops. He took them very seriously and nodded nervously.

"Where's your friend?" Trevisan asked.

"Back at the hotel, I believe," he said and drank off the vodka. "No matter!"

The cat leapt onto the counter and moved toward his glass. The Ukrainian brushed it to the floor too roughly for Marcello's taste. That man's dangerous, he thought, scooping up the cat and putting it back on the bar.

No matter, he thought. Two spies at large, a black market arms shipment underway that was certainly in violation of various international laws, money laundering, and God knows what else, and this character says ‘no matter’ about the whereabouts of his partner. Something was going on between them. If his intuition was right, Marcello thought, this guy was going to regret his arrogance.

All of them were now standing.

Marcello and Trevisan kept Kravets on the defensive.

The Ukrainian picked up his beer from the bar and held it like at a cocktail party. Marcello ordered a double espresso. Santin moved down to the end of the bar, spoke to the bartender and turned his back on them.

“Hey, Santin,!” Marcello called, “What’s the cat’s name?”

“Name? He doesn’t have a name,” Santin said over his shoulder. “He’s just cat.”

“Everyone has a name, cats too,” Marcello said. “We’ll give him one.”

Kravets watched the same scene, shrugged and muttered something in Ukrainian to himself. Santin down at the end of the bar, was temporarily in perfect equilibrium with himself.

“Signor Kravets,” Trevisan said, leaning on the bar nonchalantly, “shipping is not our field. Nor is it our concern as long as it is legal and lawful. But we ARE policemen and we’re interested in your activities in our country during the considerable number of years since you finished your schooling in Perugia. How would you define your long presence here? Extended tourism? Journalism? Search for employment? Research for a book? Or simply love for Italy? In other words, what the fuck are you doing here? You know how it is. Questions arise. Doubts.

Suspicions. A decade and no job. No income in Italy all these years. Now, I know what SBU is. Ukrainan Security Agency. Thirty thousand officers. Thirty thousand! That's a big number. Bigger than MI5. We too have our special agencies, you know. AISI, for example. And you don't want to fall into their hands. And your mere presence here looks baaaad. Better to talk to me. Maybe I can help you."

"Help me? Look, here's my updated Residence Permit! All in perfect order. I have money to live on. I'm fortunate to have a rich family."

"Same rich family that supports your colleague, I suppose?"

"Well, we're not brothers, Vasyl and I. We just happen to be of the same nationality. He has his life, that *sukin sin*, that son of a bitch … and I mine. We're actually very different."

"That's evident to all of us. Anyway, Kravets, we don't want to hold you for now. But be aware that we're keeping an eye on you. And you should be glad it's us and not AISI. Or maybe you perhaps know them already? In some capacity! Like an informant, for example."

Kravets had not said what they'd expected. But the public explosion between him and his colleague and Tarnovsky's sudden flight rang to Trevisan like the kind of dissent that leads to defection from the old.

10

Once a cop, always a cop! Marcello wondered how true the adage was. All those perks he'd had as a Florentine detective counted. Nor had he forgotten that police secretaries and clerks often resolve problems that detectives can't … or won't ... and sometimes solve cases. Now he had no one to call but Trevisan—who claimed he worked alone. On the drive back to Santa Lucia, the rain poured. And his mind wandered. The wipers click clack, click clack, ineffective against the splash of the squadrons of eighteen-wheelers headed to and from the mainland. Marcello drove, dodged the biggest splashes, and wished he'd taken the cat. If not for the rain and Trevisan's presence, he would turn around and go back for it now. Every cat has a name!

Trevisan was on his phone with the Questura, the Venice police department. He didn't really work only alone. Quickly he got the addresses of Kravets and Tarnovsky, and those of three other Ukrainians with families who'd lived and worked in the city for years. They had a connection with the Honorary Ukrainian Consul for the area, in Padua, twenty-six minutes from Santa Lucia Station.

Back in his track 1 office, Trevisan awarded him as an ex-cop a local transportation pass: vaporettos, speed boats and regional trains. They split between themselves self-imposed basic police duties: Trevisan from his Santa Lucia office checking trains from Padua; Marcello foot-tailing Kravets.

Marcello headed for Academia Bridge and the *Pensione Ponte* just behind the gallery where the two Ukrainians shared a third-floor walk-up, a two-bedroom suite. It was already dark.

The rain slacked off while Marcello was on the vaporetto. Short November days. He pictured the suite, thin mattresses, tiny bathroom and flowery wallpaper. Another place like the ones the Ukrainians had been living in for years. He got goose bumps just thinking about it. Next stop, *Pension Ponte.*

Actually, there were few places Handsome would go. But you never know. Kravets could look up other Ukrainians or contact persons in Venice. He could fast train to Padua. If he did board a train, Marcello would feel no qualms about using his Florence police agent credentials to scour their pension suite while he was gone. He would grill the pension personnel anyway. And hopefully Tarnovsky would reappear.

Since the rain had eased, Marcello stood under a ledge on the steps of the academy museum and viewed everyone coming across the Academia bridge. No sign of Kravets. But to his surprise, Tarnovsky who'd never seen him suddenly came and stood on the steps, some ten meters away. He too waiting for his old friend Kravets. Time passed and Marcello got antsy.

Suddenly, he turned to Tarnovsky and said: "I think we're waiting for the same person."

No answer. He added: "Kravets."

"Are we acquainted?"

"I was in Chioggia today too. Transworld Shipping. You didn't see me. But I was there and saw you in what looked like the end of a story between you and Kravets."

"I see … and yes, it was the end."

Marcello moved nearer Tarnovsky. "I'm not a policeman, you should know."

No reaction.

"But I was once. My name is Marcello Bolzoni. If I were still a cop today I would probably detain you for questioning. No one is charging you with anything but like my police friend said to Kravets, we do wonder what you've been doing for so many years just traveling around our country."

"No longer! That's for sure. My break with him is final. But it's chiefly for personal reasons. Andriy is ignorant. Traveling around Italy like we were supposed to—who knows why?—we were always together, like Siamese twins. Sometimes I felt like we were in a circus. No one to talk to but this ignoramus. I don't know why they had us enroll in the university but that is exactly what I wanted. For real, I mean. With no more obligations to Kiev."

"But what were you doing all these years, traveling around Italy … and paid to do it? We keep wondering. Who were you spying on ?"

"We didn't spy on anybody … well, except for a brief and indirect relationship with the AISI in Rome —Italy's FBI. Kravets might still be in contact with them But the high-level AISI man that our department in Kiev hoped to recruit as an informant was assassinated—or maybe he killed himself when his sympathies were revealed."

This kid really wants to talk. Sad guy. Still just a kid. Twenty-eight, he said. Thirty in the records. Reminds me of my kid brother back in Montepulciano. So much stored up in him that it's overflowing the banks of himself. No need to interrogate Vasyl! He poses the questions himself and then gives the answers. Either anti-Fascism has intensified his hate or he's simply a courageous man. He could be Ukrainian or he could be Russian. Like many Ukrainians, and not only in Kharkov. The choice was his. Recalls the words of the Italian-American historian, Howard Zinn, that *The memory of people behaving magnificently gives me the courage to act as I believe all human beings should act in defiance of all the evil around us.*

Tarnovsky seemed to have the same memory as Zinn. He had simply run out of patience. That's why Marcello's soft spot for him even though he'd just met him. The inexplicable things in life. Like that cat. Things that make you feel chill bumps, but which we're too hardened by life to admit they even exist.

"The ultimate was always infiltration into Italian intelligence agencies and political parties," Tarnovsky said. "I learned that our agents from Nazi-led West Ukraine had long ago infiltrated the fascist party running Italy today. So you see the spy network I was associated with did accomplish something. Ugly things like that are going on all over West Europe which is quickly turning fascist itself. What else is the European Union doing besides hatching Fascism-Nazism?"

"You're an unusual person, Vasyl Tarnovsky. I hope we'll become friends … if you don't get yourself killed like your AISI informant. Which reminds me of words I read about loyalty and love. The metaphor pertained to sexual love but the real subject was loyalty to institutions, to native countries, or to persons. The sentence read: 'In real life most people want love. Even a street walker's love will do in a pinch. However, hesitation, reason, insecurity and a sense of surviving but fading loyalty to a loved one or thing stand like disintegrating turrets of a weakened fortress in the sand of the desert of human emotion.'"

"Well, yes, that too, Marcello—if I may use your first name. In Kharkov, everyone studied Pushkin, who in his greatest work shows that you can be both patriotic and European, loyal to tradition yet receptive to the new Though Russians see him as very Russian, the Russians' Russian, he himself was drawn to works of Shakespeare, Dante, Walter Scott."

"Yes, but keep in mind though that it sometimes happens that a new set of the problems arises when the objects of your loyalty are disloyal to you."

"That's what's happening to me right now."

"Yes I hope that's the case. Meanwhile, let's go check your rooms," Marcello said, again forgetting he was no longer a cop. Vasyl too took him for a policeman. Funny, he thought, it really is like they say, once a cop, always a cop.

"I assume you won't mind since you're moving out anyway," he added.

The *pensione* was a two-story structure, covering most of its own little island formed by small canals surrounding it, canals too narrow for boats. Secluded just as the Ukrainians had wanted, the pension was accessible only by a walkway from a calle behind the Academia Gallery. No one saw Marcello and Vasyl enter and go up the stairs to their two-bed room suite. From the doorway you could see most of the flat: both rooms, bath and kitchenette and a small balcony attached to the second room and hanging over a small garden illuminated by multi-colored lamps dimmed in the rain and mist. Marcello stood on the small balcony and listened to the sounds of vaporettos and the hum of motorboat taxis on the Canal Grande. He could barely hear the light drizzle. Maybe the rain had ended, he thought, but doubted it—Roman Tempestas and Aztec Tlaloc gods of rain were the universe's greatest jokesters. They never had enough. Marcello smiled to himself and turned toward the desk in the corner near the balcony.

He turned on the computer.

Vasyl shrugged and said there was nothing of interest there.

Marcello didn't know what he was looking for either but he held his phone ready to photograph any names, places, reports, projects, hopes, delusions. He found nothing. He looked at the discs tossed haphazardly into the first drawer.

"Pictures of scenery and places he liked," Vasyl said. "One I recall of the Oto Melara arms factory. I've got the same in my phone. We visited there in the guise of buyers but they didn't show us anything. Told us to go to an office in Rome. It was a government to government matter, they said. But what did we know?"

Marcello tapped his arm affectionately. In that same moment, he thought: Pushkin! The cat's name is to be Pushkin.

"Let's get out of here," Marcello finally said. "Since you are footloose now, why don't you come have dinner with me and my wife. We've got to find a safe place for you anyway. Too many of your fellow Ukrainians around, precisely the people you have to avoid, people ready to disappear you. Word about you will be spreading. Andriy will see to that—and most likely accuse you of being a Russian spy."

There were few passengers on the vaporetto. They passed under the Rialto Bridge. The drizzle intensified. They were standing on a covered platform, following the scenery along the Canal Grande, palaces that to them seemed repetitive, even though both understood that it was beauty itself that was repetitive, for each palace-palazzo- Ca' was a chef d'oeuvre of the major architects of past centuries, works reflecting the whims and complexities of time. In better times, Marcello thought, he would learn the names of palaces along this the heart canal of Venice lined by palaces of which Shelley wrote: " *it's temples and palaces did seem like fabrics of enchantment piled to heaven.*" He chuckled to himself at the thought that Chioggia from where they'd just returned liked to refer to itself as Little Venice. Bullshit! At the most it could claim to be a southern aquatic suburb of the city. He felt that his presence here was all one extended dream: the dream that he was actually living in this city that itself was a dream.

Later, as they climbed the blue carpeted stairs on Calle di Solferino, he said: "Vasyl, you're our first real guest in Venice. I'm glad it's you."

Vasyl glanced at him ambiguously and commented: "The wall lamps and the blue carpets make the staircase a little eerie. A nice eerie though."

"Somehow, I always end up living on the third floor. The same in Florence, the same where I come from. So I've seen a lot of different staircases. Some are works of art."

"Where is that, where you come from?"

"Montepulciano, in Tuscany."

"I've been there! We stayed in a strange hotel run by two young Scots."

"I know them pretty well. They are Stuarts. Scottish-Italians. And their cousin lives here on the first floor. A writer. You'll meet him. This is a very special house, as you will see."

Marcello's apartment door was wide open. Tarnovsky looked at him quizzically.

"No problem, Vasyl. It's my wife's way. She says she can't work behind closed doors. She's a painter ... and a chemist."

"And a very sensitive person too, no?"

"That's for sure. But wait till you see her work … and her."

Marcello led the way through the *shadow hall* to Helen's studio. She was standing with her back to the window, waiting. When he saw her, Tarnovsky gasped. Then, unlike others—except for Marcello—he immediately apologized—endearing himself to her.

"Ciao, Vasyl!" Helen said. "Glad to see you here. See that picture over there in the corner, that's me too. I uncovered it to see me finished … as I see me, and as do some few others. Oh, forgive me. I'm so egocentric! Every day I think I should go back to chemistry. But I can't. Not now. I haven't finished with myself yet."

He didn't answer. He was studying the corner work and thinking, not of his ex-colleague or of black market arms sales. Nor even of Marcello. After some time, he looked again at Helen and said simply:

"Yes, I understand. And who ever finishes with himself?"

Then silence till Marcello intervened and proposed dinner in the trattoria down on their street. "We'll invite Oriana and the others too. You met her at the university, Vasyl. She'll be pleased to see you here. And there's Stuart and Sophie on the first floor. All of us exiles … and dissidents too, you might say. We're all changing lives, maybe you more than any of us. A healthy change—not one that everyone experiences."

Trattoria da Manin was just across the street. Few others present. Everyone spoke softly. Vasyl felt at ease with them. They spoke of a hideout for the Russian-Ukrainian. Spontaneously they all had the same idea: the unoccupied fourth floor just above Helen and Marcello. Oriana would transmit to him highlights of lectures and seminars from the philosophy department. And I, Stuart, had found an in-house Russian language teacher. And Manin found a new clientele to carry him through the winter of the Venetian red rains.

They ate pasta and sipped a red Valpolicella.. The bottle remained half full in the center of the table.

Their host looked sadly at the torrents smashing against the tall front windows and said philosophically: “I’m still a positivist. I believe it will stop.”

After a meditative silence during which they all stared at the window, Manin added: “Someday. Maybe.”

11

November 11

Pushkin! The Chioggia cat. He must be lonely at night in that huge plant floating on lagoon water. Unacceptable that he had no name. Where did he sleep? Where and when did he eat? The next morning he told Helen he was going back to that fake Little Venice to get his cat; he'd already named him. And she shouldn't tell Vasyl he'd gone back Chioggia. No need to scare him.

He bought a cat carrier and cat food, borrowed Trevisan's car—the loner cop thought him mad—and an hour later was parked at Transworld Shipping. Chioggia town was wine shops, grocers and snack bars along the Lungomare. The company building looked ghostly in the drizzle. The doors were open. No one at reception. *Menos mal*. He elevatored to the third floor, looked around and called softly: "Pushkin." He retraced their steps of yesterday, looking down the aisles and calling Pushkin.

He looked into an office with glass walls, called Pushkin, and literally jumped when he heard a meow.

"Pushkin!"

" Meow!"

And the cat's dark, streaked head peeked out of a box in a corner, his green eyes full of sleep. He knew his name. Marcello repeated the memorized words of the refrain of a song he liked that he'd been reconstructing during the drive down: *I've been through the desert on a horse with no name /It felt good to be out of the rain/ In the desert you can't remember your name/ 'Cause there ain't no one for to give you no pain.*

Pushkin must've been waiting for someone to give him his name. Marcello placed a plastic plate filled with prime cat food in front of the carrier door.

"Come, Pushkin. Lunchtime."

"Meow!"

He pushed the plate inside the carrier. The cat only had eyes for the food. Marcello felt guilty for the dirty trick when he closed the gate behind him.

"Now you have a name." The thing about Pushkin was that he always answered. What did it mean? That he understood? Or that out of politeness he acknowledged that he had been spoken to?

In that moment the office door opened. Santin came in.

"Detective!" he said in a low voice.

"Ex-detective. What am I doing here? I came to get my cat. His name is Pushkin. And what are you doing here in all this silence? Are you alone today?"

"Alone? *Magari!* The financial police are here in full force," he said in a near whisper. "Checking our books, our registrars. That's the silence you hear. I'm almost glad to see you. And you can have the cat. He doesn't belong to anybody."

"Cats never belong to anybody, Santin!"

"Then let's go the bar and have a drink together to celebrate Pushkin's name day. I mean the day you told him his name. Like a christening."

Marcello put the carrier on the bar and opened its gate. The cat sat there inside. Seemed to like his box. Marcello risked and ordered vodka and beer which he thought would please Santin.

It did.

"They're in that big room over there, their whole team, together with some of our accountants and bookkeepers. And that Ukrainian is with them too."

“Kravets? What’s he doing here?” Marcello said, his voice rising despite Santin’s shh’s. “Up to no-good, you can be sure of that. He’s an asshole. And a scoundrel besides. I’m certain he works for their secret police, the SBU.”

Santin didn’t care about the Ukrainian secret police; only the Italian *Finanza* scared him. “The financial police could put me away for five years, easy,” he whispered. “They brought all the mandates they need with them. For Christ sakes, our situation is critical; we have to prove there’s no fraud … or any other fiscal crimes. Right now, they’re verifying all our fiscal documents, registrars and inventories of the shipment. The problem is that someone here falsified accounts on the Mali shipment and intended skimming maybe 20% off the value of all that military stuff. Mali was to be billed for over eight million for the military hardware but our own inventories show a total declared value of less than seven million. And that guy Kravets verified both. The culprits seem to be Kravets and the accountant he bribed. You’re right. Their war up north is a real bonanza for the Ukie leaders. But they’re criminals anyway and don’t have the Italian *Finanza* to deal with And to think they get all this stuff they sell to Africa free! A seller’s dream scheme.”

“Well, let’s hope for the best, eh, Pushkin.” The cat was hanging around the carrier. Marcello believed because it held the promise of food. Or maybe it already felt like home. And each time he called his name, Pushkin looked at him and sometimes answered “meow.” The cat had learned his name in record time.

Another dangerous drink with Santin and an exchange of cellphone numbers before Marcello and his cat set out for Cannaregio where new people, several injections and a little operation awaited the cat, which worried Marcello more than arms sales to Mali.

12

Trevisan met every train from Padua that afternoon, the fifth of which had just arrived. It was deluging again. Heaven's waters crashed down on the train station's slate overhang and reddish water backed up along the magical tracks that served big trains at three hundred fifty kilometers an hour. Then he saw him. The Ukrainan was fooling with the opening mechanism of a big multicolored umbrella and smiling to himself. Kravets then ambled toward the exit, trailing a hand along the shiny green metal of a new train car. As he approached, Trevisan stepped behind a baggage cart, uncertain about the necessity of tailing the Ukrainian since Marcello had already told him that he found nothing of significance in their rooms and that Tarnovsky was living temporarily with him: Kravets followed the tourists to the Santa Lucia vaporetto station, irritating others with his huge umbrella. On the spur of the moment Trevisan jumped aboard the boat too: he thought he might as well observe the effect on Kravets of Tarnovsky's absence who had in effect defected—not only from his still unclear work relationship with Kravets and the SBU, but also from his country. Now it would be up to the police and immigration authorities to decide his future in Italy.

When Kravets stepped off the vaporetto at Academia, Trevisan followed, shielded by a group of tourists and thinking that the art of foot-tailing was truly different in Venice from any other place in the world. No streets to pretend to idle on, few shop windows to use as mirrors. When Kravets circled the darkened Academia Gallery, Trevisan opened his own umbrella, signaled a police launch stationed across the Canal Grande to be ready, and stood in the museum doorway to wait.

Fifteen minutes later, Kravets came back and boarded a waiting water taxi that u-turned and headed back toward the Rialto Bridge. Trevisan followed in his launch.

Both deboarded and walked through the fish market, winding over small bridges, through archways, until Kravets suddenly stopped, turned back and hurriedly rang twice the top button of a five-story building. The door opened instantly and he vanished inside. Trevisan waited a couple of minutes before walking away. Then five minutes later he returned to the same door. Kravets had rung the doorbells for Georgetti-Kristin. House number 11, Calle Serena, San Polo Sestiere. As he was studying the names, a couple arrived and clicked in their door code. Trevisan asked them if they knew the people on the top floor. They looked at him suspiciously and then at each other.

"I'm a policeman," Trevisan said, showing his ID.

"Foreigners, I know," the man said. "Middle-aged."

The lady said the couple had lived here for many years, "but they don't speak with other residents that I know of. All we've ever exchanged with them on the stairs is a *bon dì*. And I have heard them speak Russian to each other."

"Oh yes? How did you know it was Russian?"

"Well, I don't speak Russian but I studied it for two years. I know enough to recognize it. And I know they have Russian or maybe Ukrainian friends."

"May I ask which floor you live on?"

"The fourth, just under them," the man said. "And I think that's all we can tell you about them."

"I apologize for my insistence and thank you for your cooperation. It could be quite important." A bug in their ears won't hurt, he thought, and added: "Please don't mention my being here to other people, especially in this building. Spies do exist in real life, not just in fiction."

Since there were no cafés or public places nearby, he stood in a doorway close enough the see anyone come out of number 11. He hated stake-outs in the island city. At least it wasn't pouring rain in the moment, just the steady, nerve-wracking drizzle. As usual, the queer red color. It looked like blood. Bloodfall, he thought. Half an hour passed. No one entered. No one came out. An hour passed. He didn't really expect Kravets to leave anytime soon. The image of a vodka-beer combination flashed across his mind's eye. One just like those at the Tansworld bar in Chioggia .What a fucking job! If they were at least over in Mestre he could be sitting in a car. Dry. Why, Kravets could be up there for the night. Maybe even looking down at me now … and laughing. It began to rain hard. His feet were already wet, squishing with each step. You can catch a cold like this. The cold turns into the flu, maybe pneumonia. The Trevisan method! Work alone! Bullshit. Two hours had passed. He began to detest that pompous Kravets, probably up there in a warm, dry bed and listening to the pleasant pattering of the rain outside. All his fucking fault! "And fuck my solitary system too," he said aloud. And to himself, he added, 'And for that matter, fuck non-drinking on duty. I'm leaving you here, asshole. We'll see about you tomorrow. And just wait till AISI gets its hands on you! They don't fuck around with foot-tailing and stake-outs in the rain; they just come for you in the middle of the night and stash you away in some secret place and get the information they want straight from your mouth. You should know that. Same as SBU. Mean people—you find them all over the world. Torture or execution, all the same to them.'

He entered a pub near the fish market to dry his feet and drink something warm. Then he called his AISI contact. He had a friendly relationship with Agent Thomas Cassiano, a Calabrian, born and partially raised in Newark, New Jersey where his father and uncle ran the famous Calabria Brothers Deli—a meeting place for musicians, Cassiano said. After a reassuring number of clicks on Cassiano's safe phone and an exchange of friendly greetings, he related the series of events since Bolzoni and Stuart arrived in Venice. Gulliver, black market arms sold and transshipped from Chioggia destined for Abijan and Mali, the two apparent Ukrainian agents Oriana met at Ca' Foscari—one of whom now a defector—the infiltrator in the Transworld firm, and now the immigrant couple from Ukraine in Calle Serena, where, as of ten minutes ago, the putative SBU agent was holed up.

"Admittedly stuff far from my bailiwick and city police jurisdiction, Tommy, but which by chance fell my way."

"Now, now, Trevisan. You and I do not believe in coincidences," Cassiano said in his surprisingly musical Calabrian-American accent. Greeks all, speaking il Griko dialect in a town named Siberi. "So how do you account for your violation of our code?"

"My Tuscan writer friend believes firmly in coincidence. But he says if you reject that, then there is destiny. And however you look at it, my feet are still wet from the stake-out that should never have happened."

"Well, for now I'll relieve you of the people in Calle Serena—both the couple and the one you called an SBU agent.

And Trevisan, you might show the defector your place, ok? I'll look for you tomorrow morning . Same place as last time?"

"The same."

"Time to change for you. Even if only to another track. You've been there too long."

"I'll think about it. Wait! I thought about it. You're right. I'll move soon to the other side of the tracks ... where I probably belong."

"I'm serious, Nicola, don't wait too long. You never know."

At ten the next morning Thomas Cassiano knocked lightly and pushed open the glass office door on Track 1 of Santa Lucia Station. The Venice operative of the *Agenzia informazioni e sicurezza interna* –Domestic Information and Security Agency, or AISI—was of medium height, had dark, longish hair, the blue eyes of some Sicilian ancestor, and unexpectedly clean shaven. A tight fitting light blue raincoat emphasized his broad-shoulders and muscular physique. When he embraced Trevisan in the usual bone-crushing way the policeman thought that this man's prisoners must maintain a low profile and refer to him carefully as *signore*. Still, as tough as he appeared, for his own reasons Agent Cassiano felt protective toward Trevisan … as if he were a kid brother. Nicola still wondered why.

"So, Nicky lad," he began, eyeing Vasyl standing next to the make-shift table that Trevisan called his desk, "what's this story about black market weapons and SBU agents you're mixed up in?" Cassiano spoke as if he knew nothing about arms sales to Africa after having most likely grilled Kravets and the Calle Serena couple half the night.

"Bewildering events. Sordid stories. Many things happening simultaneously. My detective friend Bolzoni and his friends who recently moved here from Florence made the acquaintance of Gulliver, that is, Signor Gulli whom you might know—by the way, that man's one hundred and two years old! The old guy told him stories about Venice's shipping industry and black market arms sales. Then Bolzoni's friend, Oriana Alberti, ex-Florence Chief of Police by the way who's now studying at Ca' Foscari met the two Ukrainian SBU agents, they too students there. You know Kravets, and now you meet Vasyl Tarnovsky who has, er, defected from the SBU. But Tommy, however AISI handles the matter of black market arms sales, I think I'm destined to be involved in some way."

Uncertainly, the Ukrainian stepped forward and offered his handshake and said his name: "Vasily Tarnovsky." Cassiano shook hands no less uncertainly, looked him over in his police manner and told him that he now faced difficult decisions but not all of which were actually his own. However speaking with others would help immensely. "You've already taken the first step—it seems spontaneously—which in such cases might seem the hardest—though it really is not. But then no one can do everything they might want to do. In any case, your future choices might not depend on you. Since Italy has been good to you all these years, we will hope for signs of gratitude. Now as you know the majority of Italians are not fascists like our government in Rome and some of those with whom I'm associated would naturally hope that you will share our interests wherever you are. Anyway, after this break, return to Ukraine is impossible for you. You would go straight to prison or worse … unless, of course, things there change dramatically … which I doubt. Your country is now a satrapy of NATO-USA-EU. So you have to consider other options."

"As you know, I'm from Kharkov. But I am Russian. So living in Russia attracts me ... no less than living in Italy. I studied philosophy at the university in Kharkov. And now I'm enrolled in studies in that field at Ca' Foscari. In any case and wherever I am, as you say, I hope to find a place in the academic world. And that can only come about in Russia."

Part Two

13

November 12

During the Carnevale di Venezia on Piazza San Marco the observer can witness firsthand the extraordinary transfiguration of a masked celebrant into the personality of his mask. The carnival reveler dons the mask and almost immediately begins acting out its role. The powerful Venetian mask transforms the wearer's character into that of the mask itself. Unconsciously, the reveler might at first only imitate the gestures of the mask. But then something mysterious happens; he quickly assumes the mask's personality as it incorporates both the form and the interior force of the subject it represents. In the end, the mask triumphs. It is the catalyst for the carnival magic that turns the person into his mask. The mask provokes both terror and respect in us humans. It is mysterious and seems to contain something of the divine … something of the eternal. The mask role precedes also modern religion; the mask is itself a kind of god. Atavistic. It incarnates a guardian spirit and is therefore sacred. We know that Egyptians covered mummies with masks that transformed their pharaohs into gods, while Greeks covered the faces of their heroes with the masks that were fundamental also in their theater.

While living in a small central Mexican town, I frequented the shop of an elderly Indio of the Cora people. A dealer in indigenous masks and artifacts, Ignacio instructed me in the role of the mask among Mexico's ancient peoples. He was a cultured man and knew esoterics. Romantically, I thought of him as a shaman.

The five thousand surviving Coras in the state of Nayarit in western Mexico make extensive use of masks in their annual celebration of the *Santo Entierro*, the Easter Procession celebrated on Good Friday all over the country. "It's extraordinary," Ignacio told me one day in the cellar of his shop, "that the shy and reserved Coras become ferocious when during Holy Week they put on their masks—accompanied by consumption of tequila and peyote. As the Cora establishes contact with the eternal, the mask erases the individual." A very socio-political consideration in contemporary times: collectivism wins.

Indigenous peoples of Mexico use the mask as a magical means of transforming their souls by assuming the identity of a god powerful enough to control nature and lighten their earthly lives. At Cora celebrations the masked figures become the wild animals they represent; they crawl and leap, growl and howl, in imitation of their animal double. Ignacio's favorite was a lugubrious Olmec mask representing life and death hanging in his bodega: the left side of the face depicted a live person, the right side a dead one. Ignacio explained that at the beginnings of Mexican culture the shamans—who were more sorcerers than priests—wore masks to give themselves identities and to become gods. "Masks make gods," he repeated. "Or perhaps gods become masks."

The essence of Ignacio's belief was this: The mask is what we all are. We wear different masks all our lives, changing them according to the situation or circumstances. Even the facial expression itself is a mask for our interior selves, a reflection of our intelligence or our soul—of that which is eternal in each individual. It represents the person ever in change. All taken together, the different masks make up the personality. The mask also represents the society in which the *persona* lives. Thus, mask is a totality, a summing up, a macrocosm.

At times Ignacio would return to the mask in the western cultural sense in which the face covering is a disguise to "mask" our true intents. One covers one's face with another in order to simulate a personality different from the real one. The mask represents another self, which is *perhaps* the real one. Yet, forever the mystic, he could not help adding that of course the ordinary face might not be the real person either. In most cases the masker is attempting to establish momentary contact with his real self, or, on the other hand, to cut off contact with it. The riddle of which among all our faces is the real self seems unsolvable. But that was Ignacio's point: if all the faces are masks, then it is a matter of knowing which is the real one. And under that? Is that so-called real one just a shabby ordinary being? No better, no worse than you. For in the demands and compromises of our ordinary lives we do not usually know which face is mask and which is reality. Life becomes a game. A futile attempt to understand ourselves and our relationship with the universe.

Albert Camus writes in *The Myth of Sisyphus* that "a man defines himself by his make-believe as well as by his sincere impulses."

Man's desperation is that despite his reason, he can never truly know himself or the core self of others. My father was a good man. The total of his deeds and acts defined him for those around him as a good man. Yet, after he was gone, I came to realize that I never knew his core self. I never knew his heart. The most I can say is that I believe his mask of goodness was his true face. For as Octavio Paz wrote: "We are condemned to invent a mask for ourselves and afterward to discover that the mask is our true face."

One says that reality is the face. That is precisely what artists have traditionally painted and sculpted. Yet for whatever reasons, humans have always been moved to use masks in order to flee from that reality and to adopt an alien personality. I know well an extremely beautiful Venetian-Viennese painter, Helen Peterson, who arrived at what she considers her true face through a series of dual paintings of a beautiful face and an ugly face. In each iteration the ugly face becomes less ugly and the beautiful face less beautiful, swapping their exterior appearances until she arrived at a synthesis that she believes represents her and the qualities of beauty and ugliness.

But as I said earlier, also the masked face is reality. That creates confusion for philosophers, psychiatrists and artists: the mask confers temporarily a different face on the wearer, who in turn can see the world with a different face, that is, see it from another reality. From another perspective.

I once had occasion to speak at length with Marcello Mastroianni about his many roles. The actor was remarkable both for the quality and the quantity of his roles. In cinema and theater he personified lovers and heroes, artists and adventurers, and as he said, he was never so complete as on set where he only had to follow the directions of the film director. Yet his genius was his ability to become instantly his characters. Each role was a new mask. Remarkable his ability to break down the borders between being and seeming. Yet everyday life without a mask bored him. I was surprised seeing him ensconced in a chair, in casual dress, speaking in normal conversational tones, trying his best to be an ordinary man. Yet something was wrong: from time to time he kept falling into one or other of his roles—the simpatico Italian or another Fellini creation. Mastroianni was the totality of his characters. He carried them around with him from day to day. It was hard to imagine him without one of his masks. Layer after layer of masks concealed him. I now wonder if perhaps without his masks Marcello did not exist. For the actor in his choice to live many lives in one is the mask *par excellence.*

Camus recalls that the Church condemned actors because they objected to living only one life. They were heretics. They chose the hell of multiple lives instead of eternal life. Acting, like writing or painting or any kind of creation, is living again. Again and again.

On St. Mark's Square you can see how the man behind the mask becomes another. One can do wild unimaginable things behind a mask. In that sense the mask crushes our inhibitions … like drugs or alcohol.. Although through the eyes of the mask the reveler sees the same exterior, the same world outside that he has temporarily abandoned, he now sees it with the mask's eyes. His perception of the world is therefore different. That phenomenon is bound to transform also his being: permanent epiphany.

While the mask bears the assumed personality, the wearer's habitual thoughts and awareness are concealed.

His everyday attitudes are erased.

His real personality is hidden.

Unawares, his essence behind the mask mutates: he believes he has acquired the character, the powers and abilities of the mask.

The man becomes his mask.

It is easy to lose one's train of thought in discussing the elusive but omnipresent mask. It's like the search for the final answer of who you are. Your thinking process is turned upside down. Like the psychiatrist, the writer deals constantly with masks. To create his literature he is obligated to wear many different masks. Sometimes he simply observes the exterior of the mask itself and narrates its actions. Other times he peers under it and tries to identify with the personality concealed there. Often he is tempted to put on a mask himself, in order to conceal himself and to transform himself into a new personality.

One mask of the writer can be so-called "sincerity". In its most degenerate form—the word sincerity has long since lost its original meaning of pure or unadulterated—the well-known mask of sincerity has become the lie. At least since the eighteenth century, false and dishonest sincerity in literature has been recognized as the mask concealing bigotry and hypocrisy which for the writer are fatal. The sincerity mask conceals the writer's own fears—the fear of extremes and commitment and the fear of violation of established codes and correctness.

Provocatively, Alberto Moravia suggests that the writer in his most authentic mask must be extreme, not logical. The conformist writer instead, inhibited and bound, coolly and with "measure" takes on subjects that neither concern him nor interest him but that the majority of his readers or his society welcome. His conformist mask is a double one: he flees from himself in order to avoid dangerous directions and accepts the ready-made schemes his society proposes.

Inevitably the mask of falsehood condemns the writer to struggle forever on the surface of things. To battle eternally with the unimportant. With his mask of false sincerity he can never descend to the depths of human life; he is condemned to mediocrity.

Another writer may attempt to shed his masks and speak for himself. But by the nature of his activity the writer is obligated to assume diverse roles. He must be able to handle masks. For without them he stands naked and alone. Without masks he can only speak for himself; he quickly runs dry.

Defining the nature of sincerity as "philistine respectability," Oscar Wilde wrote that man is least himself when he speaks in his own person. "Give him a mask and he will tell you the truth." For him the mask was the only source of truth: cryptically, he claimed he lived in terror of not being misunderstood.

Nietzsche, with his unexpected affinity with Wilde, said in *Beyond Good and Evil*, "Everything that is profound loves the mask.... Every profound spirit needs a mask." For the renegade philosopher *any* moralizing was depressing.

Their point was that displayed sincerity is usually a negative face. The "sincere" man is often false. You never know where sincerity ends and hypocrisy begins.

Like the shaman, the honest writer—however he goes about it—is attempting to establish contact with his real self, just as his characters who in turn are all of us. Whether he writes in the third person about his invented characters with all their different masks—which are his own masks—or in the first person about himself, the writer is also hoping to determine which is the mask and which his real self.

The writer is fortunate if he is able to see clearly, not only under the mask of others, but also to see the world from the reality of those different masks. At a certain moment, the creator becomes his creation.

That moment is the dimension of his art.

It is the transcendence of the artist.

It is his special insight. His power.

The writer sets out energetically and optimistically. In his life and in his art he tries on many masks-faces. Often it seems he has found his true but elusive self. Sometimes, however, he comes to realize that his face--his mask--is alien to himself, after which he is forever plagued by the nostalgia for return to his original and true self.

In the course of the violent twentieth century the most infamous mask was that of "I didn't know." It was the mask of "sincere" ignorance. Ignorance about the huge reality in Nazi Germany, ignorance about the deportation of Venetian Jews from their ghetto from which there was no return.

Writers today face new realities. They can don the mask of ignorance or indifference and refuse to know. But those who dare to look cannot help but see the great lie enveloping us all—the great lie hidden behind the "sincerity" of our political leaders who pray for God to protect us from our enemies, who describe war as peace, bombs as security, the free market as brotherhood, imperialism as democracy, first strike as self-defense, and dissent as terrorism.

You object that the fiction writer is neither politician nor philosopher? That is true. He is not. But he still shares the world of humanity, which is conditioned by politics. He has to know something about politics. He can't hide behind art for art's sake. If he is genuinely sincere, that is, according to Lionel Trilling's definition, authentic, he cannot put on his mask of "I didn't know" and feign ignorance.

The fiction writer has ideas. They might not be immediately evident in his fiction. Yet his ideas, his themes if you like, spring not only from his mind but also from his sensitiveness. Thc world in which he lives creates the honest writer's sensitiveness and thus his ideas. The reader must scratch beneath the surface of places where the honest writer operates. If you delve into his sensitiveness, you will find his ideas.

The writer himself is perhaps unaware of the ideas in his fiction and the superficial reader might not recognize them. But they must be there, hidden in his every word. Taken together those ideas form his ideology. The ideology of the novelist, confused, ambiguous and contradictory—for he is not a rational philosopher—is the totality of the ideas and themes lying under the surface of his story.

The honest fiction writer, by means of his various masks, which are his characters, offers two readings: a story line that only hints at an ideology, or a story built around a clear ideology.

One hopes to find in his writing ideas that promote humanity and wellbeing. Otherwise, his writing will turn out to be a series of meaningless loose ends. (Stuart Stuart, Time and Space Journal).

I click send and turn back to the rain splattered window. How could I not write about ideas and where they come from? Where fantasy comes from?

The crazy red rain pummels the panes and I think. It turns nearly dark outside and I think of you. I think of darkness at noon and our blue-carpeted stairs. And I wait. Aware or unaware of ideas, they are there … bullshit ideas or not. The writer, any writer, all writers have ideas. Here in the bloody red rain of Cannaregio, some just pop into your mind by chance while you press your head against the window panes and wait for them; others you acquire by living, studying, reading other writers. They come from memory of things past. The sweetest things, the ugliest things you remember. Countless ideas are out there, looking for a taker. Like will the rain ever stop? Or how did I end up here? Admittedly some ideas are better than others. Most worse. Maybe not. But there is always a connection, one with the other. Depends on whether there are more good or bad persons among us. Or is it all the same, good and bad, like Helen's ugliness and beauty.

Now, the Greeks said it first, for Christ's fucking sakes! I read in *Ecclesiastes* of the disaster of foolish, fractious, querulous man—rebellious and insubordinate:

"All *things come* alike to all!" Solomon and Heraclitus believed about the same thing, as did Giordano Bruno a millennium later.

*"There is one event to the righteous, and to the wicked; to the good and to the clean, and to the unclean... as is the good, so is the sinner....There is an evil among all things that are done under the sun, that there is one event unto all: yea, also the heart of the sons of men is full of evil, and madness is in their heart while they live, and after that they go to the dead. For him that is joined to all the living, there is hope (*through the centuries to *John Donne—No man is an island) ... for the living know that*

they shall die; but the dead know not anything, neither have they any more a reward; for the memory of them is forgotten. Also their love, and their hatred, and their envy, is now perished; neither have they any more a portion forever in anything that is done under the sun."

These thoughts have plagued me all morning. Evil Venice rain comes down erratically in bursts that crash and fog up the windows. Not even Marcello goes out. He is at peace with Helen and Pushkin.

Vasyl Tarnovsky, installed on the fourth floor, hasn't yet found real peace; he has a stove, refrigerator, bed and table and lots of space and is accumulating the books he loves but he doesn't know the most important thing: he doesn't know who he is. Literally. His brother Andriy in his grave is not at peace either and likely wants to kill his brother Vasyl over and over again.

Nor am I at peace.

Are the philosophers right?

Is Cain destined to kill Abel forever? Over and over again? Has it always been that way?

Is who is more Semitic, Jew or Palestinian, of importance?

Will Germans kill their Jewish brothers over and again?

Will the Jews kill their Semite brothers over and over?

Do the Zionists believe Palestinians are not part of the main?

It's like the rain and the wind. Battering and pulverizing the sub-islands surrounding us, each apart one from the other. Killing and killing. Burst after burst crashing into our windows even on the lowest floor.

I watch the murderous, unceasing rain pounding against our windows.

I watch. I watch and try to separate one single drop from the main of the billions of drops. An impossible task. A hopeless struggle from the start. A Sisyphean labor. Like my night hours. Oh, even the slow, slow minutes! The sleepless hours when I live with the clock, time and the past, and sometimes a hopeful future. Just don't think, I tell myself. But who cannot think? Thoughts are like dreams. Demonic dreams. They come as they will. Will this night never pass? Like the rain, it has to end. I hang onto that conviction and count the hours. I never get up and read, nor do I lie there and purposely think of syntactical issues of yesterday. Don't think! I don't dare re-hash or consider where the chapter that I began yesterday is going—or maybe it was the day before—nor do I drink more than a few drops of water in those insomniac nocturnal hours for fear that were I to fall magically into one of my naps, the urge to piss would wake me. What then a waste of hours and effort not to think in the hope of sleep. Or I do think of that chapter after all. Positive thoughts. In those killing hours it's all clear. Constantly, regularly, I check the clock even though I always know the time: 3.30, 4.15, 6.30, maybe a little less, 7.15. Too early to get up, too late to sleep. In those too-late-to-sleep minutes I think of matters like Camus's rejection of Communism. Of Cioran's Fascism. Of the snobbish Bellow's hate for anything left. I think of an unjust God who created the Gaza genocidal world, the meaningless world and the absurdity of existence. Solomon wrote or said or sang that God saith to have a good time and to love people. So if God created us good or evil and chose you in the evil role, then it's not your fucking fault you're a psychopath. I find that hard to believe. Most people want to have a good time and love people. Psychopaths might do one or the other of God's commandments—or none. Some historians claim

Hitler was a nice guy personally, he liked people, joked around, had a girl friend or two but he had this streak of evil in him: he liked having certain peoples killed, en masse. Ceauşescu also was a psychopath and Nicolae had a few quirks too: *he* loved to tear down cities and build them back again, godlike, in his own image; he loved to sell military arms abroad to finance his projects; he didn't mind his own people starving in the dark; and besides he would have preferred to be an Italian—or any Westerner—rather than Romanian. Yet when his people rebelled and they executed him, he had the courage to shout 'Viva Communism' at the rifles pointed at him.

14

November 12

Vasyl lay on the bed in his fourth floor bedroom, his arms crossed behind his head and an expression of "how-good-to-be-in-my-own-home" on his face. His thoughts skipping around from one unrelated thing to another, he was also aware of the music of the ceaseless rain reverberating on the house and the cobblestoned street as it used to do in the late autumn in Kharkov. On his music box he had his favorite, the Shostakovich String Quartet No. 8, the "Dresden Quartet", so-called because written there and dedicated to the defeat of Fascism in reference to the Allied fire-bombing and destruction of that city of art in1945. He knew Shostakovich's work well and why the composer included a musical quotation from the revolutionary song, *Exhausted By the Hardships of Prison*, a favourite of Lenin and sung by the Bolshoi chorus at his funeral. Vasyl listened to the music and with some surprise thought that although he loved many things about his home city he did not actually miss it as happens to many people who spend their lives wandering around the world—he missed only Lyuba, the love of his life. He felt a powerful sense of nostalgia for the freedom he'd felt with her. The freedom of those times during the warm summer months when early evenings he and Lyuba took cotton spreads out to the fields of thick grass and took off all their clothes, and after hours slaking their love thirst, pointed out the constellations of stars in familiar patterns in the high, high summer skies. Russian skies, he always thought. He often thought of Lyuba. Childhood love … and more. She was fourteen years but looked older and he a boy of sixteen when they began kissing and touching each other which inevitably transformed before summer was over. After they gave each other their virginity, he came to think of her as his. That she belonged to him, a concept he came to hate ... even though he remained extremely jealous and couldn't bear to think of her with another. Nonetheless, intellectually he thought no one *belonged* to anyone else. No one was a slave to another. Anyway, there was her terrifying father standing between them. He was a policeman. A policeman in Ukraine, he'd also been a policemen when Kharkov was a major city of the Soviet Union. Some people said he was a Communist then … and a tyrant. Vasyl hoped that he was and that he had become a Communist again. Wishful thinking, he feared. If Vladimir Radovich had discovered them in the fields, he would have beaten the shit out of him and made him pay and pay and pay. Still, there was something clean about her father too, something honest, a quality hard to find in those times—in any times. Still Vasyl mistrusted him. His feelings about the man he'd hoped would become his father-in-law were mistrust, fear and admiration. Fear was over-riding. Fear of Vladimir Radovich made honest communication between them out of the question. Her father who would call his daughter to bring him a beer just to throw around paternal authority. Not a heavy drinker, he loved beer and only on special occasions, did he delve into vodka. In those first few minutes after several beers and between the first and the second vodka, they could have conversed and understood one another. But the man was in the on-drinker's rush to reach a certain point, the point at which communication ended. Instead he gave orders to her in Vasyl's presence. On purpose. She belonged to him, Vladimir Radovich thought. *His* daughter. All her links led back to him. Unfortunately for their love story, Lyuba was not an independent creature. Not a full person in that respect. She was tyrannized by him. Her father's word was a command. She would decide nothing for herself until the day she married, when authority over her would pass to her husband. And that would never be mild-mannered Vasyl, too weak and fearful of his authority to carry on a man-to-man conversation with him. Her future husband would be a bully like Radich himself. So it came about that when he was twenty and Lyuba eighteen he accepted an irrefutable offer of a three-year language school program in Italy: it meant giving up his university studies … and, in the long run, also Lyuba. The day he went with Andryushka-Andrei-Andriy to an anomalous office in a distant district of Kharkov and signed incomprehensible documents pertaining to a school in Italy and his vague future obligations to the Kiev government in exchange, he knew he was betraying his Lyuba. From Italy he wrote her letters, often including one hundred euros and telling her to buy a new dress and think of them and their love and that someday he would come for her. Wishful thinking again. She was a woman now, a beautiful woman; she married a rich man. And he had to accept that reality. But nonetheless he held to his rich dream life in which Lyuba was still his. His dreams ran deep, through his blood stream and into the hidden recesses of his liver and his pancreas. His dreams opposed the duplicitous world he lived in and sometimes previewed a new existence to come. His dreams depicted a heroic Vasyl of glory—*Slava Vasyla!*---but now also projected the smell of death from *their* arms sales and the bombing of tiny Gaza. Lying on his bed in the palazzo in Calle di Solferino, his dreamscape was all-encompassing. Hating irregularity and hating non sequiturs, he perceived his own dangerous shape-shifting personality and in his dreamscape he realized that Andriy Kravets—Andryushka—had to die and that it was his mission to execute his death. The music of the string quartet then ended, it too in death. Dreamily, Vasyl returned to the reality that his home now was in Italy, Venice, Cannaregio, Calle di Solferino, fourth floor. Lazily, smiling inside, snuggling into himself, he turned his head and took note that Schopenhauer's major work, *The World as Will and Representation,* still lay beside him, open on page 15 where he'd left it before his dreams had carried him away. The philosopher writes that "we consider the world only in so far as it is representation of each of us." He understood representation to mean anything of which the mind is conscious in its experience, anything present in the mind.Without sitting up, Vasyl thumbed back to the book's opening quotation by Jean-Jacques Rousseau: *"Quit thy childhood, my friend, and wake up."* On which Vasyl answered the question that had pestered him constantly for so many years: 'Yes, I am Russian.' That was his *identity. The identity that he gave himself in a world of representation.* The role or roles which he believed defined him. His perspective of life and what it is to be a unique individual was forever changing. He now understood that the culture in which one grows up is only one element that shapes one's beliefs: environmental phenomena contribute greatly to his identity; and the phenomena that he had experienced now seemed countless.

"Во всяком случае, I am Russian. I feel Russian. I perceive my Russianness. My background is Russian. Many of the people where I was born and grew up consider me Russian. Lyuba considered me Russian, like herself. Like my parents, she called me Vaska. Yet many others like Kravets hate me for that background and would like to extirpate my Russianness like a metastatic rot, as if it were a disease to be treated and cured. For me, proof enough that Russianness exists in me. Because of my Russian-Ukrainian parents, the Russian language in which I speak, read, write and think, Russian culture is that to which I feel I belong—and, he added, also because of Lyuba. In every aspect including the political, I am Russian. I am Russian in my nostalgias, which today in Kharkov—if nostalgias still exist—are anyway artificial representations.

"How will my individual representation and my nostalgias play out?" He closed his eyes and wondered.

How human intentions and destinies differ!

Before the war and despite his contractual obligations, his intention had always been to go to Perugia, learn the language, travel the country, and then move to a Russian university to complete his doctorate and thus enter the gates of academia. But destiny willed otherwise. How could he have imagined that the distance between him and his old schoolmate and boyhood friend would become an abyss? Andriy—that is, his old pal Andryushka—made *his* choice before Vasyl even knew what SBU stood for. He accepted the offer to go to Italy, from which moment his and Andryushka's paths moved inexorably in different, incompatible and finally in conflicting directions. A gulf divided their individual representations. Their destinies split. Andryuska was no more.

Vasyl stood at the tall window and watched the red streaked rain hammering the city and listened to the rumbling thunder and wondered what to do. What was to be done in general? He had to talk. Stuart would be at home working on his novel. To interrupt or not? Mornings, never. Now it was nearly two o'clock. Go ahead, risk. Down the three flights of stairs. Again aware of the bluish color emitted by the combination of the color of the carpets and the scarcity of wall lamps. The apartment door was closed as per the accord. Sophie opened, kissed him on both cheeks, and said lunch was ready but that Stuart was not. In the same moment, the studio door opened: "I'm here for Vasyl."

We sat vis-à-vis, Vasyl on the couch, I in my favorite easy chair that I'd shipped from Rome to Fiesole and now to Venice-Cannaregio. Barely a couple of years older than the others, my near two-meter height seems to bestow on me both the qualities and the role of a patriarch. Though I pooh-pooh the suggestion, my ego must be pleased to the degree that I have gradually, gradually stepped into the part.

"So what's on your mind, Vasyl? Have the vagaries of defection entered your dreams?"

Mind reader! Vasyl thought. "Yes and no. But betrayal and death have found their way in."

"How do you mean? That though you abandoned one life, you're struggling to enter another? Not an easy task … and after all, you've lived for years hampered by ambivalence in a mindset determined by others."

"I'm doing my best to break out."

"But why death? Have you been there … and back? I did that once in the moment I saw my friend lying dead on a lake beach. I still can't get the image out of my mind—or rather the no-look in his pale eyes and water-logged face."

"Death is fixed in my mind. Not my own but rather that of my former friend—or false friend—and now my enemy. My question is can I morally desire his death if I'm incapable of doing the killing myself? Am I capable of that? In Kharkov, Lyuba's father—my girlfriend's father—believed I was too weak for such matters."

"I remember that the philosopher of your studies spoke of death? Is that meaningful to you?"

"Yes, it is. According to Schopenhauer, dying the death is the aim and purpose of life. To live is to suffer, he maintains. The triumph of death is inevitable, and existence is a constant dying."

"Well, I can't accept death as a triumph but murder and killing seem to come about quite easily?"

"That's what I have in mind: can it ever be moral to kill another? In his *Studies of Pessimism* Schopenhauer hinted that it could be: 'If the world were a paradise of luxury and ease, a land flowing with milk and honey, where every Jack obtained his Jill at once and without any difficulty, men would either die of boredom or hang themselves; or there would be wars, massacres, and murders; so that in the end mankind would inflict more suffering on itself than it has now at the hands of Nature.'"

"The question is not easy. Are you asking me if there is ever moral justification for murder?"

"Yes. In a nutshell, that's precisely my question."

"Still, why do you ask me? You make it sound like a request for my permission to kill someone. It's almost as hard to give permission to kill—as Pontius Pilate must have felt when the people asked him to give the order to crucify Jesus—as it is to do the killing. He had Jesus whipped, but I don't recall that he ever ordered explicitly: 'crucify him.' Maybe he did. Many other Pilates do give that order and the blood stays on their hands forever. I personally am not a fan of Hoerderer in Sartre's *Les*

Mains Sales with his hands in blood and guts up to his elbows ... as I sometimes wish I were. Anyway, killing another individual with your own hands—as Marcello experienced—is a tiger's leap into the dark. It would mean abdicating your previous life and assuming personal responsibility for murder. Thou shalt not kill! Remember that commandment?"

Vasyl's eyes roamed around the small studio. His voice choked. Rain hammered the window. The copy of Klee's Angelus Novus hanging adjacent to the desk observed them. He didn't get it. You see an angel looking as though he is about to move away from something he is fixedly contemplating. His eyes are staring, his mouth is open, his wings spread. Vasyl's eyes were fixed on the image with the angel's eyes turned toward the past.

"That's how some picture the 'angel of history,'" I said. "The angel has his face turned toward the past. No dialectical movement forward toward the future. Nothing could be more undialectic than the 'angel of history' turned toward the past. But looking at the ruins of the past, the angel is blown back into the future by the storm of progress of history. Walter Benjamin writes that, 'Where we humans imagine a chain of events, the angel sees one single catastrophe which keeps piling up wreckage on top of wreckage—a complete disaster. But the angel would like to make whole what has been smashed. However, a storm is blowing in from Paradise which is caught in his swollen wings so that the angel can no longer close them. The storm irresistibly propels him into the future to which his back is turned; the storm is what we call progress.' To a certain extent, Benjamin, Brecht and Kafka go hand in hand, like Klee's Angelus Novus, looking at the past longingly but hating it at the same time. It's like Kafka's sickness of tradition—and simultaneously wishing it were so—propelling themselves forward and crashing through the present. For example, like America today—toward the future. Dialectical thinking for proclaimed non-dialectical thinkers! Here you see it all clearly, Vasily. We live in a constant state of emergency because Fascism is treated as if it were NOT the exception, but the rule. Look at Rome today. A Fascist-dominated government in a so-called parliamentary democracy: Fascist salutes say it all. We know—or should know—that Fascism is not, never has been, nor ever will be the norm. Yet in the Italy we live in, its opponents treat Fascism as if it were a historical norm. That cannot be. Most certainly it is not philosophical as Ca' Foscari University should clarify … but most likely does not. Ah, Vasyl, the great failures of academia! Busy, busy confirming whatever social-political realities exist and cutting, cutting, cutting from its programs of study whatever has nothing to do with money-making."

Vasyl stared fixedly at Klee's work. And as if Stuart's words were meaningless, he smiled and believed he understood.

"Maybe I *am* asking for permission," he finally said. "Yet I'm still debating the question with myself. And I need help. I've learned how people love to crash history, as you say. They did that in Ukraine. And maybe I've already made my decision to do the same and am asking for at least concurrence."

"You might find that minimal concurrence. But permission, well, that's something else. No human is the God of life and death."

"But you *can* take a stand. You can say yes or no."

"Hmm. Well, that's true. Vasyl. But destiny goes its own way. It's inexorable. Our friend Marcello faced that same conundrum in Florence ... and took the momentous decision to kill a man … a man who truly deserved to die, mind you. But in the same instant he squeezed the trigger, he changed his mind: he shifted his aim a millimeter—a millimeter, mind you—and shot the torturer in the shoulder instead of the heart, but then drove away leaving him lying on the sidewalk in the rain to bleed to death—the man he wanted dead. Maybe he just didn't want to do the killing himself, he didn't want to be present. Still, again he changed his mind: he turned and drove back to the dying man anyway, laid him carefully on the car's back seat, stopped the blood flow with his own shirt, drove him to the hospital and saved his life. But Vasyl, not even that is the end of his story with killing. Weeks later Marcello went to check out the healed man at his home: he saved his life once and felt he had to keep on saving it. Instead he found the man's naked body tied to a chair, tortured to death by his own gang of killers. Destiny!"

"God rest his soul!" Vasyl said spontaneously. Then he blushed, recalling Lyuba's severe Communist father. "In any case Stuart, I hope to finish my doctorate here, but I'm a lot less certain about entering the academic world when and if I ever reach Russia. I feel I'm emotionally more suited to some form of journalism. Russia has many such magazines like yours in Glasgow. Anyway, I've written some of my observations of West Europe based on my sixteen years of a rather unique experience here. May I leave an article with you in the hope you might submit it," he said and handed the three pages to Stuart as if they were drops of his own blood.

November 12

Curious to learn what an intelligent Ukrainian of uncertain political beliefs and of shaky affiliations in the homeland thought of Europe and his homeland after a unique experience of sixteen free-wheeling years in Italy, Stuart read his article-testimony.

EUROPE

By Vasily Tarnovsky

For over seventy years national elections in the EU have been determined by the 'Europe idea'. Until recently no major candidate for the political leadership of EU countries dared a clear anti-Europe program. In every political election, from north to south, Europe is on the lips of all. In peoples' minds, "Europe" refers to the powerful, unelected, bureaucratic European Commission in Brussels, i.e. the European Union. Or to that powerless 'debating society' known as the European Parliament in Strasbourg. "Europe", in one way or another, is on the minds of all.

Italians are proud of their modern passports marked "European Union" and only secondly, "Italian Republic". It is indeed pleasant to travel from Italy to Spain or France or Belgium or The Netherlands or Germany with only the Euro currency in your pocket and know what price you are paying for hotels or meals or souvenirs. Unlike my native Ukraine where everything is in change—and never for the better.

Despite such advantageous innovations, for many people Europe *is perfidious, dictatorial and impoverishing. Ukrainians too should understand this reality they so desire to join. The problem posed by one branch of Euroskeptics is that Europe has too little political power: the union is chiefly economic and financial. To all effects, Europe is a union of unelected bankers and financiers. Not the social or political union of peoples its founders had in mind. The original dream of Europe was a Europe of the people, socialist and democratic. Not a capitalist Europe of bankers filling the pockets of their caste. For many other Europeans the missing element is political clout. "Europe" does not have the power or does not exercise its power to defend its minorities, its immigrants from Africa or Asia or its Romani people--branches of the Twelve to fourteen million Sinti and Roma peoples, more numerous than Belgian--are treated as beggars and thieves. Peoples for reasons of survival forced to leave their East European origins in Romania or Hungary or Bosnia. Ukrainians in the EU would be identified similarly: a Sinti-Roma-Ukrainian coalition.One should recall that it was only a few years before the creation of the European Union that Fascists simply decided to eliminate both homosexuals and gypsies from the demographic map.*

Today, Europe decides by the discretionary use of its economic powers which countries may survive and which are destined for exploitation and eventual elimination—nations like Greece, the cradle of European and thus also American civilization. Or, to some extent, Ukraine. Short of war against Russia, the nation of Ukraine is useless; only its great land expanses of fertile earth count.

Without the use of marching troops over borders, capitalism has never before enjoyed such power as today in the EU. The EU is the instrument for the economically rich nations to control and rape weaker societies. In their attempts to unify Europe, neither Napoleon nor Hitler ever achieved such real power over the lives of the peoples of Europe as has the European Union.

Now it has become clear for those with eyes to see that not all the founders of the EU had in mind a union of peoples. A purely economic-financial union—that is, Fascism—was in the minds of many of its founders and is still in the minds of its bureaucracy. Therefore, its close relations with NATO which serves as its military arm. It is child's play to grasp that the difference between the EU and NATO is chiefly one of name.

Now one can easily understand that military alliance with the USA—in 1945 victorious and all-powerful after the fall of Nazi Germany—was in the minds of many of the original founders of the "Community" of Europe. U.S. economic aid offered by the Marshall Plan was not generosity and gratuitous. Europe paid a high price. U.S. troops were not in Europe to defend it against Soviet troops ready to take the whole continent. U.S. presence in Europe was to support U.S. interests. The Cold War ensued to consolidate that American presence.

The European Union has guaranteed the perpetuation of unity with the USA. Today the EU and interlocking treaties between it and NATO provide troops for the widest possible coalition in America's continuing world-wide wars. The small country of Denmark suffered fifty deaths in Afghanistan, proportionately the highest of any other nation of the Grand Coalition on that distant and now largely forgotten Asian battleground. One concludes that if the USA wants to count on Germany and NATO as combat allies in the coming years it will have to help the political establishments in those and other countries to overcome public resistance—not to mention the growing political-economic influence of Russia.

Therefore, the EU can dabble with the French idea of a European force de frappe. It may send a few Foreign Legion troops here or there. But I don't believe the EU has the political or the economic power or desire to even try to withstand American pressure and create a military force capable of competing with the U.S.-dominated NATO or with Russia.

15

November 13

It was mid-afternoon. Vasyl-Vasily mounted the blue-carpeted staircase. His face was dark, his mood black. He was dissatisfied with Stuart's evasiveness. Pontius Pilate! My ass! As Governor of the Roman province of Judea, Pilate—subservient, servile, obsequious servant—didn't want to disturb relations with Rome. Nor did he want to stir up more trouble in Jerusalem. Pilate was a vassal and behaved as a vassal. His concern was to keep the peace and not disturb the Empire with a minor ruckus in the provinces. On grand questions he gave to Caesar what was Caesar's, while trying to keep the fiery Judeans from killing each other. Still, Vasily recognized that Stuart was no Pilate and owed allegiance to no one. He respected that. Stuart is genuine, he thought, while my lot is indecision and suffering because I don't know who I am or what to do. Like my parents I've always been behind … or ahead of time. My father was too young for the war; I was too young when the great swerve happened in my home in Ukraine … too young to participate, too young to even understand where I was: Ukraine or Russia. It was simply home. Sometimes we called ourselves Russians, sometimes Ukrainians—but with a funny feeling. Thinking of ourselves as Ukrainians seemed unreal—like a fairy tale—even though we were citizens of that country called Ukraine. Over there in western parts beyond Kiev lay another world. But Kiev too was Russian. It was always Russian. Donetsk, our international football team, was a Russian kind of thing. Crimea is Russia and Russians took it back. Our great city of Odessa is a Russian city. Kiev and Odessa, two of Russia's major cities. Moscow, St. Petersburg, Kiev and Odessa.

Everyone I knew spoke Russian. Yet *they* said—now I know the corrupt Nazis said—that all of that is Ukraine … and you can go to jail if you dispute it. Ukraine to me is like a fugitive afterscent of something that *may* have once been but is no more. Ukraine is an abstract idea of a country, distant in time and significance from authenticity. *"Authentic belief,"* as the Italian essayist Nicola Chiaromonte wrote in *To Believe and Not to Believe* that he had recently read in Stuart's library, *"is uncertain like existence, and like existence it is already present before one is even aware of it. Explicit beliefs instead generally concern a fictitious world in which real and authentic beliefs are confused with those maintained in form as articles of faith—or perhaps as fanaticism—but are no longer alive. Therefore it is easier to say in what one does not believe than to formulate what one truly believes. And this is also the reason that one who sees and denounces the falseness concealed behind official professions of faith can be so easily accused of not believing in anything."*

An abstract madness of crazed super-nationalists of the end of the Great War took root—perhaps the Versailles idea of a nation. Tracing borders. Laying out boundaries. Reasons for feeling that lack of volition, a lack of connection with the reality of my confused situation, Vasily thought, that at some point in time I just sat back and allowed it to come over me like a net. I don't think I'm a coward but I am a prisoner of my inability to react.

Stuart instead says what he believes is right—ethically right. Obviously he stands in opposition to the arbitrary power of secret agencies in Rome, ethically evil agencies that rule that self-willed rebels must die. Nonetheless, Stuart's private conscience follows an unwritten law against a criminal public power to which he will not submit. And flight underground was his only resource. A hard road but the only road for the free person. Even though he's in hiding, he's also the freest man I've ever known. I didn't expect him to advise me to kill Kravets; but still, for God's sakes, he could have agreed—concurrence with the idea that sometimes killing is also acceptable.

The most I request is concurrence.

On the second floor landing, he saw Oriana's apartment door open like Helen's always was. Open doors are an invitation … and unsafe. Disobedience reigned there too. He thought they should be holed up like in a deep, tightly guarded cave. He started when he heard her call:

"Vasily!"

Then, when he turned: "Since we can't get to Ca' Foscari in this downpour, why don't you come in for a coffee?" Oriana had begun Russianizing his name which she knew appealed to him and he too had begun identifying himself readily as Vasily.

He hesitated, one foot on the first step, a hand on the banister, his head turned over his shoulder toward her and thinking of the Angelus Novus. Oriana was a serious student on whom he relied for language issues; she was also sexy—as she said of herself. Sex oozed from her very pores. Moreover, she had disliked Kravets from the first instant—which said a lot for her—but had taken to him instead and, after all, she was instrumental in his living here. Now she was luring him into her life like the spider attracting the fly. Her friend from Florence used to come every few days he had learned. Now weeks had passed since the last time he was here. Busy man. No Giacomo. It all went through Vasily's mind in a flash: Oriana, her big apartment, his too big apartment likewise. And Kharkov, where Lyuba no longer existed. No more cotton spreads on green, green fields, no more letters, no more money for new dresses. No fear of a tyrant father. He thought of school in Kharkov and apropos of Oriana's sexy invitation to coffee, he remembered the old poem of the spider and the fly they'd read in English class—in Kharkov, now so long ago. In Kharkov.

Alas, alas! how very soon this silly little Fly,/ Hearing his wily flattering words, came slowly flitting by;/ With buzzing wings she hung aloft, then near and nearer drew,/Thinking only of her brilliant eyes, and green and purple hue/–Thinking only of her crested head–poor foolish thing! At last,/Up jumped the cunning Spider, and fiercely held her fast./He dragged her up his winding stair, into his dismal den, Within his little parlour–but she ne'er came out again!

"Oh, thanks so much, Oriana. Yes, the rain. Like steel, the rain. We can't stop it now. But spring will come again … with fresh new rains. And things will go on and on. Is it only in Venice, do you think? "

"And summer too will return, Vasily. Also here. Meanwhile, it's the time to cuddle and hold together and listen to the rain while you explain to me the mystery of Russian names that people here don't grasp. Vasyl seems silly and Vasily formal. What else is there?'

"My parents and a girl called me Vaska, a pet name. Means also cat. Imagine. My father's name is Vladimir Vasilovich. So I'm Vasily , taken from his second name or his patronymic. So many call me Vaska for short. Easy!

On which he stepped into the spider's web for coffee and didn't come out again until the next day and found that the rain was still there as he'd predicted.

16

November 20

A week passed. Vasily held onto his own fourth floor apartment even though he had only a few pieces of furniture and some books, most of which were already in Oriana's second floor bedroom. Again he looked toward Helen's open door when he passed. He heard Pushkin's meow. The dark gray stripped little guy was standing in the hallway. Vasily stooped and called, Иди сюда, Пушкин! Come! Иди сюда. He thought the only way to speak to animals was in Russian. Most people were that way. Helen spoke her native German to the cat, Stuart spoke English. Pushkin seemed linguistically indifferent—he understood them all. Human speak. And Marcello, who only spoke Italian, swore that the kitten had recognized his name from the first instant and so it remained: Pushkin was polyglot. Now Pushkin came, meowing and the end of his tail twisting and turning, begging Russian-speaking Vasily to feed him as he sometimes did despite Helen's severe control of the cat's weight. He picked up Pushkin and cuddled and kissed him. He didn't weigh more than four kilograms. Pushkin loved the caresses but Vasily suspected the cat considered a few kisses as an advance payment for food. When Vasily entered her studio to see the progress, the cat slithered out of his arms and ran back to the kitchen to wait. Modifications of the self-portrait were on Helen's mind, he knew. Such was her sensitive art: the quasi imperceptible changes in the face, the shade of the eyes, the position of the chin, a faint strand of hair, the lips. She had a fixation on the mouth; the slightest twitch of the lips at the corner of the mouth changed everything.

Vasily saw no changes. The painting looked identical to yesterday's version. "I've worked on this for days," Helen said, "but I still can't get it right."

Vasily wanted to make a satisfactory comment but only stared at the image that was no longer only Helen. He felt truly perplexed. In lieu of the suggestion she so wanted to hear, he asked: "When do you expect Marcello? I have some information about Andriy Kravets that might be useful to him."

"Oh, I really don't know. He has no schedule so I seldom even know where he is. He usually calls me every few hours but I'm not supposed to call him. For all I know he could be in Chioggia. Or, as he says, staking out someone, Kravets or other Ukrainians like that couple near the fish market, or he's off somewhere with his detective friend, Trevisan, maybe on an official police visit to the Ukrainian Consul in Padua. But of all the places he tells me about, he seems fixated on the Academia and your former apartment as if it contained answers to his conviction that your old friend heads some kind of secret network of Ukrainians linked in some way to what he calls the 'resurgent Masonic Propaganda Lodge Two'.

"Oh yes, our gangster Honorary Consul. Only Kiev would choose such a person. A Mafioso! Very possible a link with that secret Masonic Lodge. "

Late that evening Helen's door was still open. Marcello had not arrived. He hadn't called or answered his phone. At midnight, Vasily looked in again. Helen was in the living room. The rain poured relentlessly. Marcello sometimes got home late. But tonight they'd planned going out for dinner. Helen called his phone every few hours. No ring. No answer. No contact. Nada. She was nervous .

I too came up from below, I also worried. The hours passed and the rain hammered her windows, she walked the floor, calling his number every few minutes. "*Nada.* Stuart, I'm scared." Since around eight he'd been involved in a dangerous police action. She'd called Trevisan at nine; he hadn't seen Marcello but promised to follow up. When she again asked Vasily about the man Kravets, he repeated that he was an unpredictable scoundrel.

It was close to one a.m. when Vasily and I left Calle di Solferino dressed in slickers, rain hats and rubber boots. Municipal transportation was shut down totally. We cut straight through the heart of the city, using narrow passages, crossing bridges back and forth across the winding Canal Grande. Darkness and rain and mist shrouded the Academia. The pension was dark, but the front door was standing wide open. Vasily turned on the staircase lights. The door to the suite was also open. Lights worked there too. We gaped at the chaos. Everything overturned: couch, chairs, cabinet doors open, drawers pulled out, the small corner desk torn apart. The same upsidedownness in the small bedroom. Popular music sounded from the kitchenette playing English-language songs.

"Andriy's music box," Vasily said. "he plays it day and night."

"An expert did this work," I muttered, observing the systematic disorder of the rooms. "Marcello was here. I feel him."

"Andriy was here too,"Vasily replied. "And a fight took place afterwards. Stuart, look! Blood here behind the couch. Lots of blood."

In that moment the door downstairs slammed. Someone running up the stairs. Trevisan stood in the doorway. Pistol in hand. Taking no chances. He and I had met before and he knew Vasily's story ... but sure was sure.

Once identities were settled, he holstered the pistol and began reviewing the room the same way Marcello must have done.

"In Chioggia, I wasn't sure, but now I know. This is a police story, Stuart. Very much so. And it will be treated as such. Who knows who ransacked this place earlier. Maybe Marcello. Nothing of interest remains. But not long ago two people fought to the death here. "Let's hope that's not from Marcello," he said, looking at the blood on the floor. "Blood dries within an hour, and this blood is fresh. We got here an hour or so too late."

Trevisan headed straight to the window door in the bedroom that opened onto a French-looking, meter wide balcony. The black, wrought iron railing reflected glistening individual drops of rain. The balcony hung directly over one of the small canals surrounding the island pension. There was blood on the balcony flooring and on the railing. Trevisan concluded killers had done their work here under the cascading Venice rain.

"Whether dead or wounded, the victim—or victims," he said meditatively—"ended up in that canal."

"Why victims?" I asked.

"Your friend Marcello Bolzoni is or was a shrewd man. A beginner like Kravets could never take him out so easily. We may find two bodies in that canal ..."

"Which means?"

"Which means there are other neglected killers somewhere in Venice tonight."

"Maybe Marcello was the real target, not Kravets," I said. "Kravets's enemies didn't necessarily want him dead. Marcello's enemies did. That's why he was in Cannaregio, in hiding. But he didn't keep a low profile as he should have. On the contrary."

The detective summoned the scientific police and a canal diver and lifted fingerprints from the balcony railing onto his phone. Vasily and I went back downstairs and walked along the canal, dodging places where its water was overrunning its banks. I imagined bodies lodged somewhere in the mysterious depths and at the same time I was tempted to phone Helen. But I didn't. I wouldn't be able to even hint at Marcello's disappearance—nor could I chase from my mind the thought that the mere possibility of Marcello's body at the bottom of the canal opened a whole new perspective in our lives about which I was unable to even speculate at this point..

Trevisan joined us when the diver arrived. He was dressed in a heavy rubber suit and carrying a diving helmet. "The canals around the pension are not more than three-four meters deep," Trevisan said. "The diver will find the bodies quickly. So shortly we'll know what's what. Blood types and finger prints will tell us the rest … or most of it."

"But not as much as the bodies," I muttered, my words smothered by the cold and perverse stupidity of the rainfall—uniform, smooth, each drop identical to the other, ever and forever the same, the whole as if driven by compulsive repetition.

The diver slipped into the dark water and sank with hardly a splash. A gurgle and he vanished.

"Just a few minutes now," Trevisan said. "The body or bodies have to be here. The current of this canal's water is practically nil. And Stuart, though Ukrainians may be involved, I sense this is essentially an Italian story. Marcello is the enemy of the new fascistic Masonic Lodge. He's the enemy of their

Florence city police and of the governing Fascist Party. They, those people out there, are killers. And as you saw so well, Marcello took few precautions and acted like he was still a Florentine cop. Motivations for killing Marcello are more powerful than that of angry Ukrainian agents killing a fellow countryman—unless of course there are other political reasons of which Signor Tarnovsky is unaware."

Vasily spread his arms in agreement.

"Still, Ukraine is unhappy about Italy's on and off military aid," I said, "and someone in Kiev must believe that Kravets—an apparent SBU agent—has betrayed his mission and is collaborating with our intelligence agencies. They send him here, he learns Italian, gallivants about the country for years and then betrays the homeland. Bad stuff. More than sufficient motivation for his assassination."

A few minutes later, the diver emerged with an arm around the back of the body of Andriy Kravets.

Vasily exclaimed, "боже мой! I expected it, but still, seeing his body like that is sickening."

"Hang on!" the diver said. "There's more. I'll be right back."

"Number two!" he said, rapidly reemerging and pushing toward them the body of Marcello Bolzoni, Florentine detective.

"And there's still another. A human limb rubbed against me as I started up."

His muffled voice announcing such horrible events as number 1, number 2, number 3, rang obnoxious, distorted by his dark helmet, the cloudy water, the flickering blood rain, and he breathless from the effort of surfacing bodies from the depths of the river Styx.

"Be right back," he announced again, joyfully-evilly-satanically this time, I thought, now hating the diver who had embraced dead Marcello. The diver who didn't dive; just moved bodies from one place to the other. I imagined myself standing on a waterfront and watching death-marked bodies delivered by hand one after the other from the mysterious, invisible deep, whose surface waters continually lap at you, snap at you, safe and sound on terra firma.

Trevisan laid the bodies parallel one to the other. I shivered. Neither of us pronounced the name Marcello. I stared down at the man I'd come to love as I did the ex-AISI intelligence agent friend in Rome, Ermanno Riccardi. Ermanno, who had lived in fear of non-achievement, failure and promises of happiness, a complex man who had died double deaths—first botoxed by his ex-fellow AISI agents and his body then immersed in the waters of Lake Bracciano. Looking down at Marcello, I recalled the agent's words uttered one summer day on Rome's Piazza Barberini of the difficulty of abandoning the old when the new is not yet approachable: 'Once you're on the inside of resistance, once you are involved and committed, each step becomes easier.' Ermanno took that easy step. I had stood in the circle of people staring down at the lifeless Ermanno lying flat on his back on the sands of Trevignano beach of Lago Bracciano—Did he die of botox poisoning first, or did he drown tragically in the deep Bracciano waters? I never knew. I would never understand the truth. I imagined that events happening now were mere signs, uncertain, fleeting promises of knowledge. Of the gap between life and death. The passage from one to the other. Promethean promises. That one infinitesimal fractal of a raindrop, a snowflake, the flap of the wings of a butterfly in Brazil that results in the death of three men in a miniature Venice canal, itself a small dimension of a real canal, like the original trickle of the Danube-Donau at its source in the Black Forest of south-western Germany is the same as the river cutting through Ingolstadt, the same river that splits Budapest on its fearful way to join the Black Sea. Promises, promises, promises.

Marcello Bolzoni's pale, water-logged face on the bank of a small Venice canal was identical to that of Ermanno's lying on the Lake Bracciano beach. He most likely did not die of water either—whatever the scientific police ruled—but what do I know? Strange, I thought, you can know a person for half your life and never know who they really are. You know their given name—maybe false, not even their own, never know if they are right or left politically, nor if they believe in God. Yet in a period a few months Marcello had become my spiritual brother. We told each other our most private thoughts and feelings and sometimes I seemed to perceive his unspoken thoughts … and I suspected he, mine.

In that instant the insistent emergence of another body locked in the embrace of the cynical canal diver appeared as if it were an event that would be repeated, on and on, forever.

The third body was a nobody to them. Maybe he was a masonic lodge killer who had targeted Marcello. Or, perhaps he was a Ukrainian SBU killer—*Sluzhba Bezperky Ukrainy*—whose target was Kravets.

Now three bodies lay side by side alongside the canal, their identical water-logged death masks observed from their position of life above by Trevisan, Tarnovsky and I, and their identical shoe soles viewed by the sardonic diver—he, alive but still in the water—while the red rain fell. And the three bodies seemed to be turning to the same dark blood red.

"Those guys weren't in the water long enough to be that dead," the diver ventured. still not climbing out, as if to claim the innocence of his beloved water. Then I asked the question all were asking: "So who killed this one, whoever he is … or was? Was there then a fourth man … or woman?"

Trevisan seemed strangely detached, as if who killed the third man was unimportant. I knew that was not the case. The fourth man was likely his chief interest. It could mean most anything: P2 redux, rogue AISI, Kievan SBU.

Filled with nervous trepidation, Vasily and I returned to Calle di Solferino, both still thinking about the fourth man. It was after five a.m. I knew Helen was not sleeping; she refused to even enter the bedroom when Marcello was absent at night.

I started up the bluish staircase searching my mind for the proper words, words which in any case would shatter her dreamscape of love, words which could not yet tell the story of Marcello's life. I couldn't even tell story of my own life, of who I really am today, of why I am the way I am.

Now, Helen. Her turn. Her life, though somehow charmed, seemed to have always consisted of connection and separation: part of her life with her mother in Rome, part with her father in Vienna; a year's relationship with Gudrun in Vienna-Grinzing and a short marriage with Rome playboy Romano; simultaneous liaison with Sophie and me; and finally love for Marcello Bolzoni.

I found her sitting in a straight chair near the front window. Her face was the face of her self-portrait in which ugliness had found its place. Her eyes were cold and dry. Her brain had turned off. I started to say that *he* would not be returning. Instead I didn't say a word. Helen had already understood. She'd known when his phone calls stopped. My entrance was the unwanted confirmation.

"The Masonic Lodge did not forget. I believe their killers did it."

Silence. Pushkin adjusted his position on the couch and went back to sleep. Helen's brain had turned off like mine did when so long ago they told me *she* was dead. At two years old, my daughter was no more, which after all the years since still determined my life outlook.

"Some persons you wait for your whole life," Helen began. " I waited. "He came along in time. In three months I came to love that man from the depths of my soul. And now he vanishes into the rain. How do we remember things the way we do? We're so absorbed in ourselves that we confuse our own lives with the flow of history, that it will go on and on. Solferino. Battle of Solferino, Calle di Solferino. You told me it was the chain of history, that it had always been so and would go on forever. So while I loved him and waited for him in Calle di Solferino, I worked egoistically on myself—my portrait. It seemed so important that I understand me…"

She stopped, peered toward her self-portrait, her eyes unseeing.

"And now that I do understand, I find it's relatively unimportant. He didn't say so but he didn't think my portrait so important either. So it turns out that the important thing I did was wait for him in Calle di Solferino. I am now learning another thing: although there's nothing socially useful about suffering—

look at Gaza; they're suffering but it's certainly not useful—there is theoretically something cleansing, something purgative and purifying about it. Catharsis? But is it really true? Did your suffering, your manias, your psychoanalysis, did all that heal you and make you a better person?"

"I still don't know, Helen. But it made me a different person. And no, I have no theses to nail to a wall, and no, I don't believe suffering per se is redemptive. The only redemptive suffering is that voluntarily undertaken in the cause of justice. Martin Luther in fact believed that redemptive suffering is not something we choose. But I'm certainly no Martin Luther."

In this moment, I saw a total egoistical Helen. Cold and analytical. In a way, she was already far away from here. Although she hardly listened to my words, I hoped the sound of another voice was useful. Maybe it was. *His* cat sat up and watched me. The reality was that aspects of her life not related to the subject of *his* life—not his death—were mere whiffs of an extraneity that she shooed away with the back of a hand. Or, with an exaggerated puff from a puckered mouth.

"You see, he was ..."

"Who was? Who was?" I repeated in another attempt to get her to pronounce his name.

"He was. He was the earth. Male earth. His hands were the earth. His arms and legs were nature's limbs that enveloped me. His body was like a tree trunk. Fixed in the earth and fixed in me. I loved his kisses. I sucked his saliva. I loved the taste of his cum. Earth's nectar that came straight from him into me, descended through my throat and into my organs and limbs. So that it became a necessity, a dependence, a torment of compulsive repetition, maybe the first symptom of an addictive malaise. He went off to God knows where, but he remained in me. I held onto his taste long after and tried not to dilute it. Yes, the earth. Different from the past in which I wanted to soar. Oh yes, Stuart, you exist there too … as the firmament, the stars and all those unknown bodies you search for in your dreams. Your dreamscape, your castles in the sky. His earthen realities, the cop who didn't believe in coincidences, whose soft heart killed him. So that now the mere touch of life frightens me and invites me to the same dark side where he roamed."

While Helen remembered, already reminiscing as if of the distant past in some way attuned to the increasing intensity of the early morning rain, gigantic drops hammering the windows and the berserk wind shaking the building, I stood up and looked out the window down onto a fog-ridden Calle di Solferino as an excuse to move to her, fixed stiffly in her straight chair, prompting her to move away from the window to the couch where she might sleep. The rainfall was uniform, but the darkness out there was the dark of a corpuscular thing which reminded me of the extra spaces between the words he lived with, spaces that demanded explanation, modification, limitation or expansion with those elusive, ever tempting fillers-filters.

"Do you want to sleep, Helen?"

"Yes, yes, I do. To disappear. Just never again in the bedroom and its shadows. This is the waiting room. I'll live here from now on."

"And do you want coffee first?

"I'll accept anything, Anything or anywhere to escape the incubus of this world where new starts are verboten"

I turned toward the door. Sophie had appeared with a breakfast tray. I remembered our many breakfasts together, the three of us, on the summer terrace of the villa in San Nicola and under the great cypress behind our house in Fiesole.

Helen took a sip of coffee and lifted her bare legs onto the couch, closed her eyes and immediately fell asleep. Vasily, still wet like me, came in and looked down at Helen. Oriana had tears in her eyes and held tight to Vasily-Vaska. My phone buzzed. Pushkin meowed and looked at me as if waiting for answers. The cat loved people in general but he belonged heart and soul to Marcello. His instinct told him that all these humans together at once and Helen sleeping on the couch must mean something terrible.

It was Trevisan calling from the Questura. He shouldn't relate his news by phone, he said, but the intensity of today's rain was permissive of many things that in normal times were forbidden: fingerprints on the pension balcony belonged to Marcello, Kravets and to the third victim , a Florentine freemason. Partial, blurred prints lifted from a wall near the balcony belonged to an unidentified and probably unidentifiable fourth person. The blood inside the apartment and on the balcony belonged to Kravets and Marcello.

Trevisan's instinctive reconstruction was this: Kravets wounded Marcello lightly on his shoulder. Marcello then killed the Ukrainian and pushed him over the railing into the canal to make sure; the Freemason killed Marcello and dumped him over the railing; the fourth man—perhaps a rogue AISI agent or of the fascistic super-secret international "Ring" —killed the Freemason and cloaked in anonymity vanished into the pouring rain.

Everyone but me had left Helen to sleep. After covering her, I set up a cot retrieved from the fifth floor storage room, turned on all the electric heaters in the apartment and stretched out, covering myself with my coat.

Almost immediately I too fell into a deep, dream-filled sleep. I was telling my old friend Marcello Bolzoni about the Unicorn. We were wandering through Montepulciano. I shouldn't be out here in the ceaselessly pouring red rain, I told Marcello. I felt feverish. We stopped and peered up through the spray at the arch of a massive palazzo when a man threw himself to the wet sidewalk right under our feet.

"Oh! Oh! You good people, have pity. I'm seventy-five years old. Look! Look at me! Look at my seventy-five years. I have nothing. I am nothing. I'm less than nothing. I'm hungry. Help me to eat."

Wiry and emaciated, the man had a head of extraordinarily beautiful gray hair and a scraggly beard, his eyes closed as if in prayer, he clasped his tiny delicate hands in front of him, the top of his hat gaping upward from the pavement.

"I beg you, I beseech you, help me. For the love of God, help me. I need you to survive. Before they kill me. If you've a bit of humanity in your souls come to my aid. Succor me. As Mary Magdalene did Jesus."

In fascination, I stared down at the abject figure. I squinted. Mary Magdalene? Jesus? I saw what my father would have seen. A light hovered around that gray head. But, but … was that not a horn? From the thick wavy hair, yes, a horn seemed to protrude, powerful, impudent, arrogant, swaying from side to side like the head of a cobra and searching upward toward us. It had to be the rain. The reflection from city lights. I leaned forward. I shuddered feverishly. Is he a messenger. For me? Could it be me? I must be delirious. I took from my pocket a twenty euro note and put it in the thin hand. "Get up!" I cried, grabbing at the wet hat on the pavement and pushing it into his trembling hands. "I'm sorry but you must get up!"

"See his hair? How it stands up! What pain he must be in. Oh, Marcello what pain!"

"Bless you good people. I will pray for you," the old man cried, pushing his hat on the back of his head. "I forgive you!"

His horn of onyx glistened in the red sparks of rain. Now grinning, all white teeth, he turned and rushed down the wide street in short hurried steps on stick thin legs in his jeans.

"I hate myself when I feel self-righteous," I said. Yet, I thought in my dream, thank God there's always that crack in the door of my mind left open. My father looked out that crack. Anarchist and atheist, sheet metal worker in red Sesto Fiorentino, his life was a dream. Nights, when I was small, the powerful man with the body of a boxer, a dreamy look in his eyes, told me about Jehovah—and later, to help me sleep after the tales of terror, he spoke of the Unicorn. He said it was all shiny, the magic Unicorn, a halo around its head from which extended a long black horn. It is good. The ideal. If you do good in life anyone can hope for a visit from the Unicorn. But then when in life the Unicorn leaps high and dances on two legs, pitiless hunters plunge their spears into the shiny white animal. That's why I today hate the pious. Maybe it was a twist of fate, the child re-found, that above all, I still wanted to see the Unicorn.

Rilke too wrote about on the Unicorn that never existed:

It behaved as though it were.
They always left some space.
And in that clear unpeopled space they saved
it lightly reared its head,

with scarce a trace of not being

there.

They fed it, not with corn,
but only the Possibility of Being.

17

November 24

After tramping around the sestiere of Dorsoduro under an exceptionally heavy nocturnal rainfall accompanied by a meteoric drop in temperature; after the decanalization of the three victims—victims one of the other—and after the early morning trek back to Cannagerio and the Calle di Solferino, Vasily began falling ill: a headache and a debilitating weakness creeping up his legs. The first time Oriana took his temperature, it was 39.5. His fever then rose rapidly higher and higher. When it reached 41, she called the weekend *guardia medica.* Since it was impossible to get a boat of any kind to Calle di Solferino to carry him to an emergency room, a professionally dedicated doctor came in the November morning darkness and the unrelenting downpour. Other medical persons soon arrived, specialists and nurses hand-carrying an emergency room to Calle di Solferino.

Vaska in his delirium knew that medical diagnosis was uncertain, his fever immeasurable. He was sinking into a weird world of his own. He was both delirious and super aware. His eyesight was inexplicably reduced to an agitated tunnel vision which at first fascinated him and stumped the phantom-like doctors—appearing suddenly and rapidly disappearing. The situation was curiously also frightening, from which he knew he must escape, his attempts at which were thwarted by his no less inexplicable inability to close his eyes. I don't know when it happened, he recounted to himself, but my visual field is truly strange. Everything blurred. Limited. Narrow. Bizarre. Those shapeless and dark, white, green and blue phantoms fluttered down that tunnel. My own tunnel. Dancing phantoms. Strange, those dark dancers. Surely as rare a vision as a Monarch butterfly in the Caucasian mountain range in the winter. Crazy imagination in such a moment. Monarch butterflies fluttering and dancing in the cold winds. Distorted phantasmal figures. There for an instant before vanishing in a flash into the cold of Mount Elbrus. Grotesque. Again I try to blink. I have to clear the haze. In vain. My eyes are as fixed as the absurd theater of white and green and blue contortionists appearing in and fading out of my tunnel. If they would only stop their jerking around like Italian marionettes so that I can concentrate on this ridiculous situation. But wait! What was that? Patience! It will return. A deformed red shape is drawing near. It's hovering as if searching for my ghost. Is it Death? That balloon figure with bulging eyes leaning toward me. It's jabbering something. A non-Slavic language. Maybe about me to some other form somewhere outside my visual realm. I don't comprehend a word. Well, let them babble. I will ignore them. They pull at my face, somewhere below my eyes. My face attracts them. They don't like the hair there. I feel my face wet. Then a cold something slides over it. The wetness goes away. Whatever it is, they can decide. They can decide everything. It all matters so little now. In my fixed state I just have to stay focused on the identification of the few certainties passing through my still perceptive mind. Elimination of impossible variations however is hardly consoling progress. My distant past remains the complex element. How to deal with that past is the question. Once it arrived in the guise of the present, dallied a short time, and was gone. Piff! Gone. Flying on the winds of the steppes. The only certainty is still Lyuba … my world, Lyuba, Her name too is as fixed as a name inscribed on a gravestone in one of twenty-one cemeteries of Kharkov, a veritable city of the dead, even of German soldiers who died there for the Führer. Since we were children she has been the one certainty on which I counted. Maybe she too is somewhere in the shadows lying outside of my tunnel with its gossamer walls. If so, she should step forward and explain what this is all about. This thing. The phantoms. The great red dot. This paralyzing tunnel I'm in, in which Shostakovich and his Dresden Quarter plays over and over, ceaseless, like Venetian rains. Peculiar visions. Drops of blood. The word *massive* hangs in the thickening white air. It's like being the main character in a *pesadilla.* A pantomime in a nightmare. Magical happenings. A whisper. Do I exist? Am I anything at all? Have I ever been anything? Or, or, or, am I, maybe, already dead? Of interest to scientists: the dead remember their lived lives. If it were just not for the remembrances! This should be clarified once and for all: do the dead really remember? Now I can try. I have only time. Like when I left Lyuba, I had little besides time. That was when the turmoil began. I left her. That is established. But I left part of me behind. I thought I had to *make* a career. In this tunnel I can see all my yesterdays. Dim and distorted … maybe unreal. Real was only Lyuba. So it was to Italy. And someday soon she might follow. Oh yes, I do remember. Was memory my undoing? My greatest regret? Or is my real regret not missing the other present? The one always around me? The new in the past. Missing the revolution? Yes, the revolution. And my part in it. In this mysterious present in which our brief but myriad past keeps marching across and through, marching, marching through the tunnel of my mind's eyes. Do the white and green and blue phantoms not see it too? Don't they see my memories marching? My unswerving eyes miss nothing, not the smallest detail do my eyes miss. They miss nothing within this narrow field of vision that is mine. The marching past, a potential past, a cortege headed by Lyuba. To think that I was only twenty when I too left. Now I am … I am … How old am I? Peculiar, my age escapes my memory. Memory is truly a rover. Escapes time. But still alive. Still alive. But no longer in my time. Time too is truant. Does time not live? Strange feeling, not knowing your age. Like not knowing your name. Anti-revolutionary convictions had no role in my departure. I had no such convictions. Not me! I was a believer. Seen in that light my departure was heroic: to destroy from within was my role. In order to play the hero in Lyuba's eyes … and to gain the esteem of my father who advised me that if I truly loved Lyuba, I had to fight for her. Go to Italy. Get a university degree, then come back to Lyuba and join our struggle for our Russia. I was not a refugee. Nor an exile. I was a revolutionary. Still, I had to have Lyuba like before. The clamorous clash of desires. I remember. Was her love not strong enough? All these memories: the familiar smells, the heat of the sun's blinding rays, the warm wind across the steppes caressing my face. Upwards, ever upwards, the Caucasus's highest peaks within fingertip distance. All these mountain passes and snow-laden heights. And as light fades in the mountains the warm lights of Russia beckon in the distance below, where Lyuba waits. A rose radiance colors the mountains and sunlight paints rooftops in the valleys fiery red. Oh, the splendor, the magnificence of memories. And for a moment, I see again the red roofs of home. I feel my breathing accelerate and the fever rise still higher and I regret leaving Kharkov. Russians think that way. But I have to keep it secret from the dancing white and the green and the blue phantoms in the tunnel. I don't want to be dead; I want to live my life to the fullest even though Lyuba used to mock me for that. Always she'd mocked me … that I just wanted to *be* a hero … not *become* one. That I saw life only in the present in which I didn't have to *become* anything, while only slowly, slowly the future arrived, always in the present. I could never be a revolutionary, she said. They themselves bring about change and build a new future. Sometimes I hated her for that. And I never acknowledged that she was right. Such clear insight into myself however underpins my unspoken perceptions of the overall correctness of my existential choices. Awareness of the former lucidity of my thought was elating, even in this moment sparkling in the tight, dimly illuminated tunnel of this channel vision.

Lyuba was right. Lyuba always knew. Lyuba had *always* been right. Now where is she? She was part of it all. Of this life. Though absent from my vision in this bizarre situation, she must be there in the impenetrable shadows, near but distant from this condition of living only in my eyes. Lyuba had known that what I really wanted was freedom ... freedom from restraints and limits. It was the nature of things. Strange nature, the Ukrainian-Russian. How easily he betrays. Now this tunnel I live in is driving me crazy. What's really going on?

Lyuba and her eternal love. She'd been my life. Always. Without her my existence turned black. Onyx black. Her eternal love wasted away.

No, I couldn't live without her, without what she had given me since we were still nearly children. Only to me, the snob, as she called me when I derided our provincial roots. My obsession with her drove us both crazy.

Lyuba. How to explain her? Even her name rang crazy at times. Lyuba and I loved each other: she selflessly; I possessively. We grew up together. We learned sex together while we were still children. Life without her was meaningless. But still, times were changing. There are people over in Russia who want to change things much, much faster. Change geography. Rewrite history.

Still, fathers in the provinces knew no more than politicos about what their children's generation was thinking. Lyuba and I were children when our bond was sealed. Sixteen and fifteen years old—compassionate, passionate, unlimited Lyuba. I brushed her hair and squeezed her feet when she had her first periods, in Kharkov. Oh, how I brushed her long hair. How she danced naked on the blanket in the fields of Kharkov. Our story passes before me now slowly—or maybe fast—and I keep wondering if the white and green and blue figures saw it too when we made children's love in the fields.

Ours is a story, the story I love most. Our Kharkov story. Reliving it makes it live now in this fixed state of white and green and blue confusion and the dark shadows filled with both promise and threat. The kisses, the fumbling, the touching of our mysterious secret parts on the summer evenings, in Kharkov. Our love scents filled the air. The air of the provinces, where the light breeze comes in from the steppes every passing day.

Two children –Lyuba and I—march across my visual field and then their figures too vanish into the shadows. My real self reaches for her. And for the first time I know: it has always been *my* story more than *ours*. Now it seems over. I belong to this *massive* thing, whatever it is, which has overcome me. Now my only wish is that one of those deformed phantoms would step out of the tunnel and close my eyes for me. It might be the fourth man.

It was very dark in the whole apartment house on Calle di Solferino. Except for sounds of wind and pounding rain, total quiet reigned. Vaska was asleep in Oriana's bed on the second floor. His temperature falling after ingestion of several antibiotics each compatible with the others according to the doctors, and a huge shot of demerol—just in case, the last internist said without defining 'in case of what'.

Helen, drugged with a variety of tranquilizers and alcohol, was sleeping on the couch on the third floor, with Pushkin at her side. I thought the moment proper and propitious to write an essay I had long had in mind: "On the Loss of a Loved One".

Sophie and I breakfasted wordlessly. Not one word was spoken. Just sitting there and staring, the two of us. Seeing or unseeing so long that I had the thought that some people just sit like that all their lives, fixed like in death.

We both seemed to be trying to ignore the chaos invading the five floors of our house. I started to say that this house on this street that had once possessed a special beauty had forgotten itself and today was displaying its dark side. Our house is dark, the sestiere of Cannaregio is dark and swampy, the city of Venice is rundown, things in general that were once beautiful are now less so.

The new buildings across the inlet in Mestre are ugly—people seem uglier than before: dress fashions arrive to underline the potential ugliness of people.

Not only *things* and relatively unimportant aesthetic life are in decline, but also ethical thought and behavior of the human race are not what they used to be.

Then if you shout too loudly, 'enough', and cry for a return to the higher quality of life and the genuine beauty we once knew, you risk being considered a conservative-fascist. Then there is this other deterrent: you don't always recognize true beauty immediately when it appears. Not that all beauty is as éclatant as that of Helen, and after all hers is only a limited kind of physical beauty, as she shouts to one and all and feverishly paints herself over and over.

I look at her auto-portraits and realize each is a little different. Each contains a little less of her first beauty. A little less. A little less. Is ugliness to be the final result? I wonder about that.

Her first beauty begins to fade—the skin-deep beauty which she hates out of fear it may be taken as mere cosmetic beauty. You dig deeper, deep enough to see that ugliness is less ugly and you then see that true ugliness lurking around beauty. Helen's painting intimates the decline of beauty and its coalescence with ugliness, so that the outcome appears nebulous.

You have to dig still more. Dig and dig more until you realize she is removing the excess of any hint of cosmetic beauty in search of true beauty where all is all. Beauty is truth, truth is beauty, the poet sings. Truth and beauty and you wonder if her search is the search for God. Did Keats mean that? Most likely. Or is beauty God? The point, I realize, is what kind of beauty you search for.

If mass consumption cosmetic beauty is your desire, it is there, everywhere, and gives you at the very most a momentary, seconds-long satisfaction. It is now yours. You open it, "ah'—so simple to install, attach, apply, even a child can do it. You look at your new wallpaper, your new carpet, a *mi casa es tu casa* mat, a flowered spread and exclaim 'ah, lovely.' You can view it, admire it for a few seconds, touch it, taste it, and voilà, you have consumed beauty from which you derive no durable aesthetic pleasures. Now you can relax and forget your former desire to have it. You don't even remember that you have already had beauty. It's over. Done. Like after a loveless exercise of sex. No emotion or a feeling remains to fill and excite the core you as when you finish The Scarlet Letter or a James Baldwin novel from which you take something lasting away. It has possessed you and then left something important in your heart.

Therefore, I cannot accept that life is really random. I believe that things and acts matter. I believe there is a difference between right and wrong and that morality imposes virtues.

MAN

On the Loss of A Loved One

His name was Marcello Bolzoni. He was a cop. Sometimes, in the worst circumstances humans can bear, I suspect that what is real— in the sense of 'authentic'—is not simply crushed by a sick and uncaring world—but has remained an empty philosophical concept, fictive to begin with. So that my personal feelings of being an upholder of virtue and of morality, after all is said and done are no more than the most limited of feelings. Such suspicions had lain semi-dormant during the years that my reputation as the upright defender of human morality was maturing. Therefore, nights, alone in my bed in Montepulciano, Rome, Guanajuato, Paris, San Nicola, Fiesole, suspicions that everything that haunted my insomnia was merely relative —even my dreams. Such was the dire message the night reserved for me. The suspicion that 'all was all' made me as lonely as Giordano Bruno as he traveled and spoke his heresy around Europe, the loneliness he felt in his cell in the Angel Castle waiting for his fate, his loneliness when the priests burned him on the Campo de' Fiori.

Thoughts of Bruno underline the non-fictive reality that everything changes when the intruder—death—enters your mindscape. It changed me when my daughter died of an allergy at two years and four months of age. I lived in Paris then, I had slipped on wet metro stairs and in fighting to regain my equilibrium twisted my ankle leaving me partially incapacitated. She touched my ankle propped on a chair, like her mother said 'poor thing', found a bottle of pills, took two, maybe three—maybe all intended for me—and within in two hours she was gone. All is all? All is relative? Nothing was fictive there. Nothing relative. She was gone, perhaps leaving me her loneliness that she too must have felt in her last moments.

Now there is my friend Helen, alone with her cat and trying her best to escape her loneliness but nevertheless feels doomed to be violently lonely the rest of her life. The horrible quality of loneliness is its exclusivity. Each loneliness is unique. Everyone is trying to escape from something. The outsiders, the misfits, the rebels, the ones who see things differently, those who hate rules and have no respect for the status quo, they know what loneliness is.

But there is no escape from the loneliness death leaves behind. On the death of his friend the painter Franz Marc on the Verdun front in World War 1, his friend Paul Klee wrote in his diary: "Sometimes I remember the name Marc; I am shaken and see things crumble." In the short time his illness left him after he was sixty, Klee painted the figures of angels that seem to foreshadow the next world: his Angel of History has affected me. Loneliness becomes a companion, a painful, lifetime companion. Mine, Helen's, yours.

How much strength we need to survive this life of loneliness! Somehow we find that strength, or else the human being would have gone extinct along with the Angels and the Jinn, and the Creator would have been left alone to make his greatest decision: try again, or remain, he too, alone and lonely for all eternity. Man is gone. God is at last free. He won't make that mistake again. He could just leave the mountains and say 'fuck off' to man.

Now I know that my unconscious dialogue with the purple Abruzzi mountains and the shooting stars is a permissible memory of a memory of my original place. Some of us desire the same as God. Retire to the mountains. To the mountains of the Tirol. The Alps. The Great Smokies. The Elburz. Mount Etna. Popocatepetl. The Andes. Summers of return. No powerful regrets. The sensation you feel at the sound of the final mysterious word we search for, the word that will explain all, the word that has to do with one's place in the world. It's on the tip of your tongue and you know the unpronounceable of your life is within reach. But the word never arrives.

Summer, mountains and the shooting stars forming the Eden under them live in innocence—but at times in violence and guilt. First impressions are sometimes misplaced. For mountains are not lands of innocence either. Mountain people know violence. Blood flows there too. Animal natures are vicious and easily aroused. Apparent innocence feeds on violence. And God knows that innocence is permissive. In the purple mountains, under the stars and amidst the beauty and the boredom, in the good life and in the bigotry of sincerity, innocence is a luxury. People are born, live and die, to the very end grappling at their innocence. In each man there is an instinct of innocence. An instinct of solitude, aloneness, non-involvement, non-responsibility, absolution. An instinct that is neither destructive nor creative, but the great luxury of a life lived for nothing. No role, no participation in the history of human life.

I remember: in Tuscany when evening descends amid the omnipresent purple mountains, people seem content with themselves. As in the flatlands, darkness falls slowly there in the summer. In the dusk the mind has time to register and consider the day. The cool nights are conducive to sleep. But if one is fortunate, the heart is troubled and the night sleepless. If one is fortunate, after endless sleepless nights under shooting stars, the sad pioneer, immobile and indecisive in this territory of beauty and innocence and sincerity and violence, comes to himself. It is late but he still has time to realize his life will soon be over. Perhaps he begins to cry and he asks:

"Already?"

Why did he choose not to choose? Why did he reject pain and longing in exchange for peace and security?

Why did he do it?

God knew. He had to know.

I do not envy those who sleep comfortably, free of anxiety, the anxiety which is the necessary ingredient of a life worthy of the man God may have intended. Cain was his mistake. I would not put my life in the hands of those who never look over their shoulder. For life is also dangerous. Nothing is secure. Even the perfect society is a jungle as we saw in Fiesole. In the best of conditions living life is not easy. The good life is not the easy life. Am I not right? In the worst conditions living becomes habit. Living in habit and comfort and ease you forget that you risk each day as you move inexorably towards your end which you can see clearly down the straight road ahead. But you don't see the tragedy of it. You are immersed in a mystical dream, acting as if you were living a good and normal life—day in, day out, weeks, months and years pass, and nothing except habit happens. The good life. Work each day, maybe church on Sunday, a short vacation in the summer, the children grow up and leave, retirement, old age. At that point—your last chance— you might come to realize you no longer feel soaked in life. Though you have stuck it out, you too come to feel uprooted and alone. The strange thought might occur that maybe life is not worth living.

What have you done wrong? What?

Suddenly your spouse and children and friends are as distant as the mountains. In your short "lived" years you have never seen yourself. Never considered your real you, your essence, the essence we seek, the core you. You want to reconstruct emotions you suspect you once felt; but they have volatilized. Just flown away. You awaken in the middle of the night and wonder who you are and what you have done with your life. Has it been worth it? You don't know. What are you doing here? You don't know. You are a stranger to yourself. Your life is a theater. Mimesis. Your life has been seeming. There is no recourse. It's like looking in a mirror and for the first time really seeing yourself. You look at your face each day, to shave or make-up, but if—gradually more curious—you look closely into yourself often enough, you come to see a stranger. You become aware that the person you see is different, distinct and distant from everyone else and from the you, you had thought you were. If you look long enough at any object, even a rock, you will begin to see yourself. But it's in a magical mirror that you can meet yourself as nowhere else. Mirrors create a sense of loneliness and fear. Naked and alone, concentrated on yourself, you wonder if it is really you. Left and right are reversed, confusing what you see with what you know scientifically but cannot explain. You become afraid of the confusion and the aloneness staring out at you. And the fear in the mirror causes the fear in you to grow. Yet the mirror lures you back. You can't pinpoint yourself, not the thoughts, not even the sound of the voice of the child you once were. You are staggered by the solemnity and the mystery. You wonder if under your skin you are still the same person. On the right side of your face looking back at you, you might see a hint of yourself, but also you see the face of a stranger. The reflection is alien. That mimesis? But it must be you. That is the magical way mirrors work. There is something familiar after all. It is you, but you are an alien. You tell yourself you are seeing the figure in the mirror with the eyes of others. Left is right, right is left. It is your other appearance, the one others see—eyes different from your real eyes, forehead, hair, mouth, cheekbone, beard, all different. You cannot see yourself as others see you. Rather, others don't see you as you really are. You concentrate, trying to penetrate the bunker of time and feel only a vague relationship with the alien in the mirror. You look and wait for the arrival of enthusiasm and euphoria and passion and inspiration and divine grace. Sometimes you think of cutting your throat to escape your desperation.

18

December 1

The rainfall had never been so heavy as on this first day of December. Winter thunder rumbled from enraged churning skies. The smell of meteorological violence hung in the tepid air and news spread of hurricanes from the Atlantic sweeping across north Europe. An anti-climactic blowout in the early evening crowded into a ten-mile radius of Calle di Solferino launched shiny projectiles of coin- sized raindrops. Silence reigned over La Serenissima. No one ventured out of our house.

Vaska has more or less recovered but hardly ever leaves the apartment and lets Oriana pamper him like a domestic pet. His most distant destination is his former fourth floor apartment to transfer the last of his few possessions to Oriana's second floor, each trip up the bluish illuminated stairs interrupted by a visit with Helen working feverishly in her studio day and night.

True to herself, Helen rejected the intellectual tactic of non-recognition of her new reality: she would paint Marcello just as she had painted herself: suffering. She worked in pain but held it within her; she drove forward. She worked in a fever. Lightening a shadow, darkening a reflection, redirecting a swath, studying details nearly invisible to the naked eye. And she heard everything her companions said to her. She didn't hold it against Vaska that he seldom criticized his old friend Andriy Kravets for what he had done … or for what he knew he was. "Andriy suffered from his ambitions to be what he could never have been," he said. She considered Vaska a very sad but astute and perceptive person.

Everyone being present seemed strange, as if out of sympathy with Helen. A very strange day. The former abandoned building had become a home for ship-wrecked people like Vaska, like Helen—in one way or the other like all of us. No longer just a house that I consider an artificial construction, but it was a home. Feelings, sensations and heretofore unspoken thoughts roamed around as if liberated in Calle di Solferino. Tears ran down my face in the moment the *questura* men brought Marcello to his last home. His wayward and unwanted ashes now rested in a Venetian urn in my studio making our Cannaregio house twice a home. Sophie wrapped an arm around my waist and laid her head against my chest. I spontaneously started to wipe my eyes and apologize for not controlling my emotions. Instead, I said "fuck it all!" I loved the man in the urn and I cry for him at will despite social etiquette that demands that I crush authentic feelings and leave their expression to the virtual world.

Helen's grief was unlimited; she too rejected all rules of behavior, restrictions or controls. "Sleep is a woman," she said to Vaska on one of his visits. "Night's a time to cry in." Nonetheless, she no longer differentiated nighttime from pure time. A web of sleep came over her on its own volition; it overtook her in a chair or on the floor mat and, exceptionally, on the couch. Her grief smashed its way into her art, no less real and authentic for its tubed oily colors.

Man, she called her nascent work—now a mere splash of mixed dark colors poured at random from the top of the canvas. Likewise, *Man* was the title of my essay about a Tuscan cop whose renunciation of the power of his own status in the end doomed him.

"*Ecco*!" she said as she slit another tube of paint and splattered a brilliant carpet-like crimson streak down into the confusion of colors at the center of the canvas.

Vaska followed her work which to the naked eye consisted of only invisible nuances of color and form "All the things that words cannot describe," he commented after a first view of *Man*.

"The definition of my grief!" she murmured.

A baffled Vaska stared at her. Helen had always puzzled him—not because of her feminine nature—for after all he'd had Lyuba and he saw into Helen in the same way he had once seen into her. No, it was her otherworldliness. Beautiful women in his mind behaved in a different way from non-beautiful women: they were actresses: diaphanous, fragile, untouchable, inimitable ... sometimes amorphous. And the men who knew them or loved them were also different and strange. Like Marcello, he thought. Like Stuart, he perceived. They had to be. It was not for everyone to touch a semi-goddess. His insight enabled him to shrug off her perfect beauty at first as a *fata morgana,* a false beauty. And he recalled from English literature class in his Kharkov high school the lines "Beauty is truth, truth beauty" from a poem by John Keats' *Ode on a Grecian Urn.* The poet found that beauty and truth were one and the same and that true beauty was eternal, a manifestation of the divine, and a way of accessing deeper truths about ourselves and our feelings and emotions.

Helen's work suggested that beauty and truth are truly interconnected and that her pursuit of the truth of beauty in the discarded painting standing lonely in the corner revealed also deeper understandings of truth than she admitted. He thought that for Helen as for Dostoyevsky beauty transcends aesthetics and inspires the best in us: our aspirations for what is real and authentic, good and true perceptions and the current that connects everyone one to the other. Authenticity was her god, her goal, as it had been for Dostoevsky. I think that all of us in the house on Calle di Solferino understood that Vaska was a mystic trying to see himself as true mystics do. A non-religious mystic. A mysticism in which he found refuge from the modern world in which he'd wandered during the last decade. Still, he was surprised that anyone thought of him as a mystic. From his own experience he perceived the error of believing you really know another. He'd been physically close to Andriy Kravets for a lifetime and yet only now that he was gone did he realize that he knew such a minor part of him. For the first time in his life he felt a sensation of ease, a sensation of having lightened himself of a former meaninglessness by dispossession of the Promethean baggage he'd carried for so long, and that the security he had once perceived in his Slavic ambiguity and unknowing was insufficient. He felt he too was in that magic moment of making a leap toward the marvelous in his new lightened state following the lost decade and a half of wandering in an Italic desert with his blind guide, Andriy Kravets.

I thought he seemed to have been blessed with the quality of grace, although he probably had no idea what natural grace was. Not that Vaska had claimed that his feverish visions during his illness were supernatural experiences but in his innermost self he intuited that the sickness out of which he'd just emerged had left traces of a form of grace behind, the grace of having experienced an intensified otherness, uncertainty and wonderment about his anomalous situation in the bed of Oriana and in the home of these different Westerners. Though in the passing years in Italy he had felt estrangement and bewilderment at his unorthodox situation so far from Kharkov and the world of Lyuba as well as his links with Ukraine and Russia, he now seemed aware of the paradox of his life today. During the past empty years he had become accustomed to the Italian free expression of love for others; in the homeland he had experienced chiefly mistrust and hate one for the other, among people where betrayal, heartbreak and pain were the norm. Despite his trust of each of these new people in his life, he didn't talk with anyone about his fears.

Vaska was convinced that Ukrainian killers waited for him somewhere out there in this small and restricted world of the outlying Italic province in Europe that he had come to know from east to west and from north to south. And they wanted him dead.

He knew that it was the SBU that killed Kravets and Marcello and the Freemason in the pension and he'd doubted from the start the theory that it was random or that Freemasons had killed two other men just to get Marcello. The idea seemed ridiculous.

To him it was as clear as Lyuba's blue eyes looking up at him from the cotton blanket on the summery fields near Kharkov that Andriy was the target. The massacre of three men that night in the Pensione Ponte was not random.

But then why? He didn't know the answer. The SBU couldn't know the betrayal waxing in his own heart, a traitor to what he knew was false. To Ukraine? It existed in name only. Values? None. Truth? Meaningless to them.

They could only suspect his feelings: he knew that the authenticity which he wanted to personify was in itself traitorous to today's Ukraine.

But his feelings were not the point either; he was guilty by association. If Andriy was executed as a traitor, then he too was already condemned. It was only a matter of time.

December 2

Shouts from downstairs. People running up and down the blue staircase. Windows opened wide. Overnight an historic meteorological transformation had occurred.

The rain had stopped!

I understood how Noah must have felt when his ship came to rest on dry land. The city we knew was bathed in sunshine. Radio Venezia announced the return of normal business activities. Lessons and lectures at Ca' Foscari resumed. Vaporettos and water taxis and motor launches flew their flags and literally pranced majestically over the waterways as if the mere idea of water under them were illusion. The sun was rising from beyond the Lido and Malamocco and the Adriatic Sea. Apparently the all-clear front arrived from the East and was still moving westwards; night-shift workers on the Malamocco wharves reported that at three a.m. rainfall had ceased and minutes later stars hovered in clear skies over the Adriatic. Passengers from a Red Arrow train that arrived from Rome at 4.13 a.m. reported that the last drops had fallen on the city at the Santa Lucia Station, five kilometers west of the Malamocco port but that low clouds overhead were still suspiciously heavy. Pessimistic meteorologists who loved the rain for its news value and who had predicted that the rain would never stop prompted derision among the optimists who had spoken of the rainfall as normal November showers and that since the time of Noah the rain had always stopped. People repeated God's promise never again to cover the whole world with water. Venetians hurriedly began dismantling the elevated boardwalk labyrinth on St. Mark's Square and many sold their knee-high rubber boots cheap to the doubters.

When I started outside to look at the sky, I was surprised to find our building's entrance door wide open Not only was the lock broken and partially dismantled but also the hinges of the door were torn away.

Only for an instant did the thought of dilettante burglars cross my mind before the real reasons for our being here in Cannaregio revived.

Inept burglars?

Perhaps.

But also vicious killers.

The situation in Calle di Solferino was different too: Marcello had already been brutally murdered and now a putative ex-Ukrainian spy was living among us.

I ran up the stairs to the fourth floor. Vaska's abandoned apartment door was wide open as was Helen's just under him. I checked around Vaska's apartment where only a few pieces of furniture remained. He had moved the last of his stuff to Oriana's on the second floor. In the back room a cardboard folder lay open on the table. Hand-written pages were strewn about the room. Perhaps because of his rush to transfer his life to that of Oriana and his desire to leave his old life behind, he had lackadaisically non-spy-like left such stuff behind.

Yet I knew that Vasily Tarnovsky was NOT one to forget, especially not a file perhaps containing details of the secrets of his life in Italy. I scanned the notes written in Italian and partially in Russian with additions in green ink in the margins, notes about the life he'd left behind in Kharkov.

He might have left the folder behind in the empty back room on purpose, a folder fat with all his notes and information, his hopes and disillusionments, his calculations and his conclusions, together with memories of Lyuba and Kravets, arms shipments and long-term espionage considerations. Now, he hoped all of that was behind him. There was no logical place for those memoirs in his new life. He was determined that this life would be a better one. Not just a borderline life but a life of quality and satisfactions, uprightness and hopefully rewards. A better life? Может быть! He knew it was not as simple and easy as switching apartments or shaving off his Trotsky goatee. Vaska told me that he didn't consider himself a Trotskyist but that he'd always liked the man's style: his goatee and his stare, Trotsky's glasses, his hair, and the communist jacket he wore, a symbol of the Russian Revolution.

Scanning, I read by chance his words that he considered himself a Leninist but that he found inspiration in Trotsky's image and his charisma. A style to emulate. He wrote that he had long wondered what would have happened if he hadn't been assassinated in Mexico City –Coyoacan. In any case, Trotsky sufficed to make him prefer a Russian Kharkov to a second-rate Kharkov in Ukraine I sat on the floor and read his notes with a certain surprise, less for what he included in this round-up of his life than at what he omitted: a chronicle but no deep probing thoughts about Kravets the companion of a lifetime, the SBU, Kiev. Nonetheless, these were materials for a biographic novel, a unique story of a man of our times leading a life of the past.

In any case the burglar theory didn't hold water. So, I wondered, was it a case of Ukrainians or Freemasons on his trail? Or were they only run-of the mill Venetian thieves?

I went back down a floor and looked in on Helen. She ignored the non-rain. But I asked her anyway.

"Were you surprised this morning?"

"Surprised?"

"When the rain stopped. New light for you. Different noises."

"I was just pouring a color mix when the radio DJ started yelling, 'Venetians! Venetians! the rain has stopped.'"

While she spoke there was fast-forwardness in her brushing movement with a silken cloth of what may have been dust or a quick transformation from a deep blue to a light greenish shade in an upper corner of the canvas that I knew would one day become some form of Marcello … or his world. Or was this to be The Urn itself? Her life art in this work broke through as a shiny object, a light, a luster that if you looked at it one way it showed no promise of anything figurative; if you moved to one side or the other you saw what might have been the suggestion of a person. She looked surprised that I didn't see the same thing she saw coming to life rapidly like the Rome-Venice Red Arrow Express at Santa Lucia Station.

"So what?" she said, "It had to stop someday."

Ten minutes after I'd informed Trevisan about the burglars, he was there examining the house door. "In real life killers don't necessarily have break-in skills," he muttered. "These guys were pretty crude … which points toward killers and not burglars."

Then when he saw the mass of papers and the folder in Vaska's backroom, he said, "I don't believe these guys were Ukrainians. Of if they were they perhaps saw in the papers deliberate misleading disinformation. Anyway, despite the house door mess, they're not amateurs either. They could have copied everything of interest among the papers and left the rest as if untouched. The scientific people can check this out too. The main thing is that Vasily is safe ... for now."

"Because he changed floors."

"It might be that simple. So maybe the papers were more important than they seem."

"You know, Trevisan, maybe we're underestimating the role of the other Ukraine … I mean the people. Their fake President represents bureaucratic, sold-out Ukraine here and there like at the UN or shaking hands with European leaders in Brussels or the Elysée Palace. His unceasing pleas for more money and arms. The EU's promises to him must seem like sailors' promises on departure eve. Then you read that Ukrainian military leaders are conspiring against him. But they are just like him. If they didn't want power and the riches that go with it, they wouldn't occupy their high-ranking positions today. But then there are the people … and they count. Ukraine's spies here—like Kravets was—are spies for the President's party, spies for the conspirators. Makes no difference. But still! What I mean is that there must be more than a few like Vasyl Tarnosky. A Communist. He himself says he's not alone. He says if you're not a Nazi, what are you? A fucking liberal? He says you have to believe in something. So he's dangerous for the regime. How big is the pro-Russian movement in Ukraine? The Fascists running the government have enough power to suppress dissent today. But for how long? There are those other Ukrainians here in Italy and in other EU countries also. Some loyal to the regime. Some not. Like Vaska. The US has its Euro vassals and their media; ninety per cent of them toe the US line. But for how long? Trevisan, this Ukraine affair is about over. This year will be a landmark. Russia's war with Ukraine will end. Russian generals say they could take Kiev and/or Odessa in one day, if they wanted to. American taxpayers are sick of paying. Sick of trillions going to Ukraine and the corrupt regime and maybe to Mali too. Sick of supporting Israel. Hezbollah and Hamas and the US-EU dissenters are fed up, Trevisan. Many American Jews are still hesitant, still unclear in their Aesopian in language but getting tighter with their support of their 'traditional homeland' where they have no desire whatsoever to actually live. Weak Yemen ravaged by everyone blocked the Suez Canal route through the Red Sea—to all but Russian ships because Russia and its ally Iran give them aid! Why? Revenge! That's why. Now governed by Houthi rebels, *Slava Houthi*! Yemen has twenty-eight million people, Trevisan, the size of France, and they're sick of oppression. Forgotten and sick of attacks by the world. They block some shipping and get bombed again. They wait. The US can't beat them and continue to lose face. No one believes the US anymore. Then the BRICS nations, Trevisan—Brazil, Russia, India, China, South Africa and now Argentina, Egypt, Ethiopia, Iran—are a whopping majority of the world. Tiny Europe—not even a continent—a tip of the Eurasian continent. Tiny land mass and five hundred million people. A drop in the bucket. That variegated Europe has little clout in world affairs. The EU expands its membership but its former world influence shrinks. The putative continent of Europe once seemed limitless in its extensions over the plains to the East. But now we see Europe for what it is: that tiny peninsula attached to the heartland of Eurasia. A bunch of rich but old and divided countries. As such it lacks a decisive role in world affairs today. That reality is indigestible to Europe itself; it's accustomed to a leading role in the world. Some remember that before the so-called "union" of Europe non-European visitors were charmed by the conglomeration of states of different customs and speech which in the eyes of visionary but avid state leaders like Charles DeGaulle reached all the way to Russia's Ural Mountains out there in the mists of the eastern marches of the land mass of Eurasia. As such it formed a "kind of continent" and had a voice in world affairs. In reality the Europe that Westerners—non-Europeans and Europeans alike—knew and loved is that peninsula. Its tail end pointing westwards today ... toward the Americas. The countless border controls and currency exchanges were so romantic, confusing and annoying. Suspicious French exit controls and *tout de suite après*, the lackadaisical slow and showy *tutto piano piano* Italian entry check points. The usual lines on one side of the border or the other at the money changers busily flattering the tourists and skimming on rates. But the average tourist from the new world found it all so nice and pleasantly confusing and the countries seemed alike one to the other. But they were not alike. Not at all. There were race differences and class differences, great economic differences, everybody only pretending to be the same. Pretending to be what they were not. The old disputed border zones and their mishmash of languages and peoples who only thought they knew who they were.That was the way Europe was supposed to be. That was the public image of Old Europe which in reality was corrupt, colonialist-imperialist, evil and with an irrepressible predilection for war. The tourists and the expats grumbled but loved it that way. Europe's intellectual class and artists of the world—writers, painters, musicians—felt Europe was the only place to be. That variegated multiethnic semi-continent of Europe was a world. Even the Iron Curtain that descended to mark the start of the Cold War after WWII reinforced the continental image of this incomprehensible Europe, with an enticing taint of danger attached. A fake world. Now also BRICS says 'no' to that fraudulent Europe pretending to be the world. 'No' to NATO, 'no' to the dollar, 'no' to sanctions. If oppressed Yemen can block the Suez Canal-Red Sea route to Asia again, BRICS can block the world. It's a fact, Trevisan. Like Galileo Galilei said, Trevisan—right here in Cannaregio he said it too: "And yet it moves", attributed to the Italian mathematician, physicist and philosopher in 1633 after being forced to recant his claims that the Earth moves around the Sun. Despite his recantation and the Inquisition or any other conviction or doctrine of men, he told the world that the earth moves around the sun and not the contrary."

Helen had followed Trevisan's report and our talk as had Pushkin who seemed to remember him, purring and meowing and brushing his legs. He looked down at the cat, stooped and scratched him behind his ears. I believe Pushkin smelled Marcello on him as he did on me.

Trevisan looked up and said he was off to Transshipping in Chioggia. Our friend Santin had called: a Ukrainian couple from Venice was to take over negotiations for the Mali arms shipment. They were pleased that the ship was going to West Africa and had no need of the Red Sea route.

Never has the call of Mother Africa rang more persuasively.

19

December 3

"I'm so alone, Stuart. Inside me I'm alone. Sad like your new friend, Vaska. In Vienna there was a Russian student like him in my faculty. Wanted to become a doctor. He was alone too … and sad like me today. He shot himself. I'm trying. I really am. I'm not going to shoot myself but I don't feel I'm part of things. Not even of things here in this house. I feel abandoned. Alone with my imagination of what my life could have been together with someone. This feeling goes back in time, back to Vienna. But I distrusted that image, and all the other images like that. Reality proved me right. I guess I was meant to be alone."

"Oh, Helen, stop it! You're not meant to be alone and you're not alone. But you're right about imagination. It's a power to be reckoned with for everybody."

She still speaks little, but often her memory caries her back to Vienna and then quickly returns to an image of Marcello.

"Sometimes I fantasize that one image or the other is just my imagination. Then I see it's really much more than imagination. Still, it's not real; it's pure fantasy after all. But other times when I imagine I'm fantasizing, I think it unimportant … that it's just my fertile imagination at work. I confuse the two—reality and fantasy. "I remember the story you told me of a summer morning you stood at the top of the Kuhleiten, the highest peak of the western Dolomites. I liked your description of the tired dilettante hikers standing around you, dripping with sweat but proud they'd made it to the top. Then you and the vacationers fell silent when you saw standing near a ledge three real mountain climbers wearing helmets and spiked climbing shoes with red and yellow leather laces, you said. They were checking their harnesses and their axes, readying for the final steps across a chasm too deep to even contemplate. On the other side of the abyss was the tiny section of the summit of the Alpine world reserved for the real mountaineers who laughed and slapped each other on the back. The reality of mountain climbing became clear that day. Not as simple as I'd thought. That's why I too feel I have to hang onto reality ... in defiance of my anarchic imagination. On the other hand, I'd be lost as an artist if I banned imaginary objects and unlikely events."

"Right, Helen. We need balance. We see how the media treat Building Seven in the World Trade Center like a ghost. The media say if it's not there today it most likely never existed. Like people in Mexico City I asked about the volcano Popocatepetl, in the smog invisible at the place it was supposed to be—and even climber paths to the top were closed because of invisible eruptions. Some few people scoffed and said that its existence was more myth than reality—a historical myth created by Aztec gods. Still, some people do climb it. So it exists."

"Like my two projects—first painting myself—really my synthesis of beauty and ugliness. And now *him*. I'm in a battle with that overlap between imagination and fantasy."

"That overlap seems to me even greater in writing. Fantasy implies *impossible* scenarios; creativity involves scenarios that are *possible*. But both fantasy and creativity involve the imagination—imagining *possible* scenarios. Where the two get confused is at the border between them."

"Sometimes it's a matter of opinion where that border lies."

"Because what are creative ideas for some are considered impossible fantasies by people who lack the imagination to see how such an idea could be actualized. Maybe like science fiction."

"Which interests me little."

Actually, art is resisted, I thought, examining Helen's still formless work—only Helen saw the changes in progress. There's resistance to the idea that art is useful. This kind of resistance is the problem faced by all artists: how to get their ideas realized. Most artists work on their own until their art finds supporters. The idea that the creative arts are useful and not just the fantasy of the artist is anathema to many people. Helen questions this. People think that if it's not useful in the real world it's fantasy. They ask what it is that separates art from mere fantasy? Of course it's true fact that artists *use* fantasy in their work. They use fantasy to address real life issues and not impossible "fantasy world" issues. A certain John Ross Mcglade wrote that 'sensitive people turn to art because it addresses real issues in an artistic manner That *is* the function of art. Not art for art's sake. Art is not escapism into unrealistic worlds. Authentic art highlights aspects of the world in a way we were not aware of before and integrates it into our lives. Into our brains. Creative arts creep and slither and worm their way into our entire reality. Moreover, real artists rely on reality even for their fantasies. There is a difference between imagining other worlds and believing an impossible fantasy.'

Still, I can't help wondering if my past even happened. I know that the past as I remember it today is not necessarily reality, that memory has warped those realities into fantastical childhood games. Or is that past only an illusion of what might have happened … as Helen may think in her loneliness? Only a dream? I understand her! I never seem to get things straight in my mind either. My problem is to distinguish between what is real reality and what is fantasy, between reality and what is only my imagination of what might have occurred. I sometimes fear that the things I love most in life are destined to morph into impossible fantasy in some unpredictable future. A chimera. My mind—like hers, I suppose—is in reality a bloody mess. A quagmire. A battleground where reality and fantasy fight for supremacy. I wrote in a diary that I feel like a speeding tram on the edge of a cliff. A fucking tram! A tram unaware of where it's going or of where it's coming from. It moves along repetitive rails … always in the present. So the images of the different times and events in my life easily overwhelm me and merge into my present, in the same way light overlaps darkness. Oh yes, I claim that I'm moving forward despite all those associations lingering in the shadows of my mind. Once I was cocksure of myself and the future. The world was never big enough. I had to live more than one life—two, three and more lives. Everything was so easy that I began to feel an immunity to the ills that strike less fortunate people. I often wonder if other people at certain times in their lives feel the same invulnerability I once felt. Maybe I believed that Fate—even if I claim not to believe in it—was on my side. Actually I don't claim anymore that Fate doesn't exist, but the doubt exists. Fate exists … and it doesn't. Either I'm strong enough to master my fate—if it exists—or it is more powerful than my will. Destiny is something else. There is the French proverb I often quote that people often meet their destiny on the road they take to avoid it. Like the soldier in the tale of his appointment with Death in Samarkand. The anecdote goes like this: On a square of a town, Death makes a sign to a soldier, terrifying him. The soldier runs to the king and tells him that Death made a sign to him. Therefore he was escaping immediately to Samarkand. The king summons Death and asks why he scared his captain. Death answers that he didn't intend frightening the soldier, he just wanted to remind him that they had an appointment that evening in Samarkand. It's along that precise road of apparent escape that fate can step in to give you a hand. Because though you can't change your destiny, you can challenge it. Still—and this is what is so curious about destiny and fate in my opinion—how am I to know what my destiny has in store for me? Is there really a difference between the two? Fuck it! Maybe these are the futile questions of age and circumstances. The curtain of my mind. The corners and the shadows and the otherworldly darkness of when dreams and fancy counted more than time and space—back then.

When I got back to my desk downstairs I rummaged around the drawers for the diary I'd started several times. I flipped through it looking for the word "memory". Then there it was: MEMORY OF MEMORIES, I'd headed the note that was to have been integrated into a story:

First, there is the event when it happens. The authenticity of that happening shows forth in the moment of its occurrence, even though even that still authentic event is blurred by the proximity. Second, comes the remembrance of a witness or of the one who experiences the happening. The remembrance may be very similar to the authentic event, but not the same. Then, the passage of time dilutes that first remembrance into an elusive recollection of the happening which has become a reconstruction of the now vague remembrance-recollection of the event. The authentic happening has been transformed: it is becoming legendary. It may be remembered as grander and more glorious than it was in reality; or infamous and loathsome. In the same way, your own memory of the end of a love affair first becomes a remembrance; then a less precise recollection of the rupture. Finally your recollection becomes a hazy reconstruction of what happened: you may be convinced of the infidelity of the loved one or the disloyalty of that ideal to which you were loyal. The reconstruction is your adjustment of how things happened and how they played out. You believe you have remained loyal but that the object of your love or your belief has betrayed you. And you suspect that your perception of the reality of the loved one or of the belief was misconceived from the beginning. For memory—remembrances, recollections and reconstructions—will never coincide precisely with what really existed or with what happened. Perhaps you will never grasp the true reasons of why or of the manner in which the great fracture in your life came about. For in the passing of time your perceptions and conceptualizations warp and then alter remembrances of the reality of what occurred. The defensive task of the brain must be the accommodation of the needs and instincts of your own frangible being in order to make them bearable so that you do not blow your brains out on a daily basis.

20

December 3

Carmina Burana was blasting at full volume in the front room. A Munich coral group known for its renditions in Latin filled the screen singing ancient stories that maybe the composer Carl Orff was the only person in Europe who understood. Sophie was hanging onto the TV as if trying to grasp what it all meant.

Sors immanis et inanis,/rota tu volubilis
status malus,/vana salus
semper dissolubilis,/obumbrata
et velata/michi quoque niteris;
nunc per ludum/dorsum nudum
fero tui sceleris./Sors salutis
et virtutis/michi nunc contraria
est affectus/et defectus
semper in angaria.
Hac in hora/sine mora
corde pulsum tangite;/quod per sortem
sternit fortem,/mecum omnes plangite!

"I've always loved this music," she said, "even though I don't get one single word."

Trevisan was out in the hall on his phone and acting as if he lived here. Red rain had changed everything.

"Blasio Santin," he said and closed his phone. "We need to go to Chioggia *subito,* Stuart! Breaking news! I'll update you on the way."

It was indeed a strange day. Helen and Pushkin alone together in the studio, Vaska confused by a new life, *Carmina Burana* echoing through the whole house. The only normal thing was the renewal of the steady ceaseless rain, again pounding every external surface. To the relief of many Venetians, the rain had returned during the night. Again, no white mountains on the northern horizon. No regular vaporetto service on the Canal Grande. People get used to anything.

When forty-five minutes later we arrived in Chioggia the precipitation was beguilingly minimal. But streets had their now familiar reddish tint. I looked around this normal town and saw it as a whole. So unlike Venice visible only in small parts, a bridge here, a *rio* there, a palace, a tower, a gondola, an island within an island, each marked and identified. A conglomeration of separate spaces.

Urban compartmentalization was a way of life in Venice City.

Little Venice was a concentrate of greater Venice but still different in its unity. A place where scoundrels and criminals and very rich people lived. People who wanted to live near the real Venice but not too near to run-down parts of a city that gets more and more crowded despite its decreased population. Harry's Bar and the Caffé Florian were close enough to Chioggia thanks to their high-powered speed boats. Go out for dinner. Race in your speed boat, dock at the restaurant, and step off the deck and straight into Harry's. Also the many poor—also sea-going people—who lived in Chioggia had a purpose in life: to serve the rich and their speedboats.

We stepped out of the Transworld Shipping elevator right into Santin's arms. His cheeks already had that pleasant rose-colored look of the contented man that Marcello had described so well.

We headed down the long corridors straight toward the bar. Looking to the left and to the right at well-lit workers' cubicles, waving to one or the other, Santin asked how Pushkin was doing after the tragedy.

"He really loved that cat," Trevisan said, a sad look crossing his face."

We were some thirty meters away when Santin stopped and indicating two persons sitting at the bar, said: "They're the Ukrainians and claim they've been assigned to coordinate the arms shipment: receipt of the payment from Mali and the payment to Transworld Shipping. But the reason I called you urgently is that in a routine control of final shipment papers one of our bookkeepers found a black hole down which was to go 500,000 euros from the Mali treasury for consultancy charges in Chioggia. After meetings with Signor Kravets, our chief accountant felt certain that Kravets planned to do everything as planned except forwarding the ten million euros to Kiev. Tarnovsky was allegedly sick and Kravets would have handled the entire affair. Money from Mali was on the way."

"Ten million in that scoundrel's hands," Trevisan said. "Unbelievable. Like they say, this is truly a rich man's world."

"The shipment was ready but the shoot-out in Venice took place before the money arrived. The money then arrived, but too late for old Kravets. Consequently Transworld has not yet been paid. Anyway that's what those two at the bar are supposed to handle. But Detective, I suspect they were in cahoots on the scheme from the start. I have no proof—nor does the bookkeeper—no hard and fast reason, just a strong suspicion, a feeling … and my intuition."

"Thus a strong probability," I said. In my estimation, Santin was an ok person but as a businessman his interest in the payment overshadowed the political aspects which bothered Trevisan..

"Ok," Trevisan began. "then here's something to scare the shit out these Ukrainians: our intelligence service reports—and now the world press confirms it—that Kiev is now conscripting Ukrainians abroad to their army … that is, to return home and give their lives for the *patria.* A rifle and off to the front you go so all Ukrainians abroad have reason to worry."

Blasio hemmed and hawed a bit and looked longingly toward the bar and said ever so slowly: "Transworld only wants its payment!"

"Right! We'll get you that payment right now!" Trevisan said." Better to get that part done quickly because our intelligence service, AISI, will soon take the case out of our hands. And nobody knows where the money will go."

Trevisan looked at me and whispered , "Maybe I should ask Santin to call Kiev and alert someone to take care of their problem …"

"Just not the Ukrainian police or security services," I whispered back. "And why are we whispering anyway? Everybody should know by now that the Kiev crowd is a bunch of gangsters and who run the most corrupt country in Europe. Even the Honorary Consul in Padua is most likely a crook too. And now there's nobody else to contact in Kiev on money matters anyway. With that ten million kickback their President could buy another villa in some exotic place. But that dumb bastard keeps building his future in the USA which is getting pretty sick of him ... that man is being prepared to become another patsy. Another sacrifice to US national interests. Like Juan Guaidò who declared himself Interim President of Venezuela during the election crisis there and ended up in the USA where he soon became no one. "

"Ok, I'll take care of the payment to you." Trevisan draped an arm around Santin's shoulders and said, "Your payment first and then these two substitute consultants are going to help us round up the Ukrainan agents in the area and solve the triple murder at the Academia. If not, Rome will send the whole bunch of them back home—where obviously none of them want to go … especially not these long-term ones, even though many of them are likely sleeper-spies. As for those two at the bar, I think we can scare them out of their fucking wits. Mention of extradition to Ukraine will convince them to collaborate and give us a long list of names and loads of help! No sane person wants to be conscripted into the Ukrainian army and end up in the Kherson trenches."

Georgia Georgetti and Mikhaylo Kristin were all smiles. An ice bucket with French champagne stood in front of them on the bar. Things were looking up in the world of the two Ukrainians who'd been in Italy some fifteen years. Georgia was over fifty years old, Mikhaylo Kristin, around forty. Georgia seemed to be the boss. Trevisan showed them his Venice Police ID and held it long seconds in front of each of them. "I'm from here. My friend, Signor Stuart is from Rome and you already know the director of Transworld. So we can dispense with other formalities and get down to business. But first things first. I would like to know what brought you to Venice."

Georgia snickered. Mikhaylo laughed loud, took a sip of champagne, and said, "We've been here so long that it's home. Why we're as Venetian as you. Venetians! We live very modest lives and mind our own business."

Trevisan glared at them, glanced meaningfully at the champagne, looked at Santin and me, and again stared Georgia in the eyes. He had comprehended in a heartbeat the deceit and the inherent duplicity in her position which her eyes revealed; and she knew that he knew who she really was.

"And you are not even employed," the detective added. "Before visiting your modest home, I made official inquiries. You live in a penthouse near the Rialto fish market … an expensive area. Then I stood outside in the rain there for hours. The people who entered or exited exuded well-being … if not wealth."

"You should have rung our bell and come in … uh, out of the rain," Georgia said, now only weakly ironic and quite subdued. She and Mikhaylo were both under the spell of Trevisan's police power and his mention of international laws on extradition. The couple was losing all volition and reliance on their former sense of intangibility that had developed over the years, coupled with their uprootedness that had become a way of life—fifteen years of a kind of waywardness and irresponsibility and unaccountability that became their second nature at the age most people are engaged in the ups and downs of lived life. I watched their eyes—as did Trevisan—and wondered if their behavior was normal, even though they hadn't been trapped red-handed, nor had they confessed or denied their source of livelihood. There had been no mention of corruption or espionage or Ukraine and Italy and Europe, nor any signs of lingering sentiments of homesickness. There had been no talk of legalities, lawyers and judges and courts. Their non-reaction hardly seemed that of spies once identified as such.

"Oh, I did ring, many times. But no matter. I was also there later when Andriy Kravets entered your house … and stayed. So naturally I'm curious about your relationship with him, since as you surely know that soon afterwards he was murdered near Academia. And one of the killers whom you most likely know also is still missing, at large somewhere in Venice we believe. You see what I mean!"

I stared at Mikhaylo and nodded several times as Trevisan outlined the reality of the situation of these two sleeper spies.

With a thoughtful look on his handsome face, Santin meandered to the end of the bar where the barman handed him the usual. He drained the tall, narrow glass in one gulp, wiped his mouth with the back of his hand and before turning back toward the action, he examined minutely the now empty glass as if it was at fault for its emptiness. His was a look that I understood perfectly well, expressing also my uncertainty about the real nature of inanimate objects in general and of drinking glasses in particular. I'd had this fixation on drinking glasses since I was a young man: tall glass for beer with breathing space for the beer but not so wide that the foam quickly falls flat, shot glasses for whiskey and schnapps like grappa or gin, big pear-shaped glasses for cognac … the categories and preferences were endless but I have always believed the drink itself had preferences.

In that moment I saw that Santin understood preferences too—he would have preferred a shorter glass more in harmony with the grappa he loved. And I again thought of Alessandra who in Greece on vacation fell in love with a bench at a sidewalk café at a sidewalk café on a small square in Rhodes. Now there is a connection of the bench story with drinking and glass preferences. A story that I would save for the ride back to Santa Lucia Station but will preview now:

"The bench kept looking at me," Alessandra said. Anywhere I went on the square its eyes seemed to follow me. You know what I mean?"

"Did it speak to you?"

"Of course it did ... you know that."

"And what did it say?"

"It said, 'take me with you to Italy.'"

So, she did ... in a technological way. She photographed it on her I-phone and sent it—let's say she messaged the first copy of the bench—on a cell phone to her brother-in-law in Rome—who can copy anything—asking if he could make her a bench just like the one in Rhodes.

Then when I first saw the hand-made bench in Alessandra's yard, I recalled Socrates' metaphor of the three beds in his The Republic and his warning about the difficulty of ever attaining real truth. For me, his metaphor is emblematic of the problem of the degeneration from the ideal to the banal: according to the Socrates metaphor, the first bed, made by God, is the Platonic ideal; a carpenter then makes a second bed in imitation of that ideal bed; and the artist subsequently paints a third bed in imitation of the carpenter's imitation of the ideal bed.

No wonder I sat uneasily on that imitation bench in her yard in Rome. I felt ephemeral. And I knew then that the bench perceives the same impermanence as I. But it asks for nothing. It is what it is. A wooden bench. Inanimate? I look for its eyes. And I see its eyes in each arm of the bench which I had taken for knots in the wood. They look at me. The bench in the Rome yard, a copy of the photographic copy of the original bench in Rhodes touches only a small part of the original bench. For step by step each copy is farther removed from the original, from its center. A bench may appear differently from various points of view as when you look at yourself in a mirror which keeps for itself ten percent of the original real you. And that presents the greatest problem of human nature: the recovery of that ten percent. For you suspect that one-tenth of you contains the original you, the core, the authentic you. Perhaps your soul. So painters or poets or photographers, though they may paint or describe or depict a carpenter or any other maker of things, know only part of the original craftsman's creation. Though the better painters or poets or craftsmen they are, the more faithfully their works of art will resemble the authentic original of the carpenter's bench or bed; nonetheless, the imitators can never attain the truth of God's original creation. There's always that ten percent. Most certainly it's true that in our day-to-day lives, artificiality rules ... in the world of both objects and human egos. So when I sit on that bench I look at those eyes in the bench's arms looking at me and wonder if Socrates knew what in the hell he was talking about. All this to emphasize my conviction that Ukraine is so far, far from a real country: a TV country with TV comedian as play-acting President. All a fiction.

Now I like to work the magic of the objects around us into my stories . I've always been fascinated by those poets convinced of a relationship between man's eyes and the object of his gaze, that the things we really see, see us as much as we see them. Poets have long vision. Jean Laplanche wrote of the difference between the work of thought and a poem. The author of thought takes his own language as a big palace … but he inhabits only a part of it.

He leaves parts almost completely empty. A poet tries to use his language as a whole, he tries to inhabit as much of the palace as possible; going from one place to the other, he uses new meanings of the words and new resonances. I appreciate Baudelaire's words in Fleurs du Mal: 'Man wends his way through forests of symbols/ Which look at him with their familiar glances.' I want to feel my subjects like Baudelaire did. I believe the objects around us—a table, a glass we stare into, yellow wine bubbles—also see us … as Rilke writes about Apollo. Like Rilke and Baudelaire, a new world opens for you when you convince yourself that every object around you is hiding secrets, secrets that reveal their nature. The secret that everything that passes between the spiritual and material worlds are connected by vision and words maybe speaking to you. When I think of communication with inanimate objects, I wonder if they are truly inanimate. And if they too are not filled with the passion and inspiration of Andalusian duende. Later imitators—painters, sculptors or photographers—then capture less and less of the ideal. They might graze the reality of a carpenter making a bed or of an artist painting a carpenter making a bed, but they can never attain the true ideal of the original creation. I had seen in my short bureaucratic career that the higher you go up the chain of command, the more distortion of any original idea you will meet. Yet the bench-imitation has not yet spoken to me, as did the original to Alessandra. Hopefully, the perception of sitting on an imitation bench will soon pass. And Ukrainians? Leading false lives under the presidency of a clown! And so it goes in human life. There are those who recall that in literature and philosophy even the ancient Greek gods were preordained by enigmatic Fate. It is recalled that three secret Greek gods spun a bottle in their attempt to determine the future actions and events of a life. And Nietzsche—even more complex—believed that every philosophy conceals another philosophy, every opinion is a hiding place for other opinions and every word a mask covering other words. Therefore, I felt the warmth of affection for Santin and his grappa glass.

"So what do you expect from us?" Georgia asked. "We're normal Ukrainians, moderate people. We have the proper documents and updated residence requirements."

In reality her eyes and the tone of her speech revealed that her resistance was breaking down. Relaying secret messages here and there or visiting the Oto Melara arms plant was one thing, a triple murder in the middle of the world-famous city of Venice and interrogation by the secret police another.

The rain beat against the tall windows behind the bar with renewed force. Mikhaylo Kristin looked longingly at the ice bucket. Trevisan lifted a finger as if to emphasize a point but immediately dropped it to his side. Pointed fingers was not part of his style: he aimed at breaking them completely like a lion-tamer where only the nod of the head sufficed to generate the proper response. His listing and mixing of facts and suppositions in his practiced monotone voice was a chef-d'oeuvre. His tone alone underlined the incontrovertible veracity of every word he uttered. Methodically, he shattered and erased the facade of the Ukrainian couple that only minutes before had felt indestructible. The ice around the champagne had melted like the expression on the their faces, like their you-can't-touch-me convictions. Their security in their way of life of a decade and a half and prompted Kristin's spontaneous claim that they were as Venetian as Trevisan vanished.

“I expect your full cooperation in the investigation of the murder of your fellow countryman, Kravets … and also that of my close friend whom we believe Kravets killed first. Therefore I am doubly intent on solving the shoot-out and the death of three men.”

Trevisan let the suggestion of the couple’s possible connection with the murders sink in while he looked hard in the eyes first one then the other.

Then: “And if you read the Venetian press you must know that I have a reputation for tenacity and always solve criminal offenses. Now I must again point out that you both are vulnerable… very vulnerable. And as Signor Stuart here from Rome can confirm, our intelligence service, AISI, is just as mean and nasty as your SBU. They will not interview you as we are today at a pleasant bar and drinking champagne. In any case, the minimum outcome will be the same: expulsion and in Signor Kristin’s case extradition since your government now calls for conscription to the Ukrainian army of all Ukrainian male citizens living abroad. An unpleasant prospect. So I advise you to search yourselves for the proper manner to help Italy that has hosted you all these years.”

“What do you want from us?” said a now meek Mikhaylo.

“In the first place, a little disobedience on your part would help you as much as us,” Trevisan said.

“What in heaven’s name does that mean?” Georgia said in a moment of reckless spontaneity. “Not to brag but we’ve been disobediently cutting corners and skimming for years. That’s why we’re here in Chioggia today.”

“Skimming for yourselves, you mean. That gets you killed in the end. So let’s get down to brass tacks. As the Venice police detective on this case I want to know who killed the man who killed Kravets ... there had to be a fourth person."

"We certainly don't know. There's no way that we could know. Some Ukrainians seem to suspect someone from high up came from Kiev, killed Kravets and immediately returned to Ukraine. Others think that one of the many Ukrainians spread around Italy did it on orders from above. In fact many people detested him, as did Mikhaylo and I. We were once ordered to give him our house code and provide him a safe house for emergencies. He told us that Italian intelligence agents were tailing him and he feared arrest."

"If I *had* arrested him, I would have saved his life," Trevisan said. "Ironic, no? *Academia Massacre*! Whoever coined that expression got it right. Both place and events. Now you two are not exactly safe. Not be any means. By tomorrow Kiev is going to know about the Mali shipment fuck-up. And the President's going to want his money. So it seems that leaves you and Mikhaylo open to criticism. Especially were we to announce publicly that you were caught red-handed, ready to take the whole ten million and scram. So you'd better make up your minds quick--like right now--and choose sides. For the local AISI agents are ready to grab you ... if your people don't kill you first.

"In your fifteen years here—sixteen to be exact—have you learned what real Europe is about? Or even what Ukraine is about?"

"Well, we've always wanted to be part of Europe," Georgia said.

"But of which Europe? The Europe of a genuine union of peoples? Part of Europe in the hope of becoming a world power? Do you not understand after fifteen years that the realization of such an aspiration is impossible without Russia? Have you not understood that Italy—like the rest of Europe—is a vassal of the USA? That the USA is now an albatross tight around Europe's neck? And ipso facto around yours? Ukraine membership in the EU and NATO is no choice at all. Do you understand that the real choice for Ukraine is between a Europe with Russia or a Europe without Russia? That's the decisive choice? And above all, have you learned that to choose the vassal status is stupid and that USA is a dangerous ally—that it is already betraying Europe and Ukraine by prolonging a hopeless war with Russia? A top journalist, John Pilger, praised Ukrainian propaganda machine 's success in keeping *out of the Western media the fact that much of Ukraine is infested with true Nazi extremists. The United States doesn't care a whit about Ukraine which is only a pawn in the US war to destroy the Russian Federation."*

I believe I understood Georgia and Mikhaylo. They lived the zeitgeist of post-2014 Ukraine. They must have realized their acts and intentions were ethically wrong—but not in the zeitgeist of the sinking ship called Ukraine. In their opinion they were not embezzling funds of the Ukrainan people; they were taking their share of the floods of aid from abroad, money and arms never intended for the people of their country, the kind of money that lined the pockets of their leadership elite and also those of the lower level to which they belonged. In a certain manner their actions reflected the same morality of their national president, the same as the SBU, which had no effect whatsoever on the people, not even on the army. If they didn't steal the ten million, someone else along the hierarchical line would. They were broadening the spread of the beneficiaries of foreign assistance. They forgot the conscripted part of the already decimated army, the cannon fodder, the human sacrifice, the blood of the people, the price paid to the USA/ EU/NATO in exchange for the ten million. The price of war. Their case was different. There were no limits in the spaces east of Poland where blood rain fell. Only a step removed from staging the Academia Massacre: they could have been the killers of Kravets and consequently Marcello. Suspicion churned in my mind. I'm not a policemen but I see such possibilities inside the whorl of human avidity in the deep cavern on the dark side of man. Marcello himself would shrug and consider such theorizing as amateur reliance on coincidence, a labyrinth to be entered only with the security of antiquity's ball of thread leading the way back out: the Princess gave Theseus a ball of thread, one end of which he attached to the entrance of the Labyrinth. After killing the Minotaur, he wound the thread back up to find his way out. I think there has been too little speculation about the invisibility of the fourth person who completed the killings at the Academia. Until this point in the story of Venice rain, I have simply narrated what happened. Now we will take giant steps forward into the darkness with Ariadne's ball of thread in our hands to find our way back out. I recall stories of long-term sleeper spies placed as young persons in enemy countries and called into action long after they themselves had forgotten their original purpose. Like Georgia and Mikhaylo, after sixteen years as permanent visitors suddenly called up by their masters to execute the massacre at Academia. Fantasy? Possibility? Probability?

In Greek mythology, Helen of Troy might have been a spy all that time she spent in the loving arms of Paris, her lover and/or her abductor. Originally from Greek Sparta, she was married to Menelaus. But she suddenly fled or was carried to Troy by its military leader Paris—abducted, or maybe truly in love with him, in any case, igniting the Trojan War. However, there is a third alternative which interests me: she could have been sent by Menelaus as a long-term sleeper spy to undermine impregnable Troy and betray it when the time came. Whatever the truth, when the proper time came for the Greeks of Sparta to attack Troy, from the Trojan fortress high above the plain Helen gave the attack signal to the Spartan Greeks massed at the gates of Troy. And after the defeat of the Trojans, she returned to victorious Sparta and her husband Menelaus. In the last version, beautiful Helen appears moral and just—she truly fell in love with Paris; Menelaus instead personifies the acme of cynicism who sends his own wife into the arms of his enemy for political reasons.

Trevisan told me that Venice police had turned the luxury apartment of Georgia and Mikhaylo upside down, every piece of furniture, every surface and crevice, walls and floors. It was clean. Too perfect, the detective said. Too clean, too pristine. Not a home, but merely a cold, office-like, off-putting living space even though called a penthouse. His AISI agent friend, Thomas Cassiano had questioned in depth the Ukraine Honorary Consul in Padua, an Italian of Ukrainian background, Stepan Vervega. Same result: nothing incriminating although the Consul has files on every registered Ukrainian in Italy updated and in perfect order. Only one anomaly: according to the Consul there are twenty-three long-term Ukrainian citizens in Italy; according to AISI, probably many more. And today because of the huge influx of "refugees" and immigrants from war-torn Ukraine, confusion reigns. The missing fourth person of the Academia Massacre could be lost among the new Ukrainians in Italy. Nonetheless, I personally don't think the killer is among them; I see no reasons for SBU to kill Kravets. On the other hand, Cassiano hinted about the generalized unaccountability of that rogue AISI which last year—it seems so long ago when I think back on our life in the villa in the hamlet of San Nicola—assassinated my friend, the AISI section chief in Rome. We now know that the parallel AISI ran the new rogue Masonic Lodge—Propaganda 3—both of which detested Marcello Bolzoni. I myself have begun writing of conspiracy and assassination and war as if such were a regular part of my everyday life. Nothing could be farther from reality. Though genuine reconciliation is forever foreign to human nature, enmity is indeed familiar.

Until last year, Sophie and I were living peacefully in a kind of bucolic Eden in a large villa on a former hunting estate encompassed in the sprawling Rome outskirts when the secret services invaded our territory of 'abandoned spaces' and built an underground biological laboratory, its tunnels and galleries spreading in a dark network in which were produced highly toxic chemical weapons used by Ukraine against Russian soldiers. Ukraine. Ukraine: this less than a country was on peoples' lips everywhere. Like the spaces between a stimulus and a response in which anything can happen. In the newspapers. TV shows. Ukraine. Ukraine. Botolinum toxins. Friends died around us—AISI functionaries died too—and we had to run for our lives, first to Fiesole where events soon caught up with us and we continued on to our present hideout in Cannaregio, deep in the heart of Venice. Now, my friends and I are deeper than ever before in the morass of intrigue and violence, and one of us, Marcello Bolzoni who was like a brother to me was murdered. And yet, and yet, because of the ceaseless rains, rains of blood, the world around us is as quiet as the cemetery on the island of San Michele.

Normal people, the majority of the 55,000 Venetians sleep peacefully in their beds, people go to their jobs, children to school, they read the newspapers and discuss the *Academia Massacre* in which my friend died. The rich still breakfast at the Florian, dip their croissants in coffee with whipped cream, lunch at Harry's Bar and drink cocktails through the afternoons. The MOSE water barriers out in the lagoon rise and stop some of the water in its mad rush toward St. Mark's Square and entertain the tourists from another monster cruise ship docked near the Doge's Palace. People keep falling off the elevated boardwalk crisscrossing the square into the butt-high Adriatic waters invading the famous piazza. Despite the rain, people play, drink Venetian coffee and sit on covered terraces and forget the conflagration around the corner. Nights, in small trattorias here and there accordions play carefree melancholic music and some aged couples dance, their heads together and dream of the old times and cold, lonely men come in from the rain-soaked calles and sit alone at small tables in the corners, their coat-collars turned up and their wet rain hats glistening and drink crystal-clear Bassano grappa and the ceaseless rain beats against the window panes. But as is usual one learns the truly important things too late.

So I, Stuart Stuart, dedicate myself to myself and to my friends in their apartments in Calle di Solferino. Much of the time I lecture Pushkin more frequently than he would desire, in any case better to him than to an empty room. This is only a temporary house after all. Not a home. I realize I have no home. On that Pushkin and I fully agree: home is where he is, or nowhere, or everywhere. The villa in San Nicola was Sophie's home, willed to her by her parents. This building in Calle di

Solferino belongs to Sophie also. The yellow house on the Ho Chi Minh Trail in Fiesole was a mere interlude. I admit that I am an egoist like Helen … the proof of my humanity. I have learned to care for my actions, for what I write. I assume responsibility for my acts and my thoughts. So no wonder my fears. And my anxiety. My cynicism. And my loneliness accentuated now that Sophie is drifting away, we are drifting apart one from the other. She says I saved her, the savage child in the back alleys of Rome. She has felt indebted, as I must have felt indebted to her who offered me a home that I saw only as a house. Sophie and Stuart! The drifting must have begun with Helen: we both loved her as we believed we did one another. Yet my fancies run wild as do the romantic tendencies of my nature.

"Yes, Pushkin, I'm just as quick to overrate the dangers as to underestimate them ... like you in that. I have always had the feeling that I missed my time—I was either too early or too late. It's true that I *still* call myself a Communist even though it has become a lonely word with so many meanings that it seems meaningless, used loosely by too many who speak of themselves as comrades, although their idea of what a Communist is today remains vague. Is it enough to believe in Communism to be a Communist? That's a long story, Pushkin, dear friend. Camus wrote that 'all great deeds and all great thoughts have a ridiculous beginning. Great works are often born on a street corner or in a restaurant's revolving door.' Where they also die. There is no doubt that the demise of the Soviet Union struck a death blow to the definition of Communism as our love for Helen did to the thing that was once Sophie and Stuart. And eventually the word Communist that I love has undertones of the old-fashioned. But then there are certain words and certain feelings that never grow stale. Words that hang so high over our heads that they never fade. Words as vast as the skies, like the stars out there. Such words endure time and adversity. On the other hand, not even the founder of the Soviet Union, Vladimir Ilyich Ulyanov-Lenin believed he was founding a Communist state. So what am I, a writer for a Scottish magazine, to believe? No Communist state? No Communist society? According to Lenin,: e*very* question runs in a vicious circle because political life as a whole is an endless chain consisting of an infinite number of links. The whole art of politics lies in finding and taking as firm a grip as we can of the link that is least likely to be struck from our hands, the one that is most important at the given moment, the one that most of all guarantees in the long run possession of the whole chain. On the other hand, the essential words to seekers—*unity, union, unify*—recall Lenin's formula as recorded by the writer Maxim Gorky: 'Whoever is not with us is against us. People independent of history are only imaginary. They cannot exist. They would be useless. Everybody, down to the most unimportant man, is drawn into the vortex of the reality dangled before them.' Although firmly entrenched in the present, 'Lenin was always trying to pierce the veil of the future,' Trotsky wrote. Lenin's second outstanding quality was his tenacity about his main idea. *Bulldog*, his wife called him. He was a man of a single idea, to which he dedicated his life: Revolution! Which in the words of Mussolini, 'possesses bayonets.' Pushkin, his genius was flexibility and vocabulary: proletariat and bourgeoisie, capitalism and Socialism, greedy capitalist exploiters and oppressed toiling masses, class struggle, revolution and capitalist reaction, flunkies and lackeys of capitalist exploiters, imperialist war and socialist war. Sorry for that, Pushkin, but some words need repeating. They are constants of the vocabulary of the bulldog revolutionary and social-political visionary activist and interpreter of Marxist theory. Lenin was the motor of the seizure of power in Russia in November, 1917. Though disappointing to some purists, according to Bertram Wolfe pragmatic Lenin said on the eve of the Revolution: 'The point of the uprising is the seizure of power; afterwards we will see what we can do with it.' No worry, Pushkin! That second phrase just exemplifies his Russianness and his recognition of the role of destiny and chance in the history of men. Uncertainty and destiny were ever present in Leninist thought; yet when the historical climax arrived, it seemed to have been inevitable."

When I lecture Pushkin so assiduously, he seems to read my thoughts before I pronounce them … and then meows at pertinent passages Though the cat sleeps nights to the left of Helen on Marcello's place on their bed, he has transferred many of his day-time attentions to me: I think he detects Marcello's spirit in me. But who knows the depths of the feline comprehension of man's soul, the genuine self?

I found it strange when one day Vaska entered my studio while I was holding forth to Pushkin, he seemed aware that he was interrupting a preferential line of transmission. But then, Vaska was Russian! And he wanted to speak of Russian matters. He dreamed of the day he would have his university degree and could settle in his country of Russia.

"I only hope I will find a real Russia. Not a Russia still copying the West. Look at the mess that desire has made in Ukraine. I've experienced the results of that kind of thinking. I know the difference. Russians are something else. Something different. Look what happened to Andriy Kravets. He so wanted to be a real Westerner. And for that he needed money. Lots of money. But what do I know? Communism! Doubtless, a fine thing. And revolution too. But again that is Western thinking. We Russians did all that a century ago. That's done and over. Stuart, I've changed my plans. I don't want to spend these next years with Schopenhauer and Kierkegaard. I want to be in Russia where the great swerve in social thinking is due to take place. Russia is finally turning its back on the West. The real revolution is beginning. It took over a century to mature but it's coming. Russia's error has been its overriding desire to be like the West. Peter was wrong. At least he was wrong for today. Even our great Soviet Union was infected with the same sickness. Now we are learning. Strange, but we had to be rejected first. We didn't turn away from the West willingly; we were forced to, lied to, scorned, disdained, scoffed at, sanctioned, ostracized, then attacked, invaded, our people killed. And we still wanted to go with the West. We still wanted to be accepted, to be friends, allies. Exit visas were hard to get in Soviet times, my father told me. Ballet dancers went to perform in Milano … and then stayed and became stars in the West. To the West! To the West! Writers went to a conference in Paris, and didn't return home. When the USSR ended, many left Russia … but many too returned. They learned reality. The West lied to Russia and finagled for its fall. NATO pushed right up to our borders and its military bases surround us. Until finally, Moscow drew a red line; you cross this line and we become your enemy. And now we are learning that we are sounder and richer without that stupid desire of our ruling classes to be like the Westerners. Here it's pouring rain, the streets, the calles, the rios' are empty, not even fresh vegetables arrive in the stores, the bakeries are flooded and there is no bread. But in our cities it is snowing, street lamps create charm and warmth, the restaurants are packed, the metros are filled with people reading books, oligarchs are dying out and the people are living better lives than here in Cannaregio. Russia is looking eastwards. Social development is to the East. Go East, young man, go East! And westerners are clamoring to move to Russia. Foreigners now everywhere: not only Moscow and St. Petersburg, but Ekaterinburg, Nizhny Novgorod, Tver, Kazan, Samara, Vladivostok, Crimea. Why, I would go back to my real home—Russia—just for a loaf of real bread, real country black bread."

While Vaska spoke, I understood that he was a Communist and I thought of my own life in a different way. Life was indeed complex. We're all dependent on the desires of others, like Russians on their leaders: Tsar, Party or President. Sophie wanted to return to San Nicola in Rome—to return to the past. For the moment, Oriana was dependent on Vaska, who was headed east in search of a new future. Helen had a fixation on a Vienna-Grinzing that no longer existed. Suddenly, and to my immense surprise, in fact astonishment, Vaska said, both a question and a proposal: "Why don't you come to Russia too? The future is there," Vaska the Red said. But is that true? Is the future here? For Westerners, I mean? For Communists? Did Vaska have in mind an act that would revoke his past and aid him in a search for transcendence? Would Vaska appear as another person there? Shape-shifter, indeed. Who would I be there? If I feel stateless here, would I be another step further removed from life there? Or when I pass through all of Germany, through Poland and Ukraine and cross the border into that new land, would ordinary life finally begin? I am European to the core. Our traditions: Humanism, the Enlightenment, the French Revolution and Socialism. Yes, Socialism. Especially Socialism. The Russian masses always believed Socialism was a concern of the West, that it was foolish to speak of Socialism in Russia. Anti-Fascism, ok. But then, stop! That great writer of the end of the Austro-Hungarian Empire, Joseph Roth, noted that like Jews always turned to the east to pray, revolutionaries turned to the right when they came to power. Only the Revolution itself remained on the left while the revolutionaries turned to the right. Compartmentalization at the extreme of human consciousness. If Lenin himself said, "Ok, let's make Socialism and then we'll see what we can do with it," I wonder about that twenty per cent of Russian members of today's Communist Party and the over half of Russians who favor a return to the Soviet Union. Why is the figure always twenty per cent? Are they the same twenty per cent, over and over. A sect? Shouldn't there be some coming and going? And are all the Communists Westernizers? Then what about the rest of Russia? The non-communists? Are they the real Socialists? So in Russia, I, a western Communist, would I become an anti-Communist bureaucrat? Who then would call me Tovarisch there? Would I change to fit the new circumstances? Since I do not want to become a Russian Westernizer, I would hope to feel as a Slavophile, an anti-westernizer. In such a case I would be estranged from my comfortable Communism which here in the heart of the hopelessly anti-Communist West I am not. Or is it true that nothing in the world changes except nomenclature? Such thoughts make you feel hot and cold at the same time, like the crucial moment in a game of chess when any move you make can lead to disaster. Stateless in Cannaregio, stateless in Russia.

The ceaseless rain pounds on my window and I ponder my situation. Vaska looks at me askance. Pushkin meows at Vaska, then at me, as if he too wanted answers. Actually, he wants to eat. Like Bertold Brecht said, *"Erst kommt das Fressen, dann die Moral."*

Vaska says: "I remember reading of the intellectual idea of two types of cultures—one horizontal and the other vertical—proposed by the Russian art historian and intellectual, Wladimir Vedle. Although there is a great variation in culture and ways of life across Russia, the variation is minimal when compared to the vastness of the territory, Vedle said. The Russian people of the forests of the north and the steppes of the south, in the near west or the distant east, have in general lived a similar life, have similar beliefs and moral ideas. The population of the country of Russia has never been dense, so the question of extension is predominant as Russia's misguided invaders have learned the hard way. Because of that extension coupled with a similar life style, its horizontal culture, that is, the similar culture that emerged from the masses as in other countries spread over that enormous area.

"Vertical culture instead—the culture of genius and the true great works of art—demands that its foundations not be too vast. But that great homogeneous horizontal culture breeds also the vertical culture that produces the great art originating as a rule in Russia's tiny intellectual elite, as happened, for example, in the explosion of the Russian literature of the nineteenth century. Anyone who has read Gogol, Tolstoy, Dostoevsky, Lermontov, Chekov and a host of other writers who literally erupted in the world almost together recognizes that the sudden literary flowering was a unique cultural phenomenon in the entire world of arts. That culture—the pictorial arts, music, ballet and lyric opera, but above all literature—finds its origins and back-up in the horizontal culture, the art of a people of continuity, firmly attached to their lands in a uniform fashion unknown in other parts of the world—that too as experienced by those foreign invaders: the Mongols who after centuries were absorbed; Napoleon, defeated ignominiously and sent home to Paris and into exile; the Nazi-led Germans defeated, routed, captured or slaughtered at Leningrad and Stalingrad and chased the one thousand miles back to Berlin.

"It is incontrovertible that the Russian Revolution meant political, social and intellectual revolution. Likewise, Russian society was transformed into a uniform Soviet society. A Soviet man was born. A Soviet culture was created. Despite Russia's enormous land expanse and great variety of ethnic and cultural strains, the Soviet Union too became a remarkably homogeneous land that had one official ideology: Communism. In society, one class dominated: the Communist class. And though workers and peasants were represented in the Communist Party, intellectuals came to dominate and in turn became a new class. Intellectuals created Soviet culture, responsible for forming the Soviet Communist person."

"Vaska, that's an absolutely brilliant analysis. I'd never heard this vertical-horizontal culture comparison of Russia and the West. And yes, you must move fast. No need for Schopenhauer for you now. No need for Kierkegaard. You're needed at home. Home-Russia."

21

December 4

That night I dreamed a variation of an old dream of a journey to Russia. I was together with Russians who lived somewhere abroad and some non-Russian Westerners who had settled in a big city in Russia who thought I should see the real Russia. The President had agreed to spend the evening with us. We would carouse the city together during which Prez promised to show us *the dark side.* I kept asking the dark side of what? Each time he answered *die dunkle Seite*: he wanted to practice his Dresden-learned German even though I and a German Blues singer were the only persons who spoke it. And at certain moments during the revelry he sang *"For he' s a jolly good fellow, for he's a jolly good fellow, that nobody can deny, that nobody can deny, for he's a jolly good fellow"*, and he encouraged everybody to sing along while we were on our way to the finals of the dog sled races, after which he proposed we all take a sauna and a dip in the city's icy river. He promised to perform his famous dive from his favorite bridge and everybody would sing *For He's A Jolly Good Fellow.* Everyone thought it was a fine evening. Everyone liked the song we sang, but strongly objected to *die dunkle Seite* and the German he spoke the whole night. They repeated over and over that the President of Russia should only speak Russian but the Blues singer and I thought it was a fine thing to have a German-speaking President despite the catcalls of the others: 'Westernizer, Westernizer, Westernizer'. "If that's the way things are," I told the President in German, "then I will stay in your new Russia" on which he began singing *for he's a jolly good fellow* again.

Pure folly! A stupid dream. Or futuristic. I didn't tell Vaska my dream of his country. Did the dream mean anything positive? Like a German invasion. A new diplomatic non-aggression deal. Or anything at all? I felt time racing, time running out. Life was again winding down.

While we drank Russian vodka and swam in the cold river and sang for he's a jolly good fellow, I kept thinking of Joseph Roth's summing up the Austrian's idea of the final results of the Russian Revolution in his anti-Communist Trotsky novel that like Jews who turned to the east to pray, revolutionaries turned to the right when they came to power and that only the Revolution itself remained on the left among the people.

December 6

In the late morning AISI agent Tommy Cassiano entered Detective Trevisan's new office on the opposite side of the tracks of Santa Lucia Station, gave him a bone-crusher handshake and congratulated him on his handling of the Georgia and Mikhaylo case. He too wanted to grill the Ukrainian crooks in his own hardline style but agreed to allow them to remain a few more days in their penthouse apartment near the Rialto fish market—under twenty-four hour surveillance. Who knows who might show up there? Kievan killers perhaps, or the Master of the new Florentine Freemasonic Lodge?

Cassiano poured a cup of water from a bottle of San Benedetto and sat down in the chair behind Trevisan's desk. "I see you're deeply committed in this Ukrainian arms shipment affair. You a Communist, or something?"

"I'm nothing now. But I think of myself as a Communist … like my father. But our Communism changed while I remained the same."

Tommy the AISI agent coughed and water dribbled down his chin and he wondered what the fuck that meant? Was his friend a Communist … or was he something else? "Without those two Ukes," he said, "we at AISI haven't got a case of national interests. In that event our interest in the case would cease."

"They're the key and I think they're ready to negotiate a deal. They certainly don't want to go back to Kiev and face the music."

"You're right. But our Fascist government in Rome is breathing down our necks to protect all those Ukrainians in

Italy—not even the Prime Minister knows how many of them there are."

"Our Minister could query their President on one of her trips to Kiev. She's spends half her time up there in these times. Anyway, no need to worry, Tommy. I'll get copies of that missing half million euros document in the Transworld accounts and then our two Ukrainians will have to talk. That woman Georgia must have high-ranking sources of information in Kiev. I just don't want the SBU to kill them before we resolve the Academia Massacre case and put a stop to Italy's role in black market arms sales ...which is AISI's job anyway."

"Do you believe those characters actually thought they could steal the whole ten million euros and no one would notice?" the AISI agent asked. "Maybe their free and easy lives of the last sixteen years made them feel immune to fiscal controls."

"Who knows? But when they see their government leaders raking in billions and buying magnificent villas abroad, they get big ideas, grabbing what they can before the bonanza peters out."

"Listen, Trevisan, what about Italy's aid to Ukraine and sanctions on Russia? Just because Hungary gets away with stopping aid to Ukraine and sanctions on Russia, it doesn't mean Italy wants to do the same. Italy wants full and unconditional acceptance in the European Union though. Because our government is officially Fascist, we have to toe the EU line more than others in Europe. Why, Italy is more EU pure than even Holland and Germany. But crazier still, the EU agrees with the Italian Fascist Party line, not Hungarian dissidence. Better a real Fascist Europeanist in power than an extreme right-wing nationalist like the Hungarian President. Better to call a spade a spade in this case. Otherwise, the EU risks stopping the whole fucking war which would upset considerably our US masters."

"Right! They're not going to stop the stupid war, Tommy. Not over this. Things are going too fucking good to stop now. The well's not yet dry. Dig a little deeper and annihilate anyone too greedy is the Ukrainian philosophy—anyone except the President himself, that is. One bad egg out of the loop comes along and can fuck up a smoothly running system. Bureaucratic corruption is the name of the game."

"In AISI too! Always keep that in mind."

"Meanwhile let's grill those two Ukes while they're still cocky," Trevisan said. "Good cop, bad cop. You be the bad cop, I, the good one."

Cassiano called his AISI office hidden behind the police department. The Ukrainians should be picked up. "Scare the shit out of them," he said into the phone, "then put them in the interrogation room to stew until this afternoon."

"They're nearly ready to make a deal anyway," Trevisan said. "They'd much rather deal with us than their bosses in Kiev. A little bit of jail in Italy is preferable to punishment by maddened SBU people at home."

They crossed the canal in front of the station and circled the police department to a discreet, industrial-looking building that housed the Veneto branch of AISI, Italy's FBI. The simple entrance door reminded Trevisan of the entrance to Transworld Shipping in Chioggia. Cassiano nodded at the receptionist and indicated a door in the rear. They descended two flights of stairs to a dimly-lit corridor and stopped at a one-way window through which they observed Georgia and Mikhaylo, sitting rigidly on straight cane chairs behind a barren table in a completely barren room. They were looking in opposite directions as if they didn't know each other, their nerves at the bursting point.

"Yeah, they're ripe," Cassiano said, fondling a baton hanging from his belt.

"Who wouldn't be in this setting? I'm scared myself. The designer of this place must have gotten ideas from the former Lubjanka in Moscow from whose cellars—according to an old Soviet joke—you could see all the way to Siberia."

"*Buon giorno, Signora Georgetti, Buon giorno, Signor Kristin,*" Trevisan said almost gaily as they entered the room together and simultaneously blinding bright lights flashed on.

Cassiano frowned, fondled his baton, and said nothing. The two policemen sat in comfortable chairs carried in by another employee who exiting slammed the door loudly. Mikhaylo started; Georgia smiled wryly as if she knew the psychological tricks of interrogation methods. Both tried to shield their eyes with their hands. Contemporary Venice style of torture.

"Now that you have had time to consider your new situation and understand the alternatives, I hope you will share your decisions with us," Trevisan in a pleasant conversational tone.

"And we mean now!" Cassiano said, raising his voice to a pitch barely concealing threat. "We're not here to negotiate. I am an agent of our secret police, AISI, and you are occupying space and time of the Italian state. So I will tolerate no pleas for bargaining and expect the information we desire from you."

"First of all," Trevisan resumed: "who killed the Italian policeman and your fellow countryman, Andriy Kravets? And secondly, who was the fourth person on the scene, the one who mysteriously vanished?"

Their faces blank, Mikhaylo and Georgia looked at each other; he shrugged and looked down at the table. Georgia said: "Our answers remain the same because they are true. We believe an SBU killer sent from Kiev shot Kravets for his scheme to rob the state; the others died by chance in the shoot-out. That fourth person may have been the SBU killer. Maybe not. We have no way of knowing. Then again, I repeat, maybe the target was not Kravets. Maybe the detective was the target and he and Kravets shot each other. We believe the third person pulled out of the canal is the real mystery. Was he really a Freemason? Or maybe he was from your secret services? We don't have the answers."

"You're very well informed," Cassiano said, standing up noisily and walking around the room behind them, grazing Mikhaylo's shoulder on each passage. "But we expect much more than your suppositions. Or else you're going to be on your way to Kiev tonight and we will also tip off your bosses about your cooperation with us. They will not be pleased! Am I not right? Embezzlement and ripping off the state of Ukraine! No, they're going to be very upset. They showed how angry they get over financial matters when they sent your putative killer from Kiev. Of course, that fourth man—or woman—could be one of your immigrant Ukrainians and if so then it's my job to find him ... or her. So I count on your cooperation."

"But we have no sources among Ukrainians in Italy. We sometimes meet one or the other at the Consul's house in Padua but we were never part of any Ukrainian immigrant organization—although I assume one likely exists. But I *can* tell you that the Honorary Consul belongs to the SBU … as do we. I think your investigations should start with him. Transworld Shippers accountants have ignored an unexplained handling expense of one hundred thousand euros: it's there and it's destined to our Honorary Consul himself."

"Ok, no sense beating around the bush," Cassiano said. "I know an immigrant organization exists. That's my job. We too follow such activities. Furthermore, we're convinced there must be some core group—with direct links to the SBU. In fact, you two may belong to such a parallel group and can tell us about it. If that is the case, we have the start of a deal. We also expect from you information about the ring of SBU agents among the thousands of Ukrainian immigrants. We need much, much more. So you two have to talk. For that reason we would prefer you here in Italy … as our informants. You have to be clear on this: your physical existence, your very survival, is now in our hands—whatever you decide."

22

December 8

Vaska's illness must have been contagious, for Stuart soon fell ill too and for days lay in the big bed and listened to the delirious Venice rain drumming on Calle di Solferino's cobblestones outside his window. He rested. He slept an entire day. Occasionally he had a peaceful, comfortable dream. But he dreamed also of Marcello's dying and Helen's pain. He revised his dreams, embellished them, or allowed barbiturates to subsume them. When half-awake he rearranged his dreams … he was aware that he was in a dream state.

In the late morning he heard footsteps. Not part of a dream. He had heard real steps. Then silence. He looked out from the covers. Helen suddenly stood in the doorway. Through the dark net covering her she appeared more ravishing than he'd ever seen her. But he could never say that to her. It was still verboten.

"Ciao, Comrade!" he said hoarsely.

"Stuart! What are you and I going to do?" the apparition said.

"That's all I think about," he said to her shadow which was all she left behind when she vanished.

I will tell the real her what we will do as soon as I finish this battle in my roaming mind, careening as it wills, left and right, back and forward. Feverish thinking. The Battle of Solferino, the battle that should never have been fought, was being fought again. A ghost battle in his mind, a non-battle that was destined to be fought over and over.

That morning Sophie was again out in the Cannaregio rain, a relentless drop by drop refrain which Ihe followed. Clouds darker than usual hovered lower than usual. A storm on top of the storm brewed. I perceived Klee's storm brewing in paradise and wondered where she went. I slept a deep sleep. In my delirium a voice coming to meout of a whirlwind told me that I was nothing; Ie was incapable of devising a watercourse to absorb the overflow of the lagoon waters over the banks of St. Mark's Square; I was incapable of drawing a line beyond which the water could not advance. Stuart, you are incapable of fathering the rain, the thunder and the lightning. I liked his free-wheeling, unfettered mind with which I travelled again through the cities Ie had once visited … or those he'd never even seen. But at the same time he hoped for redemption for his inadequacy. He would try to perform better. He saw the Unicorn tapestries of his dreams in the Cluny. He saw life acted out on the stages of London. He read of world-shaking events in the great newspapers of Berlin. He sipped the coffees and liqueurs in the cafés of Madrid. He visited darkened poor peoples' taverns in Cannaregio in a kind of serendipitous dream state and drank grappa from Bassano in tall slim glasses and watched sailors from Malamocco dance with wet-haired street-girls . He frequented the lecture halls of the world. He watched people preparing for war marching on the streets and squares of Europe. People with hands and fists lifted toward the heavens marching as if there had never been a war but who followed commands from on high to be ever ready. And all the time in bed, he relearned what loneliness in Cannaregio was. Each time the dawn broke through the tenebrousness and the blood rains of Venice crashed high over the rooftops of Calle di Solferino, he sighed with relief: the world had not ended while he slept away his fever. He was still alone. No shadows. No ghosts. He crept to the wall mirror to observe the physical traces of the illness he had, of what he felt deep in his guts he still had, had always had, and would have forever: loneliness and an unnameable displacement. His insatiable, unsatisfactory and unsatisfying *Sehnzucht*, his longing for something indefinable, for another place that was not the hamlet near Rome, not Fiesole hanging over Florence, not Cannaregio, the place he had never found in his travels, maybe a place that had never existed. In some moments it seemed it didn't matter and that there was no cause for worry because it would all be over soon. Too late, or too soon. He looked out the window and wondered what it all meant. As usual Calle di Solferino was empty of human life: only the augmented force of the rain and the red flickering of a neon Cinzano advertisement sign—colors that seemed the center of the conflagration announcing the end of time—hanging opposite the corner where Gulliver would later sit on his straight chair and observe the hydrous mini-world of Cannaregio around him. Strange that Gulliver seldom looked upwards; he must know that there was never a break in the patch of heavy sky hanging overhead nearly reaching the rooftops of anonymous Calle di Solferino. Where had everybody gone? He was mystified. He would crawl back into his bed for another round of delirium-inspired thought … if need be. Maybe something useful would come along. He had just thought of Helen when occurred to him clear as a Rome August day the myth of the *Kugelmenschen*—'round people'—as told by Plato in his *Symposium.* Stuart recalled the detail that the fictional narrator is the comedy poet Aristophanes who at the banquet makes a speech about Eros. According to the myth humans originally had spherical hulls and four hands and feet and two faces on one head. In their wantonness they wanted to storm the sky for which Zeus had punished them by cutting them in half. The halves are people who suffer from their incompleteness, and spend their lives searching for their lost other half. The longing for their former wholeness is shown in their erotic desires … their whole lives aiming at physical union. Some spherical people were entirely male, others entirely female, still others—the Androgynous—had a male and a female half. The entirely male ones originally descended from the Sun, the entirely female ones from the Earth, and the androgynous ones from the Moon. He told Helen that she came from the moon. Yes, most definitely, someday he had to show her the Unicorn in the Cluny. She had looked at him like he was *loco-ludo* when he repeated what his father had said: the Unicorn was only a children's story. That it never was. Where's the Unicorn? Where's the Unicorn? His father smiled. The Unicorn didn't exist. The boy cried. His father did it on purpose.

Stuart understood that he and Helen would stay together forever, somewhere in the world.

Then, as a grown man, he found it in the book of *Job*, in verse 39.10.*Canst thou bind the unicorn with his band in the furrow? Or will he harrow the valleys after thee?* The Unicorn existed. The Bible said so.

When my fever abated, Trevisan came to inform me of how the two cases had worked out. It was the Trevisan of always. Secretive Trevisan from his new office on the quai on the far side of Santa Lucia Station. And I was returning from those curious places my double had frequented.

"What do you have anyway?" he asked.

“A modern plague. Thomas Mann’s character, Gustave von Aschenbach, had it in a cholera-infested Venice in his time—Our Vasily caught it. And now me. Lots of fevers, lots of dreams … but this too will pass.”

“Well, little has changed in the days of your fever. The three murders are now popularly known as the Academia Massacre since they occurred in the apartment of the two Ukrainian men where one Ukrainian Andriy Kravets and A Florentine detective died. The scientific police established that Kravets shot Detective Bolzoni. A killer of the reborn Propaganda Freemasonic Lodge shot Kravets dead before he himself was shot three times in the back of his head—he was executed—by a still unknown fourth person. Stuart, it seems the fourth person—who will probably never be found—was either a killer sent from Kiev or a rogue AISI run directly by the fascist government. A professional killer.”

“Of course, Kiev is quite capable of it but I still believe the rogue AISI version! I saw them in action in Rome. Their major activity seems to be killing people!”

“And so do I. They’re the same people who bombed the Bologna Station now years ago and killed eighty people. Killed a Prime Minster to keep Italian Communists out of the government. Ran Gladio and Italian terrorists of right and left. You name it, they did it. ‘Rogue cops’ is too little; they were fascist rogue rulers.”

“Marcello Bolzoni believed that criminal instinct is criminal instinct and political ideology is its justification. Marcello didn’t usually speak much but he chose his words like Plato and what he said was always pertinent. So anyway, Trevisan, you can go back to normal police work now.”

"Not completely. I still have Georgia Georgetti to run. I've spent considerable time with her in that un-homelike penthouse near the fish market. I think she's the perfect infiltrator into the Ukrainian colony. A self-centric person walking a thin ideological line between loyalty to a country she doesn't love and a way of life to which she aspires. Maybe I'm granting Georgia a prescient quality that she lacks but I think she's a master of the ambiguous message. Circumspect. People would never take her for a plant or even an informant. People take her for whatever line she uses in any given moment. But she's more selfishly motivated than Kravets ever was. Hers is more than the survivors instinct that infected Kravets in the end; he was so egocentric that he didn't even take Transworld accountants seriously when they showed him the swindle errors in numbers and dates and bank accounts. He didn't realize that though bookkeepers live quietly in their world of numbers, they can come up with bombshells to explode the most ingenious of fraud schemes like his. Cops like me eventually see into people like him. It turned out that Kravets was all machination and obsessed with money. He dreamed money. For him, the beginning and end of all things came down to money. Georgia instead wants it all: money and the power it brings, a new life. She has an agenda; Kravets only had lust and an overdose of daring coupled with ignorance. He met his destiny right there in the Transworld Shipping bar in Chioggia. But he didn't recognize it. When he slapped the cat with no name off the bar, cowardly limited nature began to erode and his false self shone through. But Stuart, I'm not reporting such analyses to anyone. Especially, I'm not about to reveal my controller-informant relationship with Georgetti. Actually Tommy Cassiano, my AISI friend, knows something about Georgetti ... but he's not talking to his superiors about it."

"Oh, man! You too better stay away from dark places and out-of-the-way canals."

"I'm sometimes scared myself. But I'm careful. Why do you think I got the reputation of a loner? Trevisan! He always works alone! I stick to my Santa Lucia Station office and let the young uniformed cops take the initiative. I've got no great desire for recognition, promotions, money. Let others get such rewards. But still, I sometimes get involved despite myself."

Since the Academia Massacre has been resolved—except for the fourth man—and the hidden side of 'aid to Ukraine' exposed, life under Venetian red rains moved on. I felt like shit but Trevisan's visit revived me long enough to review and submit a new article to *Time And Space* that I had been stewing over for weeks. My feverish self told me to gather my courage, get off my ass and click *send.*

WAR

Nothing New Under the Sun

The world goes round and round and human beings say and do the same things again and again. So that it seems there is truly nothing new under the sun. Man's perplexing unchanging behavior and the ways of the world have again led me back to the ancient Greeks. And what do I find there? I find the same warmongers and pacifists of today, identical war parties and peace parties, arms industries and anti-war writers, the generals who predictably "just love war," and, as one might expect, the same identical massacre of women and children as every day in the Middle East ... now called "collateral damage." We are used to that military euphemism dating from the Vietnam War. We nearly skip over those terrible words and pronounce them as meaningless words. Someday collateral damage might be called by its real name: "Crime against humanity." For this reason I have begun examining Greek classics for confirmation that human beings are not as innovative as we like to think. A recent look at Greek ideas on Power subsequently led me step by step to considerations of how Power in the time of the Greeks of 2500 years ago led inevitably to war, as it does today.

The Trojan Women

Euripides' tragedy of 415 B.C. is still considered one of the greatest anti-war plays ever written. That conclusion is truly astounding, considering the number of major wars fought in the world's major civilizations since those times. But wait! Before going further I should situate this literary work in its proper framework: First of all, it took place in "peacetime", in the aftermath of the fall of Troy to the victorious Athenians. Moreover, centralizing Athens had just brutally sacked the island state of Melos to force it into the Greek Federation, a military action that had shaken the people of Athens itself much as each new slaughter of civilians in Gaza City stuns us today: as was customary in those times all male citizens of Melos were massacred and women and children enslaved. At the same time, the peacetime Greeks were preparing an unprovoked war against Sicily (read Iran for today), which in the long run did not work out well at all.

Such was the international atmosphere when playwright Euripides staged his protest.

Euripides' tragedy is set in Troy in the period between the fall of the city-state of Troy and the departure of the Greek fleet for home. The same thing happened there as in Melos: again the innocent civilians suffered most. The Trojan men were slaughtered, or escaped, while the Trojan women were distributed among the victors. But as happens time and time again throughout history, the villains, the hated Athenian Odysseus, pretty Helen over whom the war was fought, and her former husband Menelaus, survived.

The focus in Euripides' masterpiece is on the defeated Trojans. For a change the warlike Greeks are the bad guys. Men of both sides fought the war and suffered, but, as usual, the defeated suffered the most. Hecuba, the former Trojan queen, goes to Odysseus. The prophetess, Cassandra, Hecuba's daughter, is given to Agamemnon. Andromache, wife of slain Trojan hero, Hector, goes to Achilles' son, Neoptolemos. Helen, wife of Paris, is returned to her former husband, Menelaus. So fearful were the Athenians of reprisals for their terror that they killed also the infant son of Hector.

First element: the hopelessness of war. One sees the hopeless despair of the women survivors in Troy, their fates as slaves and concubines of the victors. In our times we recall the despondent Mothers of Mayo in Argentina, the Iraqi mothers and wives and daughters, and the wives and mothers of American soldiers killed and maimed in Vietnam and Iraq and Afghanistan. We recall the napalming of Cambodia. Cambodians for whom that napalm reality was so immense that as a Rome friend on his return to Italy after many years in post-war Cambodia relates that the people have pushed the reality of war so deep into their subconscious that they cannot even relate to the word 'war'. When asked about the war, they do not answer. They simply leave the space.

War is a vacuum in the survivors' minds.

Bertold Brecht wrote:

"When the leaders speak of peace the common folk know that war is coming. When the leaders curse war the mobilization order is already written out."

Again Brecht:

"What they need round here is a good war. What else can you expect with peace running wild all over the place? You know what the trouble with peace is? No organization.

"Any veteran of battle will tell you what war is: War is hate, torture, cruelty and death. War is children and women and old people wailing in pain and quaking in fear and trying to bury dead fathers and mothers."

War today is not the Aztecs' Flower Wars, artificial wars to collect victims for their religious-power inspired human sacrifices on the killing stones atop their pyramids where no one understood the brutal reality underneath. Brutal reality, though sometimes hidden, is a reality still happening to the victims.

Second element: the inhumanity of war. The lack of compassion on the part of the Greek warriors recalls the same degeneration of humanity as seen in Abu Ghraib and Guantánamo. So great is the savagery of the Greek victors that even the gods Athena and Poseidon turn on them and destroy many of their ships on the return voyage home.

Third element: the writer's sympathy for the defeated. The tragedy by the Athenian playwright is pro-Trojan which would cause bewilderment in a tongue-tied American, anti-war critic of America in the Middle East today. One wonders why we of today are not capable of the same self-criticism Euripides was 2500 years ago? How many of us pronounce ourselves pro-Iran today?The uncomfortable truth is that the world of the Greeks was upside-down. It was ruled by tragedy and ruthlessness and disregard for human lives; war and death and destruction reigned. Yet all who have read the classics know that its men of culture resisted. The great Greek tragedies—of Sophocles, Euripides, and Aeschylus—were expressions of cultural freedom directed against Power in all its forms. Though the Greeks were a male-dominated, martial society, the writers were the ethical conscience of mankind.

Euripides' message to people and to gods and to all eternity was that war scars the defeated and the victors alike. What remains, he said, is that not even the post-bellum cleansing can remove the stain of blood and guilt. Still today America speaks of undigested Vietnam. We can well wonder how long it will be before official America speaks of the guilt of Iraq.

Fourth element: the victims of war. Statistics of war dead are always misleading. In Greece, chiefly soldiers died. The women of Troy and Melos were enslaved. In our times, the great majority of dead are instead civilian, the collateral damage: in Vietnam, ninety per cent of the total dead were Vietnamese civilians as opposed to 59,000 American dead and its hundreds of thousands mutilated. In Iraq, probably ninety-nine per cent of the total dead are civilians.

Fifth element: Who profits from war? War profiteers are nothing new and should be recognizable by all of us for what they are. In Aeschylus' Agamemnon, the Chorus, standing at urns filled with the ashes of young men warriors (recalling the body bags and caskets bringing the dead back from the Middle East) recite: "For war's a banker, flesh his gold." The makers of swords and spears and helmets and shields of the time censored all talk of peace. Generals like two-gun General Patton singing of the "joy of war" and "crazed for sweet human blood" cringed and sorrowed at the very mention of the word "peace" at which ordinary people always rejoice. At first also the Greek wars seemed glamorous and righteous and heroic ... young men off in adventure to see the world. But those wars too ended in slaughter. Men and gods now know that winnerless war always hurts also the innocent and pillages man. Conquerors never conquer completely and the defeated are never defeated completely. Vietnam and Iraq and Cuba and Nicaragua, to name a few, are the proof. But in the attempt, the innocent pay.

Sixth element: the absurdity of war. I offer this little très modern gossipy aside about Helen of Troy to lighten a heavy read. The Athenians and Trojans allegedly fought their bloody ten-year war over the bigamist and two-faced Helen. Helen or Helena, first Athenian as the wife of Menelaus, then Trojan as wife of Paris, then again back to forgiving Menelaus. Helen, it was said, had great hair, bland manners, a cute little wart between her eyebrows, little mouth and perfect tits. Menelaus erupted into

Troy to kill her for her marital betrayal but he only had to take one look at her bared breasts before he dropped his sword. In her life, Helen apparently did little more than display her body ... and betray. We do not know what she thought. Apparently she had no virtues. Most certainly she brought disaster to men. She has been defined as "an irresistible sorrow." As Hecuba says in The Trojan Women, "a man in love once is never out of love again." Perhaps chastised by conscience but still a slave of her passions, she, Helen, once referred to herself as "bitch that I am" and "whore that I am"—which I find somewhat redeeming. She must have been capable of self-examination in a way that men warriors were not. Yet, for the Greeks too she was the confirmation of Horace's cutting words that even before Helen "the cunt was the cause of wars." Another story of Helen that I encountered in Thomas Cahill's Sailing the Wine-Dark Sea *was that when she found her sister with her throat cut, her mourning consisted of trimming the tips of her beautiful hair ... but not too much.*

Seventh element: the position of woman. It has been generously suggested that fabled Helen was just a victim of the gods. We might remember that in all her duplicity she was the subject of two Euripides plays: Helen and The Trojan Women. So maybe the words about woman's role in ancient Greece are understandable even though hardly justified. For Greeks, woman was forever the "opposite", the "other" of man, a non-man, defective, playing a negative role in relation to the male who was the first principle. The male was man by virtue of the exclusion of his opposite. Man and woman, the positive and the negative. Therefore man needed woman to survive. Down through the ages the male has always needed two things in women: the Mother and the cunt. Men admit it. Woman is the nature he wants to suppress but cannot live without: woman, fickle, beautiful, unknowable, mysterious, desirable, necessary.

Eighth element: patriotism. This is the difficult obstacle for modern Americans. The Athenian Euripides resolved the problem in this way: he was less against his Athens than opposed to all war makers. The purpose of his Trojan Women was apparently an attempt to shock and shake people to their senses as their leaders continued on their warlike path of conquest and the spread of their empire with the sword. The same dilemma goes for America today: in my mind opposition to war, rejection of Washington's Cold War-terrorism bugaboo, convictions of a Washington-organized Twin Towers tragedy, are not unpatriotic principles. On the contrary.

Who in his right senses is not in accord with Euripides who screamed across Athenian stages 2500 years ago the same word pacifists cry today: "Enough!"

23

December 9

Helen returned to her diary in which no new entries had appeared since the day she fell in love with Marcello Bolzoni in Fiesole. The presence of Stuart and Sophie stand out in her last entries. The meaning of their presence then and their enduring presence today are significant.

Now she writes: *The portrait of Marcello stands forlorn on the easel across the room near the window. Each day I add and detract something. I sometimes add a detail so that* im Grossen und Ganzen *his image to be—or not to be—may seem unchanged. But there is an infinitesimal difference in his image. This same thing occurs every day. Perhaps it will be that way forever. Perhaps Marcello is irreducible to a portrait. This bothers me no end. Artists willy-nilly paint both monsters and angels. That Marcello was neither is not the point. His essence is the point. I'm always searching for the essence of the subjects I paint. If you are fortunate, when you touch on that essence you will hear a click somewhere inside you, telling you that you are near. You likely have not yet arrived but you are on the right path. And you feel encouraged that you heard that click, and not discouraged by its minuteness.*

I look back over the events that occurred in our lives during the last year and have the peculiar feeling that they cohere. I studied chemistry in Vienna and became a chemist in Rome. Unknowingly I worked for a chemical warfare project. Since then I lived in the Rome villa with Sophie and Stuart. Given my inclinations it was normal that we ended up as lovers, all three of us, but separately, I mean. It seemed we were in far too deeply—Sophie and I on the one hand and on the other, Stuart and I—for me to be able choose one or the other. The odd thing is that although I said I loved Marcello more than Stuart and Sophie together, I knew in my heart of hearts that I would never love another man as I did Stuart alone—and likely do still. It embarrasses me no end to admit this because I fear that I hurt him deeply and confused both when I ran away with Marcello.

Now I fear I will soon have to choose again: Vasily—our Vaska—wants to head for Russia. and has asked Stuart and me and others to accompany him. I know that Sophie intends to return to her home in Rome and that Oriana feels she is too Italy-dependent for such a venture. What this means for me, I don't know. I can head east with Stuart or return to San Nicola with Sophie. I know that one day soon Stuart will walk up those blue stairs and ask me to travel east with him. He has always said that in any case he has no country to call his own and prefers to think of himself as a stateless foreigner wherever he is. But why to the East?

December 10
Some unedited thoughts for my other love—time will tell if she is my real love.
To: Helen Peterson
From: Stuart Stuart
E-mail no. 1*: It's now 07:45. I'm sending you this by e-mail, for fear of losing during day the veracity that morning freshness offers. The single most terrible recurrence of recent years occurred this morning, the pain almost eclipsing that of the day she died twelve years one month and twenty days ago. Over the years I have memorized and re memorized instant to instant each irrevocable step, each unchangeable passage to the horror of reality. Because of my illness I suppose I woke up later than usual this morning. As often happens, fragments of the incubus were still passing through my mind. The scene, the whole dream state, was an intermingling of errors of words and actions and people leading up to the tragic finale. She, the young mother, the doctor, the distances, and the weather regularly return in my dreams in which I uselessly and futilely attempt to change the past. In that moment I heard the knock on my door clearly—in my dream. I ran to the door. I held onto the doorjamb to remain upright. I checked the house entrance door and looked up the blue stairs. As each time no one was there. Who are they? What else do they want from us? Again I understood that I couldn't change the past. The horror was there. The immutability of the past remained. Even though the cost was fearful I had to live with it: the pull of memory and unchangeable loss. Love often works that way.* Bis später*!*

The darkness of the bedroom helped. The rain never let up. Its steady beat could have eased a reassuring rhythm into my life. It might do it yet.

I had already eliminated dangerous pharmaceuticals from the bathroom so that I didn't kill myself after such dreams.

Despite the high ceilings, the walls seemed protective. The inviting bed more so. I pressed myself into the bed, covered my head and made my one meter ninety-eight tiny, tiny and the world the darkest dark. From the darkness, the thunder cracked and the flashes of lightning remained invisible.

My thoughts became strange there in the maternal blackness. I remembered: I was eight or nine back there in Montepulciano. I was small compared to my schoolmates. Signs of incipient tuberculosis, they said. One summer they sent me to a German-run preventorium on the sunny slopes of nearby Mount Amiata where the emphasis was on the beneficial effects derived chiefly from rest, a well-regulated regimen and good nutrition. The fresh air fetish had disappeared since Kafka's condition worsened following his stay in a Meran sanatorium. I was small but too active, they said. They force fed me, forced me to stay in bed many hours a day and spoke German to me like part of the treatment for my smallness.

The preventorium was neither negative nor positive but I hated it with a passion. The bread and butter at three p.m. and eighteen hours a day in bed nearly killed me. However that may be, I had never thought of myself as a sickly kid and anyway the next year I started growing and never stopped even though I ran all the time.

To: Helen Peterson

E-mail no. 2: *In San Nicola when your mind was occupied by your duties at the botox lab and mine by my metaphysical wanderings, we spoke of the Dreamings and dream state that fascinate me no less now than then.*

For me it happens like in this iteration that I wrote by hand a few moments after waking. In the moment I wake but my dream continues—independent of sleep for sustenance—my dream state begins. Ancient peoples like the Aboriginals believed the Dreamings—their idea of time before time existed—was a continuum of past, present and future. And it was during the Dreamings that the land, mountains, hills, rivers, plants, life forms of both animals and humans and the sky above were formed by the actions of supernatural spirits. Aboriginals referred to the world creation as the Dreamings because they had no word for time. A shaman in Mexico where I was searching for an answer as to why I lost a two-year old daughter told me that I, Stuart Stuart, am only a dream image, an insignificant part of a dream within a dream—yet the dream continues and I am condemned to continue to lose her, day by day, to swear at doctors and nurses and the medical profession every day that passes, that I would hate the all for ever and ever. Like Sisyphus, I will be condemned to lose her over and over for all eternity.

In my Dreamtime I am aware that I am awake but I know that I am also still in the dream. It is alluring there in my Dreamings where time does not exist. Perhaps that is my real life too. Fantasy and wild imagination. Maybe. For it is bewitching, Dreamtime. When it occurs, I not only participate, I edit it and change the script, I direct its continuation in a mystical state of consciousness. I become an integral element of my dreamscape—the landscape within the dream. I, the sleeper-dreamer-creator-director, hold it together: I hold onto the remaining fragments of sleep; at the same time I live the unfolding dream.

We merge—my dream self and my wake self—and become one. In that moment I am in existential no-time, as the Maya believed. The Dreamings—as it always was and always will be—on and on and on.

Ancient peoples believed that everything that comes into the world—a song, a story, an idea —is created in the Dreamings; everything derives from the Dreamings. Individual lives are creations of the Dreamings and will return there when the body dies.

In all people there must be an eternal part born through the mother in time from the originals of the Dreamings.—of the time before time existed.

And some faraway peoples dream of return to old places that existed only for their eternal, indestructible souls.

24

December 10

Rain hammered ceaselessly against the windows along the stairs infused by light from the mysterious blue lamps that because of their enigmatic connection seem to change shades according to the intensity of the eternal rain. My color superstition most likely: dark blue means ferocious rain. Light blue means the pleasant drizzle we'd come to love. Red is the deathly unstoppable blood rain.

Helen was sitting on her usual straight cane chair looking up at Marcello on the easel. She'd told me by phone during my illness that his figure had been there for some time. A stern expression marked his face but his eyes smiled as if about to promise new but as yet indeterminate adventures … perhaps in the region of love.

"The eyes are wrong, Stuart. His face is wrong. First, I tried a laughing face and stern eyes. That was worse."

I pressed my face against the window pane and felt the cold and heard the rhythm of the rain's steady beat. I said: "I read that the eyes express the soul."

"Yes, and I wouldn't want to paint yours."

"Nor would I. My fear is surely written there. I feel it. The fear that has accompanied me all these years since I lost her. By now it is nearly a homey feeling."

"Stuart, I now know that kind of fear too. Not yours of course, but the same kind. The finality it expresses. When did it happen, Stuart? You've told me the event, but how long ago? How long does it take to get free?"

"It takes years and years while you relive it over and over again, forever. You never get away free. Everything reminds you."

Helen closed the entrance door for the first time.

It clicked.

She sat back down and waited.

"You know when I fear the most? Crazy, I know. It's when the memory is *not* there. Its infrequent absences scare me. Even momentary lack of panic causes more panic. It's like an incurable disease. A whirlwind. Does it mean I'm forgetting her? Or that I'm becoming insensitive? Helen, I'm more apprehensive about fear's departure than I'm afraid of the pain and the panic itself. Helen, Helen! Imagine what it's like to be constantly monitoring your body for signs of panic! My paranoia is fear of the pain and fear of its absence. The upshot of all this? Chronic fear. Chronic ambivalence."

"And dreams of new places, places where you can start over, like I did. Dream a new life, as the Dreamings you told me about suggest. Who doesn't do that? Sometimes you might think you're alone ... but you're not really."

"Anyway, Helen, I came up to ask you this point-blank: If I do head east, will you come with me? I believe that over there our lives will discover new dimensions—when we move east."

"I'd be crazy not to say yes. Some people you wait for your whole life. Besides, I've come this far with you—in a way. From the underground tunnels in San Nicola, to the Fiesole jungle, to the pouring rain on the cane fields of Cannaregio. So you can't abandon me now. It's too late. The trains departing from Santa Lucia are on my mind too. And my bags are packed."

“When you left Fiesole with Marcello, I wondered if there would be a next time.”

“The same thought lingered in my mind too.”

“Love works that way,” I said.

“What way do you mean?”

“Love doesn’t let go easily, Helen.”

“So also falling in love.”

“But at the moment of beginning to fall in love you still have a choice.”

“Not much, Stuart. Not much. It’s usually too late by then … but yes, sometimes you choose too soon ... at the wrong time.”

“I’ve always hoped for some kind of transformation in which you would come back to me. Maybe not this way. I don’t know. But when I felt it was happening this morning after the nightmare dwindled away, I stayed huddled under the bed covers. I wasn’t sure.

“I read about people who say you also die a little,” Helen said.

“A little, yes. That’s the way we might feel. But ours is more complicated. I mean, there’s Marcello … a real dialectic.”

“Dialectic?”

“Spiritual. And there’s also Sophie. She is still of me and I of her, but we both are of you.”

“That *is* complicated,” Helen said. “And I don’t know if I get your meaning.”

“It was a peaceful setting back in the hamlet of San Nicola until they dug those tunnels under us, brought the crows for testing their poisons, produced their botox and killed people. And you the chemist ended up with Sophie and me.”

"We were pretty wild back then." Helen said, the familiar crazed look invading her eyes.

"Still, we've travelled a long road together since—emotionally, I mean. And it's not over … not yet at least."

"No, not at all: I feel good about moving eastwards. But Vaska doesn't fit in with us. He's red, yes. And he wants to go home, to Russia. I like him very much, but his is another world. I realize I don't really know him or his Russia and sometimes I wonder about those sixteen years he wandered around Italy with the violent man who killed Marcello. Did Vaska never wonder about him? Is he so saintly because he's an intellectual and reads Schopenhauer? Does he feel smug that he is now a good guy? Or is he really so good? And Russia? You've been there. Do we really want to live there? It's far from us, maybe from our kind of life too."

"You're right about those sixteen years of that other Vaska ... the Vaska we don't know. Of course, those years count. But Russia for him is another thing. Remember he's never lived there either. The Kharkov he knows is officially Ukraine: Kharkiv. Not Russia. People in the southern Ukraine, Donetz in the Donbas , are Russian too. But most want to stay where they are. It's their home."

"Strange how we keep talking about a home for others but don't really have one ourselves. Do you think of Montepulciano as home? Would you go there to live? I lived in Rome. I lived in Vienna. Neither were home."

"I told you once about Erich Auerbach, a German Jewish exile from Nazi Germany, who wrote of the perfection of the person who finds the whole world a foreign land. Maybe we're like that. Unbelonging is a liberating sensation. But is it a goal for us? Is it freedom to be unfettered by race or people or language? I don't know the answer. Maybe it's the answer. Maybe not. But still I've never been at home in the world. Not yet. Yes, isolation brings pain but your life can still be creative, a quest for something different. The exile that you and I live in is like traveling. It's being away from any homeland. It's being strangers in the world … or also strangers to ourselves. I was touched by the words of Nobel writer Czeslaw Milosz's that his native Polish was his home and his glass coffin.

"Some families are anchored to a solid core, like an indestructible axis around which its members revolve. Such families seem to be marked for life by the reliability of regular recurrences and ritual. Parents and children have secure roles—birthdays and holidays. Education and behavior proceed according to familiar patterns and codes. That's part of the normality most people seek. It's part of what is considered happiness. Other families are decentralized, each family member skewing off in diverse directions, rejoining only for emergencies … or tragedies. When I was little, my family in Montepulciano was of the first type; yet with time, it too lost its core feeling around which I revolved. I fled from it. Now, I feel empathy for immigrants and exiles, the uprooted of the world … emblematic of the human condition. That's why I'm attracted to rail stations and often visited them in my favorite cities—Termini, Gare de Lyon, el Retiro, Kazansky— just to check on them. At train stations one best sees the cross sections of a country. I found them in big numbers at Retiro Station in Buenos Aires: the Indios and mestizos, the half-breeds and quarter-breeds. Some of the Indios from Bolivia and other neighboring countries but most are homeless, I believe. I love those people forced to abandon their present … and their past. I look at them and wonder if they think in terms of a nebulous past and a lost present too. Do they think of their former homes and schools and their friends? Is the place they left still *home*? Do they hang pictures of back home on their walls? Do they long for the past? Immigrants must be the same people they were at home but what they left behind becomes their former world. Where they're from. Most are courageous but it's still surprising that not more of them are suicidal. Most certainly loyalty and allegiance can't exist in the vacuum in which immigrants live. For them—for us too—the question is: loyalty to what?

December 10
E-Mail number three: To Helen Peterson
Thoughts On Departure.
I realize that I don't understand my life. No plan, no schedules, no system. A laughable notion. Nearly everything in my life is chance: *searching for the marvelous and encountering tragedy.* (*Letteratura Come Itinerario Nel Meraviglioso,* Angelo Maria Ripellino) Though I don't go for this 'all is all' thing, Helen, everything—lies, distortions, cowardice or heroic actions—it all has meaning. Nothing goes wasted. But who can understand it all? It's said that not even the gods are hostile to the Jinns and the demons inhabiting the world. And that they count. All together those variegated elements make up individuals and communities and cities and nations and states and continents and worlds of people. And you know what they are all together, Helen? They are unpredictable—that's the great fear: unpredictability. You believe in Destiny … and you don't. You reject it as superstition but you read astrology, pay fortunetellers to look into your future, and you read the little paper-wrapped messages in Chinese restaurants. Yet if Destiny exists, you don't want to know its certainties.

Have you noticed that men of learning are extremely careful when quoting the great names, for example Dante or Shakespeare; they tremble for fear of making a misquotation. That fear creates a lot of formalism and resistance to true truth and the tendency to never call things by their true name. We see a tribute to the euphemisms of our language. One literary historian wrote about the impossibility of committing a foolish act arbitrarily or intentionally: "It's always a mistake and unintentional. There's nothing arbitrary in the psyche's life."

But according to Freud, "we can't even perceive of the powerful determinism the psyche is subjected to in life."

Outside our official public lives, a residue hangs on. And that residue is the secret, inexpressible thing that only you know or want to know: it is the great secret. For who can answer the question: "Who am I?"

Maybe the secret is simply too banal for words: we are born, live, die, and that's it. Like the time in Düsseldorf I saw an old girlfriend, once beautiful now standing on a street corner, drunk, and whorish. Was that all? Or was there really a great secret? Her secret? My innocence? I thought there had to be more. Like the secret meanings contained in the senses of smell and sound—the smells of manure in Bavarian villages and the sounds of winters muffled by ice and snow and oars splashing, waves beating against the sides of a fragile black gondola in the lagoon of Venice.

Much goes on inside you but you're unable to define in words what it is. And it is precisely that—the dark pit that is in your dream state—that you want to pinpoint and describe with words. Helen, we seem to live in a dream, a house of images and compulsions and manias and obsessions and forgotten things that are still there deep in the well, the *pozzo scuro*, that is us. I live with the hope of experiencing everything, of touching everything, believing that contact with everything is accessible, the everything which is my engagement with life: to see it, touch it, hear it, feel it, speak it, do it. I believe you too share that hope. Yet I continue to feel the perplexity, the despondency, the hopelessness of when I wake from a dream and wonder who in the hell I am. That happens. After living a life that may seem adventurous, I sometimes feel for a moment the disillusionment that I am the same person I've always been. That perception seems amazing ... and belittling. After loves and break-ups, successes and failures, after wandering here and there in search of that elusive thing, at this moment when it seems I have led many lives, sometimes distinct, sometimes simultaneous, I realize that I can't find the words to describe what it is I want to describe. Everything has its own dimension. Everything is one and everything is separate. I can hardly believe that the child I once was ages and ages and ages and that I must die. And I'm both sad and afraid I won't have the time to complete what I know is impossible to finish. What is both interminable and eternal.

Yet there arrives a time when candor needs a new chance, Helen. I want time to give it a try. One thing is certain: the attempt to say what is true is a liberating sensation. In the midst of it you feel freedom rising up from your guts. Or is it, as Sartre and Benjamin meant, that truth lies only in death?

If I knew music better I wouldn't be as surprised as I am by its resemblance to literature, especially by the recurrent themes and motifs in both; but with this difference: in good literature those themes and motifs easily morph into ideals. The motifs, the objects or settings, situations or recurring structures lurking behind the theme symbolize the idea which can become the ideal, toward which goal the creator with his narrative theme strives. Such motifs are the landmarks in music and literature like in life. Sometimes in music it seems so simple: I listen to Rachmaninoff and wait until the motif-nostalgia returns, and I sing under my breath *full moon and empty arms* and smile to myself. Then, immediately after arrives the regret.

Departure! When choice is possible, people choose between evasion and staying fixed. What moves them to choose one or the other is a mystery, since, on the one hand, some form of escape is on everyone's mind; on the other, roots are a powerful force. Those who leave are looking for fulfillment in another setting; they feel the need and desire to escape the labyrinth. Those who stay, willy-nilly accept their situation; they either feel no need for more fulfillment than their place in the world offers them or, in the worst of circumstances, they do not even pose the question. They feel no need or desire to escape. They reject dangerous changes. Just no changes! I tell myself that it's a matter of instinct. Everything must move forward, just as the life of your father and his father before him. The voyagers, the seekers of new paths, criticize the stayers-behind. Stayers-behind cannot understand the motivation of the defectors. They no longer understand each other. Nonetheless, something from the original place of your formative years, good or bad, beautiful or ugly, remains. Wherever I am in life, I perceive that something indistinct, something truly mysterious about where I started out in this life—Montepulciano—must have cast a spell on me, like a first love, a spell forever challenging me to journey back to see how it is doing without me, like a salman returning to the place of its hatching.

Now I know that my unconscious dialogue with the Tuscan mountains and the cypress trees and shooting stars overhead is a permissible memory of a memory of my original place. Though I feel no powerful regrets, I feel the sensation of the sound of the final mysterious word we all search for, the word that will explain all, the word that has to do with one's place in the world. It is on the tip of my tongue and I know the unpronounceable of my life is within reach. Perhaps it will arrive with my last breath.

Meanwhile, the hills and the cypresses and the mountains and the stars and the Eden under them have always been alive in all their innocence ... and in their violence and guilt too. My impressions were misplaced. For these are not lands of innocence. The sophisticated people have known violence. Human blood once flowed here like in the useless battle of Solferino—war and pestilence. Their only apparent innocence feeds on violence. And we know that innocence is permissive anyway. Here in the marshes or in the mountains, under the stars and amidst the beauty, cypresses and vineyards, and in the boredom; in the good life and in the bigotry of sincerity, innocence is a luxury. People are born, live and die, to the very end grappling at their innocence. In each person, it seems, there is an instinct of innocence. But also an instinct of aloneness, solitude, non-involvement, non-responsibility, absolution. An instinct that is neither destructive nor creative, but the great luxury of a life frequently lived for nothing. No role, no participation in the history of human life.

I find it strange that people seem content with themselves. In the dusk at the end of the day the mind has time to register and consider the day ending. The cool nights are conducive to sleep. But if one is fortunate, the heart is troubled and the night will be sleepless. If one is fortunate, after endless sleepless nights, the sad prisoner, immobile and indecisive in this territory of beauty and innocence and sincerity and violence, comes to himself. It is late but he still has time to realize his time will soon be up. Perhaps he begins to cry, Helen, and he asks: "Already?" Why did he choose not to choose? Why did he reject pain and longing in exchange for peace and security? Why did he do it?

Helen, it must be obvious to you that I do not envy those who sleep comfortably, free of anxiety, the anxiety which is the necessary ingredient of a life worthy of man. I would not put my life in the hands of those who never look over their shoulder. For life is after all dangerous. Nothing is secure. Even the perfect society is a jungle. Living life is not easy. But still, the good life is not the easy life. Am I not right? In the worst conditions, living becomes habit. Living in habit and comfort and ease you forget that you risk each day as you move inexorably toward your end which you can see down the straight road ahead. But you don't see the tragedy of it. You're immersed in a mystical dream, acting as if you were living a good and normal life—day in, day out, weeks, months and years pass, and nothing except habit happens. The good life. Work each day, visitors on Sunday, a vacation in the summer, the children grow up and leave, retirement, old age.

It's a frightening experience, Helen. It is for me. Actually I know it should be encouraging. Eventually you might understand that you are you, different from everyone else. You are the nonconformist. For you are alone. It's a shock each time to consciously see yourself as an elusive stranger. You see yourself in a photograph and involuntarily you say that it's a good or a bad likeness. But it is not you. Yet maybe it is a mask of the real you, the great mystery of your life. You could be just as well looking at a dead you—gone and turning to dust. If you look long enough at your simulacrum, you blush. That happens. You begin to sweat. The reflection looking back at you is a mysterious object. Incomplete. You try to penetrate along the unifying threads you know are there under the surface. Hopeless endeavor! The reflection is of another. Almost with relief, you think your reflection—the simulacrum—looks older. And then you think of time. Oh no! Don't! But you do. It is passing, passing, passing. You tell the stranger that in this moment *he* is ageing, ageing, ageing—and dying. And you're afraid. You wonder about your own relationship with the universe. There is that too. And with the absolute. But how can you know? You're less than a granule of mountain stone. An atom. But how lucky to have arrived at the profound thought that everything is chaos. Makes you realize that you understand nothing. And you want to bellow your rejection.

No wonder the beauty of the Dolomites now invisible on our also invisible northern horizons evades us. No wonder we fear and respect them in the same way we do invisible god or gods. Nevertheless, the mountains are remote and threatening because they are inhuman and free of contradiction. Free of time. Immortal. Mountains make us realize that we are human and mortal. That in the end it is impossible to forget our human selves. They make us think that I am myself and I must die. That's what I think, Helen.

25

December 10

I found Vaska waiting for me in my study. Even before he speaks, I understand that he's ready to leave for home. To his "true home", he says, Russia. He says Russia has been calling him for the past sixteen years.

"Remember, I was young when I arrived in this country. Now it's strange to realize that after so many years here that I know the physical country better than most Italians. But I don't know the Italian people. I know the layout of their homeland but not the people who live in it."

"Well, now you know me and Oriana and Helen. That's a start."

"I can tell you the distance from Torino to Siracusa and how to travel around the country by plane, train or car. I can tell you the population of Milano or Napoli or Vicenza, where they make the best pottery, the cheapest and the most luxurious summer or winter resorts, where the armaments plants are, the names of the American military bases. I know the structure of the Rome government, the electoral system, the names of the intelligence agencies and what they do … but I don't know the Italian people. Crazy! I've read the Constitution but I don't know the people it affects. And now that I have the chance to know Italians, I can't wait to get to Russia."

"You've made that clear. And Helen and I have considered joining you there. Anyway, that's for the future. I was wondering about residence documents for us … as well as for you. Do you need a visa or a travel document?"

"A new law lifted visa requirements for Ukrainians. So I can get there with my Ukrainan passport … and as an ethnic Russian, I'll become a citizen almost automatically."

"It's different for Italians. We would need visas just to get there. Meanwhile, we're thinking of taking the train from Santa Lucia Station for Belgrade. We'll just head east, then we'll see. We might like Serbia and stay there. Helen's still got this fixation on Vienna but that will pass. But in light of what has happened, she doesn't really care where she is."

"I imagined how exciting it would be, all of us arriving in Russia together but passports and visas make that impossible."

"I felt the same. Romantic! A Russian and two vagabonds discover Russia."

"I could go to Belgrade too but now that I'm free, I want to go home. To Russia, I mean. I'll head straight for Moscow and the university but I might have to settle for less. The Russian Consulate in Milano told me there are perks for Ukrainian Russians … including student scholarships. Makes me feel like a hopeful immigrant making a new life."

26

December 11

Gulliver's birthday luncheon turned out to be a tragedy. From the start an atmosphere of things winding down had hung over each of us. Not because of Gulliver's old age—we thought of him as ageless—an age which you don't celebrate with funny hats and a candle-lit cake. Nevertheless, time played a role at the long table under the art nouveau window of the Trattoria da Manin. Since it was his party and his age, Gulliver seemed to feel obligated to somehow sum things up. Was his century worth the candle? Did things add up? Was it after all a beautiful life? Without rising, without any spoon tapping or throat clearing, the tunnel vision of his glaucoma veiled right eye fixed on the beyond, he began in a rambling manner a cultural summary of Venice art: "In this city, genius produced art and architecture over several centuries, developed it and exported it until after time it withered, dried up and died. Habsburg-sponsored art was not the same ingenious art; it was art to further the empire. In my time, big business sponsored art. And with the advent of business, genius was evermore rare. FIAT converted the magnificent Palazzo Grassi—an architectual work of genius—to display pre-Habsburg art and publish huge one- thousand-page tomes *about* artists and art: Rubens and a rare Marcel Duchamps, and breakaways like Expressionism and Futurism. The sad end of the story is that Venice today produces only false art—even the annual film festival on the Lido features cinema stars walking on a red carpet in lieu of cinema worth preservation."

A meditative silence fell.

For each of us—each for vastly diverse reasons—the time was now, Benjamin's *jetztzeit* … present time. Some of us were still eager to crash history and do something extraordinary with our lives. At the same time, even though we felt the immense differences between us and genius, I believe each of us felt we were somehow linked to creativity. That we too mattered. Is that not what we all desire? That our life has meaning. As Umberto Eco said, that we reject participation in the falsification and lie as an instrument of power.

Gulliver's dinner should have been an animated party considering it marked the long life of a remarkable man, a living testimony of real history while it was being made.

It was not.

The *Academia Massacre* and its effects was on our minds.

We live in our small community, locked in our dark industrial building … and blood rain falls. Helen is still mourning Marcello. Trevisan and Cassiano are still chasing the shadows of the *fourth man.* Meanwhile in Venice, a generalized desire for the return of a higher authority is emerging. Like dreams of the Habsburgs. One mystical reporter wrote in a front-page commentary of a cry for an alchemy against the sick red rains spreading like the plague through the city, a virus, he suggested, created in secret laboratories on a small island in the under-explored waters out beyond Torcello. Mysticism and alchemy, red rain and December darkness reign.

A kind of anticipatory silence overcame Gulliver's guests as Manin served them the b*igoli,* a long thick Venetian pasta doused with white wine, anchovies and onions. The director of Transworld Shipping, Blasio Santin, leaned forward as if to examine the pasta, in reality attempting to hide his pervasive fear.

His good life of excessive authority and an unending supply of grappa was sliding into uncertainty and misgivings. Things of the world were crashing down on his head. 'Like being guillotined over and over,' he might have thought. 'If it only hadn't been for those two Ukrainian crooks! One of them at least got what he deserved.' He turned to Trevisan perhaps to ask him about the search for the fourth man but he couldn't find the words. He closed his eyes. I guessed he was thinking about the missing ten million euros from Mali wandering around out there in the ether. When he re-opened his eyes, he faced the disillusionment that the ten million were still missing. He fixed his eyes on Vaska whose presence was confusing. Wasn't he assassinated at the Academia? He felt enough desperation to chugalug a tall, thin glass of his beloved Bassano grappa. He put down the glass and smiled as temporary relief hit his stomach.

Santin was not the only one surprised by Vaska's presence. Cassiano made no secret of his distrust of the former SBU agent. As far as he was concerned Vasily Tarnovsky should be sent back home, preferably however as a double agent under his supervision, or if not, then extradited with a recommendation of his fitness for service in the Ukrainian army on the Zaporizha front. Yet here he was treated as a hero and on his way home … but not to Ukraine at all. He was headed toward Mother Russia. Flabbergasted, Cassiano shook his head and clinked glasses with Santin.

Trevisan had warned me about Cassiano's hang-up and advised me to get Vaska out of Italy quickly … before AISI got their hands on him. I took his word and urged Vaska to move fast, which in turn saddened Oriana who in her sexual heat thought she could simply hide him and the affair would soon blow over.

I was sitting at the far end of the table, Sophie on one side of me and Helen on the other. Like the good old times, I thought, mocking myself. In fact at that moment I wasn't thinking of us at all … or hardly of Vaska. I'd been watching Gulliver and his little attentions to Giacomina his so-called housekeeper at his side. Young-looking and more attractive than I'd remembered from the first time I saw her, Giacomina occasionally put her hand on his in response. A touching scene indeed. At half his age, she seemed to sincerely care for him. Although most people are capable of such genuine tenderness and authentic attentions one to the other, their particular relationship was by no means an everyday affair: she was there to oversee his departure from this world.

In my own case, I see volatile and independent Helen in that faithful companion role in her later life more clearly than that of vulnerable and potentially unpredictable Sophie. Yet another image of Helen calling, calling, calling flashed across my mind. "Be careful of what you seek in Helen," I warned myself, "for what you think you have may again slip away in the night of her impermanence ."

Manin had just served a Venetian Tiramisu and Gulliver ordered espressos for all when Vaska abruptly stood up and excused himself; he'd thought of something urgent to take care of in his apartment. He would be right back. Gently he pushed Oriana back down; he would only be a few minutes. I too had a funny feeling that afterwards I was to recognize as a premonition of more evil yet to come. Dessert and coffee were served and half an hour later the party broke up.

Vaska had not returned.

Everybody split in various directions: Gulliver and Giacomina to their corner apartment, Santin in the company speedboat back to Chioggia, Trevisan to Santa Lucia Station, Cassiano to his secret office, and the rest of us to our apartments vis-à-vis the restaurant.

I saw right off that something was amiss in the house on Calle di Solferino. The house door was only semi-closed which I thought meant that Vaska really did intend to return to Manin's. I ran up the blue stairs. The door to Oriana's apartment stood wide open. As soon as I stepped through the doorway I saw Vaska's body practically at my feet lying flat on his back and his arms outstretched. Half of his face had been blown away.

27

December 11

Trevisan was furious. The team assigned to protect our house in Calle di Solferino had flopped. "One stupidity and see the bloody result," Trevisan said. "Our tail man simply lost the one major suspect: Mikhaylo Kristin."

"Foot-tailing in Venice must be difficult," I said.

"Yes, but this guy, this city cop, took time out to eat. Can you imagine? You're tailing a suspected pluri-assassin, but take time out for lunch! Christ Almighty! Fingerprints? None. Muddy footprints? Always dubious."

"What makes you think Kristin did it?" I asked. "And why kill Vaska?"

"There are three plausible theories here: Kristin is an agent of the Ukrainian SBU and available. Or if not Kristin, then a killer hired by the Florentine freemasons. Or it was an AISI agent. But still, an SBU killer makes the most sense to me. Since Vasily Tarnovsky cheated the chiefs of their booty and besides was Red and pro-Russia, he had to pay. And Kristin was available."

"I still wonder why they didn't simply recall Vaska to Kiev long ago and decide his fate there."

"Right! They had to know that he was on the run. Italy was no longer safe for him. Neither P2 nor AISI loved him the Red. Besides he was of no further use to either of them."

"I know that his decision to go to Russia was the result of much soul- searching," I explained. "And he wanted our company. Helen and I might have ended up there … because of him. I was coming to love him like a little brother and I'll never forgive myself for not taking better care of him. Vasily-Vaska was a nobody and he knew it. He knew it was ending. Sixteen years of nothing. He didn't know who he was or where he was. He didn't know what he should do. But when he saw that pistol steady at his eye level, perhaps for a conscious second of the flicker of a butterfly's wings he knew that it was over."

The next morning, Oriana found a note Vaska had written several days earlier: *I am writing these words just in case: especially nights I fear that I will never see Russia. I have a premonition that I will never even leave Italy. My gratitude to all of you who adopted me like a prodigal son. I learned a lot about real people and real life from you who have cared for me despite my past. But now I know that's what love does. Love is funny that way.*

28

Helen wore a dark red velvet dress that day, red pumps and a yellow scarf. Stray drops of water glistened like diamonds in her fiery red hair. Out of this world! For those who witnessed her entrance into the Hotel Moskva restaurant that day time stopped. Silence fell. She seemed unaware of her impact. But I knew she was aware of what people were thinking. 'So what!' she is thinking: 'I'm not beauty … and beauty is not me. Beauty is not a quality. Beauty lies only skin deep, they say.' Again, I read it in her eyes: her beauty embarrassed her. Yet as I have said since we met in San Nicola, Helen is doubtless the most beautiful woman I have ever seen. Forbidden words. Our pact: I am never to pronounce those words. 'I am a chemist,' she was thinking, 'I am a painter. The critics confirm it.' She preferred being known as a chemist. Chemist or painter, yet even her gait, her very walk was a manifestation of beauty and sensuality.

We have lived the last five years in Belgrade. Both of us fell in love with the city at first sight and our vague ideas of moving on to Russia vanished long ago. We think alike on our decisions: leaving Italy was the right thing to do. Coming here also. We do not consider our home here temporary, a stopping-off point like other places in our previous lives. Nor is Belgrade a kind of safe-house as was Fiesole or Calle di Solferino in Cannaregio. We live in a pleasant third floor apartment on Palmoticheva *Ulica*, a quiet residential street not far from the Parliament. It goes without saying that we were happy to be free of the ceaseless rain in Venice, romantic overtones of which we feel today when rain falls in Belgrade … like an echo from the past. At the same time, we have also come to love the Danube and the Sava rivers, so that water continues to be an integral part of our shared mindscape. I am now forty-three, Helen thirty-two. Two years after our arrival, Helen became pregnant and we have a two-and- a-half-year-old daughter, Elisabeth. She is our joy.

Our work takes us to the distant corners of Europe, from Bulgaria to Finland, from Portugal to the Ural mountains. Helen has exhibited her haunting portraits in many places while I have had unexpected success as a political commentator. We usually train to Italy, making several obligatory stops along the way. The route along which we lived months and years is now traversed by the Red Arrow Express trains traveling at breath-taking speeds of three hundred-and-fifty kilometers an hour. Our story of the events that occurred along that Rome-Fiesole-Venice- Belgrade axis encapsulates the joys and the tragedies infecting that part of Europe in our time.

Trevisan maintains his office in the Santa Lucia Station and each time meets us on the quai. We usually dine with him at *da Manin* and talk about our short time in Cannaregio, memories of which are almost as difficult to talk about as it was to experience the events. For we left two of our own there in the San Michele Cemetery with its forest of sanguine-colored tombstones. Trevisan updates us with reports on his investigations: he has not solved the Malamocco Massacre which remains among the police cold cases of mysterious, rain-beaten Venice. Transshipments of war materials from Ukraine to Africa has all but stopped in Chioggia.

On one of our trips, Trevisan told us the story about Gulliver. He died at the age of one hundred and four and was buried in the San Michele Cemetery. Although he had still been working on a history of Habsburg Venice, he was the real owner of Transworld Shipping where work had slowed to a near standstill. Reluctantly, he had fired Blasio Santin--whom he had long treated as a son--for his sloppy management and constant drunkenness. Gulliver was a very rich man and willed everything to his companion and housekeeper, Giacomina.

In Fiesole, we visit Pierluigi's wife, the Argentine-Chilean Matilda, who usually has a live-in boyfriend and seems all the happier for it. We visit Sophie in Roma-San Nicola. She and I have never divorced—for no specific reason—and that is all right. I still love her in the same limited manner as before. And if now only spiritually, our three-way relationship has survived. The entrances to the subterranean labyrinth of tunnels under the hamlet have been sealed but the structure is still available: the tunnels are intact and I assume the underground train is still usable. The former AISI-run chemical arms laboratories on the hill opposite San Nicola have been removed from the peoples' sensitive views. But in any case bigoted San Nicolians never speak of such things.

On our last visit, we found Sophie in a shoulder cast reaching to her elbow; she had a bad fall when she slipped on flagstones down in the villas gardens and had suffered, almost unable to move until someone on the street heard her cries for help. Though she seemed undaunted as was her way, we saw that she had an Indian from Kerala as a live-in helper. Her only comment was that Onkar was a good Communist and was working on his phd in psychology at Rome's Sapienza University.

Helen occasionally mentions Marcello, although his name, like that of Pierluigi from Fiesole, calls up already fading distant times and other lives.

Time and distance work that way.

Our day-to-day life in Palmoticheva reflects the life of a whole invigorating cityscape which is anything but humdrum: the city, the culture and the language which we continue to learn. Moreover, after our lockdown in Cannaregio, the Fiesole jungle and the botox tunnels of Rome-San Nicola , the sense of freedom in Belgrade is inebriating.

I work mornings; Helen works anytime so that the pleasant smell of oil paints permeates our home. Most days and some evenings we try to live in the whole city in an effort to crowd a lifetime into a short period.

Pushkin ignores the reality that he lives in another country. He sleeps at our feet, and seems to feel responsibility for Elisabeth's well-being. He loves mornings when we are all at home, and in general lives and acts as if he were still in Calle di Solferino. For all the running around of humans is meaningless to him.

Yesterday, Helen was surprised to receive an e-mail from her friend, Gudrun Rudiger, with whom she'd lived that year in Vienna-Grinzing, a period which once had seemed to both haunt and mystify her, but which had also apparently vanished in the passing time and the changes in her life. Though Sophie had once been a reminder of Gudrun and Vienna-Grinzing, Marcello and I had erased it. If once she always specified Vienna-Grinzing, now she speaks only of Vienna as her original home.

Gudrun had married a Munich lawyer, had a two-year- old daughter, and at Munich's Ludwig Maxmilian University continued her Islamic studies she had begun in Vienna. Her message describes a perfectly planned and ordered life, "actually," Helen said, "just as it was in Grinzing, which I didn't realize then." It seemed the e-mail liberated binds buried in Helen's subconscious: her obsession with ideas of home, the significance of beauty, and her unswerving steadfastness in rejection of my unconscious attempts to intellectualize her art. I was nevertheless surprised by her openness about Gudrun's role in her life. Now she understood Gudrun's many absences during that year in Grinzing, which underlined the fleeting nature of their relationship and at the same time the sameness of their sexual natures. Though their togetherness did ease the tensions in their lives, Helen had been too young and too inexperienced to perceive the absence of even a hint of permanence in their relationship. That acquired knowledge changed her ideas about how life should be lived: she felt no qualms or fears about her feelings of the permanence of her attachment to me today.

"And Helen, I have never returned to Grinzing," Gudrun wrote, "though I have many times wanted to. Circumstances obstructed me as must have occurred with you. However, I like to think back on our period together there where you began your art. Several months ago I was overwhelmed by memories of you when I saw your series of paintings of yourself in an exhibition in Berlin. Absolutely stupendous art ... and for obvious reasons meaningful to me in a different way than to other admirers of your art. I think I understood what you had in mind. I recall so well your hang-ups about your beauty and your secret desires to de-beautify yourself—and despite your crazy idea, I think of you as the most beautiful woman I have ever seen.

"I am concentrating on Iran in my Islamic studies. Both its history starting from ancient times and the language. You will remember that I started Iranian language studies in Vienna. Before Hannah was born, I spent a month traveling around the country of Iran. A very hospitable people even to me, a European … and a German. I found I could exchange amenities in the Iranian language, but not much more. So I plough ahead in my studies.

"I recall your curiosity about ancient legends and I too have become aware of how much they tell us about a people and sustain the sense of permanence in our lives. The writer Sadeq Hedayat recalls the legend that the bird of truth ate three grains each day which belonged to the weak and the unprotected and each night he cried and cried until three drops of blood fell from his throat. Then, I recently encountered another legend that defines Iran's place in the ancient world: The Legend of Arash the Archer goes like this: When the war between Iran and Turan ended, the leaders fixed the boundary between their kingdoms: the defeated Iran was to shoot an arrow toward Turan. Where the arrow landed would mark the border. Arash, the most powerful Iranian archer, said to the king: " I'm strong but the moment I release the arrow all my power will leave my body and will go with the arrow. One morning Arash climbed Mount Damavand, faced Turan lands and pulled his bow. The arrow flew the whole morning and fell at noon—2250 kilometers distance, on the banks of the Oxus River in Central Asia. The river remained the boundary between Iran and Turan. When Arash let his arrow go, he fell to the ground and passed away but his body was never found. Travelers lost on the mountain today claim they hear Arash's voice which helps them find their way back. There is a poem, Arash the Archer:

He climbed up Alborz Mountain/ And tear drops would follow him

At night/ … / With a bow and no arrow Yea, yea, Arash put his life and soul in the arrow/ He did the job of thousands and thousands of arrows.

Now about you: What a coincidence! I read in the prospectus at the Berlin show that you and your companion have a daughter, Elisabetta. She must be the same age as my Harriet. One day we will get together and see how we have become: our men and our babies! So much change has been crammed into our lives in the short time of a few years. Changes occur but that does not mean that we are at the end of history. Life just works that way.

Mit Liebe

Gudrun

29

Helen's friend Gudrun seemed to counterpose her fixedness with our rootlessness. Not that she implied that her fixed life in her home town of Munich—a lawyer husband, her family and her university studies—was a better *way of life.* She meant it was her way.

While Helen and I are detached and socially unbiased—not anonymous or incognito—we like to think we are inhabitants of the world, free, yet without a particle of 'cosmopolitanism'. For now, we are enamored of our life in Belgrade. I think of Nagib Mahfuz, the Egyptian writer who hated to travel, hated to leave his native Cairo—he sent his two daughters to Stockholm to receive the Nobel Prize For Literature in his place. I think of him and I understand why he loved Belgrade—the only foreign city he visited.

Now I have always believed in the role of coincidence in life. The coincidences that have governed our new life in Belgrade would have shattered Marcello, the cop, who only in extremis would have admitted that the unknown factors that come our way are spawned in some vague manner by *destiny*, a word that he pronounced no less begrudgingly than *coincidence*.

Coincidence. And an immense one. Gudrun and Helen, ex-lovers in Grinzing, now each with daughters of two-and- a half-years. And at the same time, I am still grieving the tragedy of the loss of my daughter of so long ago, at two-and- a-half years. I wonder what it all means.

What is the connection? There must be one.

More than destiny and, as our Russian friend Vaska concluded, more than easy acceptance that life just works that way.

There is a connection.
There always is.
That's how things work.

Also by Gaither Stewart

UNDER THE CYPRESS

THE HAMLET

SAN MARINO BLUES

THE TROJAN SPY-1

LILY PAD ROLL-2 EUROPE TRILOGY

TIME OF EXILE-3

ASHEVILLE

THE FIFTH SUN

ONCE IN BERLIN—STORIES
SIGNS OF THE TIMES—STORIES
ICY CURRENTS, COMPULSIVE COURSE
TO BE A STRANGER—STORIES
BABYLON FALLING--ESSAYS
RECOLLECTION OF THINGS
LEARNED,REMEMBERING SOCIALISM--ESSAYS

Printed in Great Britain
by Amazon